She was visibly trembling and because he could not turn his back on her in pain, he hugged her yet again.

"I'm sorry," Briony said, brokenly. "I don't mean for you to have to hold me up all the time. It's just—"

"Shh. Don't apologize. The world's upside down right now. Our world, at least. And..." Greg hesitated but then realized she deserved the truth even if it was a bit uncomfortable for him to admit. "It helps me, too. To know I'm not the only one feeling like this."

She didn't respond, but she moved, her arms coming around him to hug him back. Once more. And after a long silence, she finally did speak again, low and clearly heartfelt.

"They'd want this, wouldn't they? Want us to help each other, be there for each other?"

He thought of Rick, the prankster he'd been as a kid—and the trouble it had gotten them into—and Wendy, who would have backed Rick in anything he tried, and suddenly he was smiling.

"Honey," he said, putting on his best exaggerated drawl, "they probably planned it this way."

Dear Reader,

Idaho! Just reading that in the proposed storyline for The Coltons of Owl Creek sold me. It's one of my favorite states, and every time I visit, I wonder, *Why am I not living here?* And Owl Creek is very much like a place or two I've been, making it even more fun to write.

As usual, wherever you drop the Coltons, turmoil will follow. It's just who they are. In the case of Greg Colton, he just wants a quiet life on the family ranch and thinks of himself as a rancher, not a hero. But when it comes to stepping up for his best friend after a tragedy, there's never a doubt that he'll do what has to be done. Colton, you see.

Becoming a part of the Coltons team has been a learning experience for me, even after having written dozens of books before my first Coltons story years ago. As a writer, it's a fascinating process, trying to write your own complete story while at the same time having it fit as one part of a much larger picture. So credit where it's due—to the editing/coordinating team who work so hard at pulling these stories readers love together!

Happy reading!

Justine

A COLTON KIDNAPPING

JUSTINE DAVIS

HARLEQUIN

ROMANTIC
SUSPENSE

Special thanks and acknowledgment are given to Justine Davis
for her contribution to The Coltons of Owl Creek miniseries.

ROMANTIC SUSPENSE™

ISBN-13: 978-1-335-59410-5

A Colton Kidnapping

Harlequin Enterprises ULC
22 Adelaide St. West, 41st Floor
Toronto, Ontario M5H 4E3, Canada
www.Harlequin.com

Printed in Lithuania

MIX
Paper | Supporting
responsible forestry
FSC® C021394

Justine Davis lives on Puget Sound in Washington State, watching big ships and the occasional submarine go by and sharing the neighborhood with assorted wildlife, including a pair of bald eagles, deer, a bear or two, and a tailless raccoon. In the few hours when she's not planning, plotting or writing her next book, her favorite things are photography, knitting her way through a huge yarn stash and driving her restored 1967 Corvette roadster—top down, of course.

Connect with Justine on her website, justinedavis.com, at Twitter.com/justine_d_davis or at Facebook.com/justinedaredavis.

Books by Justine Davis

Harlequin Romantic Suspense

The Coltons of Owl Creek

A Colton Kidnapping

Cutter's Code

Operation Homecoming
Operation Soldier Next Door
Operation Alpha
Operation Notorious
Operation Hero's Watch
Operation Second Chance
Operation Mountain Recovery
Operation Whistleblower
Operation Payback
Operation Witness Protection
Operation Takedown
Operation Rafe's Redemption

Visit the Author Profile page
at Harlequin.com for more titles.

Chapter 1

Greg Colton was sound asleep when he heard the pounding on his door.

It wasn't the mare's fault. The sorrel with the flaxen mane and tail was one of the sweetest horses on the ranch, and the fact that she was Dad's favorite meant if she needed help, they'd be all hands on deck. Even on a Friday night.

The ranch foreman had sent his nephew Mitch to get Greg when, on a routine check of the pregnant animal, he'd found her down in the stall, apparently in labor but with no sign her water had broken. Greg scrambled up, pulled on his jeans and told the kid to go get his dad at the big house.

"Mr. Buck?" Mitch looked almost scared.

"He won't bite," he assured Mitch. "And he'll want to be there. Lily is his girl."

Mitch nodded and left. Greg pulled on his boots, grabbed a shirt and ran, pulling the long-sleeved thermal on as he went. He snagged a jacket from the rack beside the door without breaking stride and headed for the barn. From here he could see the light on in the bigger foaling stall.

When he got there, Mitch's uncle, Marty Gibson, was outside the door with the case of medical and veterinary basics. Lily was down, her breathing elevated. Horses had such a wide range of what was their "normal" gestation that this was early but not unheard of. And it was her first pregnancy, so entirely unpredictable.

"You had to make it complicated, didn't you?" he crooned to the horse as he knelt in the straw beside her. She snorted inelegantly. He laughed back reassuringly.

But he knew forty minutes of stage two labor was the magic number, that after that the chances of foal mortality went through the roof. Since they didn't know how long ago this had started, he had no idea when to start worrying.

Save time, start now.

His brother Malcolm's joking suggestion, usually referring to his search-and-rescue assignments, went through his head and made him smile inwardly.

"Boss? It's starting, but this looks weird."

He moved to where Marty was watching for the emergence of the foal, which had begun. But he saw not the expected amniotic sac but what looked like a bumpy red mass. He swore under his breath and his instincts instantly went into overdrive.

"Hand me that," he snapped, gesturing toward the case of medical gear they kept on hand. He was no veterinarian like his cousin Ruby, but he knew what he was dealing with. A red bag delivery. The placenta had separated prematurely, and the foal was essentially being born inside it. Which explained why her water hadn't broken. And unlike the normal sac, the foal couldn't break through the much stronger placenta.

Which would mean the baby wouldn't be able to breathe.

He heard a sound behind him but was utterly focused on what was happening in front of him. He'd never dealt with one of these firsthand but he'd seen one once, and knew every second was critical. He hastily gloved up and grabbed at the first tool at hand that could do the job, the utility knife he always had in a sheath on his belt. He swiped the blade quickly with sterilizer, then cut through the placenta, ignoring the flood of fluid to examine the foal. Saw head and both front feet first, normal delivery position. He gently made sure everything was aligned properly, then reached out to press on Lily's belly, urging her to go to work. The mare seemed as eager as he was to have it over, and soon the foal was sliding the rest of the way out.

Greg immediately cleared the baby's nostrils, and he—it was a colt, Greg noticed—was quickly breathing on his own. Greg grabbed the battered stethoscope from the case, but realized he didn't have his watch on to time the pulse.

Then someone was crouching beside him. Dad. "Go," was all he said, holding out his own left wrist, which did bear a watch. Greg applied the stethoscope, and once he had the heartbeat steady in his ears, he began the count.

"Hundred and ten," he finally announced.

"A little high, but not abnormal," Dad said. "We'll have to monitor him for a while. And maybe have Ruby come out and verify everything's all right."

"Good idea," Greg said. "Although he looks fine."

The colt was wiggling now, trying to get free of encumbrances both biological and human. Greg went about the last details of cleanup, clamping and cutting the umbilical cord and sterilizing the cut. When he was done, he sat back on his heels, watching. He was certain now the little one was going to be okay. The foal's head was up and he was looking around curiously at this strange new place he'd been deposited.

Greg knew he probably looked like he'd survived some kind of bloodbath, from knees to chest. The arrival of new life was wondrous, but nobody ever said it was tidy. He remembered his best friend, Rick Kraft, talking about when his son, Justin, had been born.

"You know intellectually it's messy, but until you see it live and in person..."

He'd ended with a bit of a shudder, and Greg had laughed and gotten him another beer. By the time little Jane had come along, Rick was a pro with the dad stuff and barely blinked.

Greg felt a steady hand gripping his shoulder, taking him out of the memory, and for the first time he actually looked at his father. Who was smiling, widely.

"Proud of you, son. You did what had to be done and saved this little guy. You're a true horseman."

Greg felt a sudden tightness in his chest. Funny, his father was never stingy with praise, yet every time he earned some it still made him feel this way, even at thirty-seven. A measure of the man his father was. The man he admired beyond all others, for the way he loved his family more than himself, the way he never dwelled on the dark times Greg knew he'd seen in the service, the way he was ever and always fair, and even for the silly jokes he told that made them all groan. Steady, solid and stalwart, the man would die for any one of his children and they all knew it.

Unlike their mother, who had walked away from them when Greg was ten years old, betrayed them all completely, gone off to have an affair and two other children—that she'd stayed around to raise—and never looked back.

That the affair was with Dad's brother Robert was the bitter icing on a very sour cake.

But Dad had stepped up for his children, and Greg had decided long ago they were better off without her. With a father like this, they didn't need her.

"Thanks for trusting me to do it," he said, his voice tight.

Buck Colton met his gaze steadily and gave him another squeeze of his shoulder. "I trust you with a lot more than this."

Greg had to wait a moment before he could speak again. "She's your special girl, and I know you've been eager to see what she and that fancy stud produce."

"That spendy stud, you mean?" his father said with a wry grimace.

He grinned then. "Yeah, that one."

He got that smile again. "Thanks to you, I'll find out." He looked Greg up and down. "And now you'd better go clean up. Go back to bed, I'll take it from here."

"Thanks, Dad," he said, rising to his feet. He started to head for the door to the stall, then looked back. "For everything," he added, meaning it completely.

"Get on with you," his father said, but Greg saw in his expression that he was pleased with the emphasis and the emotion behind the words.

Greg headed back to his place, which was the guest house on the ranch, not too far from the main house. It was small, but enough for him. And since it seemed likely that it would always just be him alone, he didn't think about it much anymore. He'd been close to marriage once, but it turned out ranch life wasn't for her, and he couldn't leave. Or, according to Jill, wouldn't. The commitment to his family and this land was something the city-raised woman just didn't get.

Just as well. He had work he loved, a big family—complicated and recently even bigger not only with cousins and a brother finding their life partners, but with the revelation he had two half siblings they'd never known about—good friends, and he got to play uncle to Rick and Wendy's little ones. It was enough.

It had to be enough.

He hit the shower smiling, remembering the moment when the colt's head had come up and he started inspecting his new surroundings with wide eyes and swiveling ears. There was definitely something about helping a new life into the world that felt good. Really good.

The shower felt good, too, and he lingered longer than he'd planned. He finally got out, dried off, then ran a towel over hair that had gotten long enough to tickle the back of his neck. He went back into the bedroom, wondering how much sleep he could get before he had to roll out again. It had been nearly midnight when he'd headed for the barn, and he was guessing it was now after two. He could get maybe four hours before his regular workday had to begin. It would still be fairly dark out at six, but sunrise was late this time of year in Idaho, not until nearly eight, so the first couple of hours of work were usually done in the dark anyway.

He yawned, stretched and slid back into bed. And was sound asleep when the second interruption of the night came. The annoyingly loud ringtone of a phone call, which he'd often been tempted to change but never had, afraid he'd sleep right through anything gentler. Because he had, which was why Marty had sent his nephew in person.

Groggily, he reached out for the phone, knocking the earbud he always used to avoid that ringtone, spooking a critter off the nightstand in the process. He opened one eye enough to swipe the screen to answer.

"'Lo?" It was all he could manage.

"Greg, it's Chase."

He rubbed at his eyes, wondering what on earth his cousin was calling about at this hour. "You okay?"

"I am."

Even as half-asleep as he was, he couldn't miss the implication that someone else wasn't. He wasn't sure he could handle another emergency. "What is it?"

"Rick and Wendy Kraft."

That sent a jolt through him. He was instantly wide-awake. He sat up, half-afraid to ask for fear of what would come next. For fear of why his cousin who barely knew them would be calling him about Rick and Wendy.

"What? Are they all right?"

And then Chase said the words that would change his life forever.

"I'm afraid not. I'm sorry, Greg…"

Chapter 2

Briony Adams was a little amazed she'd gotten here without crashing.

Even as she had the thought, she recoiled from it. How could she, even jokingly, be thinking about crashing?

She wanted to see them. Had to see them. How else could she believe the impossible? Wendy and Rick, dead?

No, it couldn't be. It just couldn't.

She tried taking some deep breaths but couldn't manage it yet. She'd been beyond revved up since the call had come, and the drive to the hospital in Conners had seemed to take forever. She'd had to work her way through three staff people, insisting vehemently she was Wendy's emergency contact, before she got to the ER doctor who had finally, gently, even though she was obviously harried, broken the news to her.

"You're related?" she had asked.

"No. B-best friends." She could barely get the words out.

"Someone will be out to talk to you soon," the doctor promised. "We'll need some more information."

And so she was left standing here, feeling more at sea than she ever had in her life. Which was saying something, given her painfully shy nature that made her uncomfortable in any gathering of more than a half dozen people. The last time she'd tried going to a big party, a few months ago, she'd been exhausted and practically nonfunctional the entire day after. Her business had suffered, since being an accountant and being exhausted did not mix well.

That party had been Wendy's birthday.

Today—or rather yesterday, since it was now 4:00 a.m.—had been Rick and Wendy's wedding anniversary. So it couldn't really be true, could it? The universe couldn't really be that cruel.

Of course it can. Hasn't life proven that to you from the day you were born?

"Briony!"

She spun around at the sound of her name. She knew who it had to be. Wendy had listed her as her first emergency contact, with Rick's best friend, Greg, next, and Rick had done it in reverse order.

She saw him striding across the waiting room—which in her opinion would be better named the torture room, or simply hell—toward her. He moved like the strong, powerful man he was. Someone who could wrestle a cow or a horse and anything else that needed wrestling on a ranch. She hadn't seen him since that party, and he looked as if he hadn't had a haircut since. She liked the slightly shaggy look. But then, she liked most things about Greg Colton.

Memories suddenly flooded her, of all the times Rick and Wendy had tried to set them up. She and Greg had both laughed it off, saying they were only doing that because they were the only single people the couple knew. She knew Greg thought her work boring and probably her as well, while she had no idea how to even talk to the sometimes-gruff cowboy. She couldn't read him at all, and she imagined he liked it that way. After all, why would he, or any strong, competent man like him, want anything to do with her?

But that hadn't stopped her from developing a little crush on the guy. What woman could look at the rugged rancher, with that strong jaw, warm dark brown eyes, that pure, solid man, and not feel her pulse kick up a bit? That he was kind, funny and a loyal friend only made him more attractive. But they had nothing in common, on any front. He had a big family he was close to and loved the challenge of managing the family ranch, working with unpredictable animals she knew nothing about and was wary of. She had no family, at least that she knew of, preferred numbers because they were consistent and knowable, and quiet nights alone to read were her favorite times. It would never have worked, even if she'd had the nerve. Or if Greg had shown the slightest bit of interest.

And then he was barely three steps away. He stopped abruptly, staring at her. She looked up at him, his face a little blurry now as tears welled up again.

"You know?" She could barely get it out.

"Yes. My cousin…he was there. At the scene." His voice sounded beyond gruff, almost hoarse. As if his throat was as tight as hers.

Greg crossed the distance between them in one long-legged stride. His hands came up and gripped her shoulders, gently but firmly. As if he wanted to steady her, which, surprisingly, worked.

"You haven't seen them?"

She shook head. "Not yet. They won't let me yet."

She saw his eyes narrow, saw the very slight wince, and knew he'd reached the same conclusion she had about the probable state of…the bodies.

"The kids," he began. His voice audibly broke this time.

"Mrs. Matson is staying with them for the night," she said quickly, guessing he was fearing they'd also been in the car. But Wendy had told her about the kids' reliable babysitter staying with them overnight right before she and Rick had left for their night on the town here in Conners.

Their fifth anniversary celebration.

And now they'd never see their sixth.

The reality of this, standing here in a hospital, with Rick and Wendy's other best friend, staring at each other, suddenly overwhelmed her.

It was true. Dear God, it was true.

They're dead.

Something must have shown in her face, some flash of agony, because Greg moved suddenly, wrapping his arms around her, holding her in a fierce, tight hug. He was so strong, so warm, she actually took some comfort from the embrace. He was feeling this, too, she reminded herself, or some version of it. He and Rick had been friends since early grade school, after all. Not quite as long as she and Wendy, but that was because they'd both ended up in the foster system together and had first met as wary, untrusting eight-year-olds.

"Ms. Adams?"

The quiet voice came from close behind her, and if she'd had the energy she might have jumped. But it had all drained away, and with Greg's arms around her she didn't even need strength enough to stand up. She only turned her head to see a small dark-haired woman in business clothes and a hospital name tag, carrying a tablet and smiling at her gently.

"I…yes," she finally got out.

"I'm Barbara Crane." She glanced at Greg, then looked back at Briony. "Would you come with me so we can speak privately?"

"Greg has to come, too," she said quickly when she felt Greg tense.

The woman's expression changed. She glanced down at the tablet she held, then looked up at Greg. "Greg... Colton?"

"Yes," he said, his voice still rough, but with a note of challenge in it now. Whatever this was, he wasn't about to be shut out of it if it involved Rick. And if his last name and the standing of the Colton family in Owl Creek eased his way, so be it.

"All right, you're the other person on the list, so you should come, too."

Moments later they were in a small room with a table and several chairs, one chair on one side, the rest on the other. Clearly the hospital worker was meant to take the single chair, and did. Greg politely ushered Briony to one of the chairs on the other side of the table, then he pulled a second one up close to hers and took a seat. In her dazed state, all she could think was that that was typical Greg—polite, thoughtful and handling it.

When Mrs. Crane spoke, her voice was still quietly gentle. Briony wondered if this was her job, dealing with people in horrible shock, and if so, wondered how she did it.

"First, I have to confirm, neither of you is a blood relative of Rick or Wendy Kraft?"

Briony only realized she was clenching her fist when her nails dug into her palm. "As good as," she said.

The woman looked thoughtful, but before she could speak Greg did. "Rick only has his father, and he's had no contact with him for more than ten years. The man's a..." He ended with a grimace and a shake of his head that managed to express his opinion of Rick's father perfectly.

While Mrs. Crane made a note, Briony added, "And Wendy has no family. She was orphaned at a young age." *The same age I was when my so-called parents abandoned me.*

"I see." She studied whatever form she was filling out. Then she looked up at them both. "So there's no other blood family for either of them?"

"No," Rick said flatly. "*We're* their family."

Briony felt a sudden tightness in her chest as he put into blunt, firm words exactly what she was feeling. Wendy had been her sister-by-choice most of her life and when they'd married, Rick, bless him, had embraced her as if the relationship truly was one of blood and DNA.

"Can we…see them?" Briony asked, bolstered by Greg's strength.

"I'll look into that," the woman said, and it came so quickly she knew it had to be a practiced answer to a frequent question.

"Do that," Greg snapped. Then, as Mrs. Crane gave him a rather startled look, he drew in a breath and said, "Sorry. I just can't wrap my mind around this. Since the kids came Rick was such a careful driver. He was a pain in the ass sometimes, even, so I can't see how this could happen."

"Me, either," Briony said quietly. "I don't think we'll believe it until we see them."

"I understand," Mrs. Crane said kindly. "If you'll wait just a moment?"

Alone in the little room now, Briony consciously tried to slow her breathing, hoping that would ease the hammering of her heart. Her well-trained logical brain tried to tell her it was all true, that they wouldn't make a mistake like this, but her silly heart couldn't help but hope. The conflict made her more than a little shaky.

Then, to her surprise, Greg reached out and took her hand. The warmth, the gentle but firm grip, steadied her once again. And her mind darted for refuge in the oft-wondered thought—what would have happened if she'd had the nerve to tell him they should give in to the Krafts' matchmaking efforts? She'd even worked out how to do it with the least embarrassment to them both, by telling him that then they could tell their friends they'd tried, so maybe they'd then back off. Behind all that Briony harbored the harebrained hope that something else might happen instead, that they might find that Rick and Wendy had been right about them being good together.

Rick and Wendy. Who were right now lying lifeless somewhere in this building.

A light tap came on the door in the moment before it swung open. Briony looked up, expecting Mrs. Crane. Instead, she saw a man she would have recognized even without the uniform. Police Chief Kevin Stanton had been all over the news when that story of the serial killer had broken. She'd paid more attention than she usually did to such horrific things, in part because Greg's FBI agent brother, Max, had been involved.

Greg stood up as the man stepped into the room. Briony didn't think she could; she was too wobbly.

"Chief Stanton," Greg said, rather neutrally.

The man's brow furrowed, then cleared. "You're one of the Coltons, right? One of Buck's boys?"

"Yes." She didn't think she was wrong about the edge that came into Greg's voice when he added, "I'm Max's brother."

The chief looked at him appraisingly. "You as stubborn as he is?"

Greg never flinched. "When necessary."

And Briony suddenly realized that, along with everything else he was, Greg Colton was a man she would not want to cross.

But he was exactly the man she would want to have on her side.

Chapter 3

His brain was acting like a skittish calf at branding time. Darting this way and that, spinning and running back the way it had come, all trying to avoid that smoking black hole in the middle.

Rick was dead.

Rick. The guy who had been at his side ever since they'd joined forces to stop those two jerks who'd been tormenting a puppy back in elementary school. The two had been older and correspondingly bigger, but the whimpers of the puppy had galvanized Greg and Rick into action and made them pretty much unstoppable. It had been the beginning of a friendship that had been solid for over twenty-five years.

Until now.

Desperate to do something, anything, he zeroed in on the chief. He already knew the basics from Chase, but he wanted the official version. "What happened?"

Stanton hesitated, glancing at Briony. Greg glanced her way, too. He saw her almost visibly pull herself together as she got to her feet.

"Don't sugarcoat it on my account," she said, her voice remarkably steady. It would seem there was more spine to Briony Adams than he would have thought. He'd known she was a good friend to Wendy, and that they'd been friends for even longer than he and Rick, and thanks to that connection he'd been around her a bit, but he'd never seen her under stress like this.

Stanton nodded. "They went off the road and wrapped around a tree." He hesitated, then added rather quietly, "They never had a chance. Their car was bent almost double."

Briony let out a tiny sound but stayed upright.

"There'll be photos in the news," Stanton said, as if in warning. "Just be prepared, it's not pretty." He eyed Greg a little warily before saying, "We're waiting on the blood alcohol results on Mr. Kraft."

Anger started to spike in Greg, but he held it down. *It's routine. You know they have to.* "He won't be over the limit. He never drinks much." *Drank much. Past tense.*

"I'm not expecting he will be," Stanton said. "From what I saw at the scene, Mr. Kraft's driving was not a factor."

Greg went very still. He sensed rather than saw Briony look at him, but he kept his gaze on the man in uniform as he asked, as calmly as he could, "What was?"

"They were sideswiped and pushed off the road. As far as we can tell—so far anyway—it was a hit-and-run."

Greg stared at Stanton. "And the other car?"

"A black something. Big, judging by the height of the paint transfer. We'll be sending that to the lab, see if we can pin down a make and model."

"Did anybody see it happen?"

Stanton shook his head. "We don't even know exactly when it happened yet. It was called in by a passerby just after 2:00 a.m."

"Were they…?" Briony began, but her voice faded away.

"They were already gone, Ms. Adams. I'm no doctor, but I'd say on impact. I'm sorry."

It registered with Greg that the man was being pretty kind. He hoped it wasn't from lots of practice. He wouldn't have thought the chief of police would be involved in something like a traffic accident, but Owl Creek was, at its heart, a small town. Quiet, for the most part, especially if you took the tourists out of the equation and stuck with the locals.

Things like this didn't happen often. Thankfully.

"Now, excuse me. I'll go let them know you can make the positive IDs."

He left the room quietly. Silence spun out for a while, until Greg, taking a deep breath, turned to Briony. "Are you sure you want to do this? I can…verify for us both."

Her head came up sharply. "Of course I do."

"I just thought…maybe you wouldn't want to carry that image around in your head forever. Maybe you'd like to remember them…the way they were."

She just looked at him for a long moment before she said, softly, "Wouldn't you?"

He laughed, and it came out the harsh and bitter sound that matched what he was feeling. "Of course I would. But it's not an option. Besides," he added, his voice more under control now, "you were right before. I don't think I'll truly believe it until…"

She continued to look at him, as if studying him. "Thank you," she finally said, her voice soft, and with an undertone of…something. But he wasn't sure what she was thanking him for.

"For what?"

"Being willing to carry that image alone, for my sake."

He had no idea what to say to that, so he only shrugged. Which for some reason made her almost smile. As much as either of them could, he supposed, under the circumstances.

Ten minutes later they were standing outside the hospital

morgue, both of them shaking. Greg knew he'd been right. Those were images he would carry forever. Briony reached for him, and once more he hugged her, but this time it was to share the blow, because he felt as rattled, as devastated, as she looked. They'd both lost their best friends, friends of decades, and if she felt anything like he did the fact that she was still standing was amazing. The only reason he was still on his feet was because he couldn't bear to collapse on the floor and cry in front of everyone.

Another person in hospital attire, a man this time, approached them, accompanied by the chief again.

"The kids... They have two children," Briony said, sounding a bit numb now.

"We're aware," Stanton said. He looked at Briony. "You provided that contact information? For a—" he glanced down at a notebook, apparently still going old-school "—Lucy Madison?"

"Matson," Greg said as Briony nodded.

"Ah, yes. She's been advised of the situation but hasn't told the children yet."

He cringed inwardly. Clenched his jaw against the reaction. Then said what he had to say. "We should do it."

"Of course. We're their godparents," Briony said at the two men's looks.

Stanton seemed to relax a little. "I see."

Greg only nodded. It was all he could manage. Somehow Briony's instant agreement that they should be the ones to deliver this devastating news, together, helped him get past the realization that he didn't think he could have done it alone anyway.

And that he was glad she'd been there with him when they'd had to identify the bodies of their friends. He'd made the offer to do it alone genuinely, but now that he had that image in his head, he was truly glad he wasn't the only one who would be lugging that memory around. Shared misery, maybe.

They walked down the hallway that seemed chillier than it had been.

"What do we do now?" She sounded so forlorn he wanted to hug her again. Maybe misery really was lessened by sharing.

He glanced at the watch he'd remembered to grab this time. "I need some caffeine before I start trying to figure that out," he said. "This place must have a coffee shop or something. Someplace where we can…think."

They found the listing on a board near the elevators and made the trip and the walk down another hallway in silence. It wasn't just the hallway that felt colder. The whole place did. Which told him it wasn't the surroundings, it was him.

After Briony had ordered some fairly complicated-sounding coffee drink, he asked the young woman behind the counter, "What's the most opposite of decaf?"

The barista smiled at him. "We have an espresso machine, if you'd like that."

"Doubled," he said. "Straight."

He sensed rather than saw Briony cringe slightly and gave her a rueful grimace. "For the hit, not the taste. I'm going to need it. It was already a long night, and now…"

Now that night was going to last forever.

"What happened…before this?" she asked as they found a small table and sat for a moment.

The first part of his night seemed eons ago. "Nothing that matters now." *At least it had a happy ending.*

"I just need to think about something else for a few minutes." She said it as if he'd accused her of something. As if she felt guilty for wanting to escape the horror, even if only for those few minutes.

And so he told her about Lily and her foal, focusing less on the complications of the birth and more on the fact that the baby would be all right. He saw the faintest of smiles curve her mouth, as if it were all she could manage. But at least it was there, so he counted the diversion worth it.

"It must be so different, living on a ranch," she said.

"It is. That's why I love it. Plus, it's my family."

He thought he heard the faintest of sighs. He wished he hadn't added that, wasn't sure why he had, except that it was true. But he knew Briony had no family, had grown up in the system, because Wendy had told him that's where they'd met and bonded as children even younger than he and Rick had been when they'd connected.

She was staring down at the table as if it held some fascinating design and was more than a chunk of ordinary laminate surface.

"When they got married," she said, so softly he had to focus to hear it, "I was afraid I'd lose Wendy."

"She'd never let that happen," Greg protested.

"I know. I should have known then. And now…now…"

And there they were, back in the morass of reality, sitting in a damned coffee shop while their friends lay dead in the hospital basement. Greg's gut knotted fiercely, and for a moment he thought he was going to lose what coffee he'd drunk.

"They looked…so peaceful," she whispered.

Greg guessed the hospital staff had made an effort to see to that, because from Stanton's description of the accident it was likely they were a mess when they'd arrived. He'd witnessed a much less serious accident once, and it had been bloody enough. He didn't want to think about what this one must have looked like.

"Their worries are over," he said, a bit more harshly than he'd intended, because it hurt so damned much.

Briony looked up at him at last, and he saw the sheen of tears in her eyes, a sheen that made them seem even more green than usual. She drew in a long, deep breath before she spoke.

"But ours are just beginning."

Chapter 4

Briony watched Greg toy with the keys on his key ring. She knew when he'd found the right one, because he clamped his fingers around it as if it were trying to escape. Or maybe he just needed the pain of the metal digging in to distract him. She could understand that.

They'd left the hospital together in his truck. She wasn't even sure why, since now her car was stuck back there. But he'd suggested it, and somehow the idea of staying together for this heinous task seemed much more preferable than driving to Wendy and Rick's house alone with her thoughts. At least with Greg there, she'd feel compelled to hold herself together. Without him, she was afraid she'd fly apart into a million pieces. So here she was in his truck, trying not to stare at the rifle in a rack above their heads.

For the first time she let what had been brewing under the surface since they'd learned it was really true bubble up to the surface. Justin and Jane. They were going to have to try and explain to a four-year-old and a fourteen-month-old that their parents weren't coming home.

Ever.

And what would happen to the kids now?

One thing at a time.

Owl Creek was quiet this time of the morning anyway,

but this time of year especially so. It was still dark, the first hint of light not arriving until after 6:00 a.m., and full sunrise not until nearly eight. Snow season and hence ski season would not really arrive until next month, when they went from maybe an inch or two to a foot or two of accumulation.

Briony had called Mrs. Matson when they were on their way. The woman told them she could stay until noon, if necessary, before she had to leave to see to her own family. She knew them both, at least, and knew they were the kids' godparents, so had no problem about them coming for Justin and Jane.

Briony remembered with a jab of agony the day Wendy had asked her to take on that title.

"First thing, we are *not* trying to force you and Greg together again," she'd begun.

"I'm glad. I'm not his type, and vice versa." She'd managed to say it evenly, and—she hoped—to hide any trace of the lie that was on her part. Because she'd always thought Greg Colton one of the most attractive men she'd ever met. But clearly the feeling wasn't mutual, and she wasn't about to set herself up for that kind of humiliation. Again.

But that didn't stop her from being delighted Wendy had found such joy in her life. Even if it wasn't in the cards for her, her kind, wonderful sister-by-choice deserved it.

"That said," Wendy had gone on, "we want you two to be the kids' godparents."

She'd been pleased. Flattered. And thrilled to have a special part in her best friend's children's lives, even if it was mostly ceremonial.

Or was supposed to have been.

"Damn." Greg said it softly, more in the tone of somebody who'd just thought of something than anger.

"What?" she asked.

"I just remembered something. Rick gave me an envelope to keep, back after Justin was born. Then after Jane came along, he asked for it back and gave me a new one."

She tilted her head slightly. "What was in it?"

"I don't know. He just asked me to keep it locked away, and…only open it if something happened to him." He sucked in a long breath before adding, so bluntly it startled her, "If he died."

Briony's breath caught. "You don't think he expected something to happen, do you?"

"He was a little…odd about it," Greg admitted, "but I think it was a just-in-case kind of thing." He frowned slightly. "But it was also something he didn't want only in digital form."

"Could be a few reasons for that," she said, but it still made her edgy.

She studied him for a moment, in the faint light inside his truck. In profile he was just as handsome, jaw strong and masculine, his nose straight and perfectly shaped. And as they stopped for one of the few traffic lights in town, she saw him close his eyes. It was for barely more than one second, but it was enough to draw her gaze to the thick, dark brown sweeps of his eyelashes, something she'd always thought unfair when she required mascara to get even close to that. But right now, all she could think was that he was hurting just as much as she was, and that his blunt statement about Rick dying was probably just him saying it out loud, trying to get his mind to accept it. She'd done that herself, after all.

"Do you think you should look at it now, before we go to the children?"

He glanced at her, an almost startled look. "I was… kind of thinking that, yeah. Not sure why." He grimaced. "Maybe I'm just stalling."

She was a little surprised he'd admit that, but then realized she shouldn't be, because on top of everything else, he'd always been one of the most honest people she knew.

"I think it's a legitimate concern," she said. "Maybe there's something in there about the kids you should know first."

The light changed, but in the moment before he looked away and hit the gas, he gave her a smile that was both sad and grateful at the same time.

"Yeah," he said as they rolled through the intersection. "Maybe. So you don't mind if we stop at the ranch first?"

"As long as they don't mind how early it is."

To her surprise he let out a short laugh. "It's after six now. Dad's likely been up and at it for an hour already, and most of the hands almost that long."

"Does he know where you went?"

He went silent, then nodded. "I left him a note. He'll cover what I'm supposed to be doing."

"With time out for cooing over the new baby horse?"

This time the glance and smile he gave her were better, more solid. "Yes. Lily is really his girl, and he's been looking forward to this foal a lot."

"Good thing you were there to help, then."

"I'm just glad I realized what was happening in time."

"Do they do cesareans on horses?"

"They do, yeah, but since the birth had already started, the foal would have been dead by the time we got a vet out. But he—"

He broke off suddenly. She saw his jaw tighten, the muscles there jump a little. As if he were biting back fiercely whatever he'd been about to say. She started to speak, then hesitated. What did she know? Either about what he'd been through last night, before the news came about Rick and Wendy, or how he was feeling now?

He and Rick had had that kind of guy relationship she'd sometimes admired. Even if they hadn't spoken in a month, the other would be there at the drop of a hat if needed. She always felt as if she had to stay in touch constantly or be forgotten. Or maybe be reminded no one much cared if she was around or not.

Except Wendy. Wendy had always cared.

Memories flooded her, and somehow converted to a literal flood from her eyes as the tears won out again. She quickly swiped at her eyes, hoping he hadn't seen her about to turn on the waterworks again. She swallowed, steadied herself, and when she thought she could get the words out, spoke quietly.

"There's nothing wrong with welcoming a new life, even as you have to say goodbye to others."

His head snapped around sharply. "How did you...?"

So she'd been right. She'd taken the chance, and she'd been right. It was a nice feeling, amid all the pain. "You just looked as if you were feeling bad that the baby horse you saved made it, when Rick and Wendy didn't."

He looked back at the road ahead. They were out of town now, in the countryside and headed north. Then, in an almost wry tone, he said, "For a quiet little thing, you're pretty observant."

"Maybe I'm observant because I'm quiet."

This time when he gave her another look, it was a kind one. "Point taken."

She realized with a little jolt that this was likely the most time she'd ever spent alone with him. She'd always thought of him as gruff and hard to read, but that was with the knowledge that she sucked at reading, understanding or having any kind of close relationship with anyone. Wendy was her sole true friend, and Rick had accepted her as that and always been incredibly kind and welcoming, but Briony knew that was because of Wendy.

She'd known the two had found such comfort in each other, Wendy who'd been orphaned even longer than Briony, and Rick, whose father was the worst kind of grifter, tied to that awful cult thinly disguised as the Ever After Church. Rick had cut off all contact with his father a decade ago, and she could only imagine the kind of inner strength that had taken. But he had especially not wanted the man anywhere near his children and had made sure it never happened.

Maybe that's what whatever was in that envelope was about. Making sure it stayed that way, even if—

She cut off her own thoughts sharply. It wasn't an "if" anymore. It had happened. The impossible, the unbelievable, the horrible had happened. Wendy was dead. Dead.

She wondered if she repeated it in her mind enough, her mind would wrap around it, process it, accept it. Ever.

"Briony?"

She gave a little start. "What?"

"Are you okay?" He seemed to instantly realize how that sounded under the circumstances and added, "Aside from the obvious, I mean?"

It was a question she would normally answer with a short, "I'm fine." Because she knew people who asked that generally didn't really want to know. At least, not about her. But Greg was in the very same boat she was, so maybe he really was interested.

"I'm just trying to batter my brain into accepting the reality. That she's gone. They're both gone. Really, permanently gone."

"Hope you're having more luck than I am," Greg said, sounding exhausted. "At this rate it'll be summertime before I get used to using the damned past tense."

"Yes," she said, fervently. "Exactly."

A strange sort of warmth blossomed in her, at a time she would have least expected it. The warmth of knowing it was true, that he was in the very same boat, and so was interested in how she felt. More interested than he ever would have been before, anyway. Odd how knowing he was having trouble with this, too, knowing this wasn't her pain alone, made it...not easier, but a tiny bit less overwhelming.

Briony had only been to the Colton Ranch once, for a surprise birthday party Greg and Wendy had conspired to throw for Rick. She'd helped a little, although not much since it had been tax season and she'd been buried, but she hadn't actually set foot on the ranch until that day.

And she'd been overwhelmed.

She was used to open spaces—this was Idaho, after all. And she loved it, loved the quiet, the expanse of trees and rolling hills up to mountains, and always had. But there was something different about this big, sprawling ranch. Maybe it was the difference between it being a grand vista you enjoyed and a vast expanse you were responsible for. The very idea of being responsible for so much land, let alone the animals that grazed upon it, was nearly over-whelming. There was a reason she'd bought her compact, tidy condo in town. Eight hundred square feet was a lot easier to handle than eight hundred acres, which is what Greg had said the ranch was.

But when he'd followed that up with "So, not that big," she'd choked on her lemonade.

He'd laughed. "Hey, big is twice that. Texas-big would be four times as much acreage."

He was grinning at her, all his usual gruffness vanished on this day of celebration for his best friend. And of all the times in her life when she'd been laughed at, this time she was certain it wasn't really aimed at her. And looking at his smile, and the way that trace of a dimple appeared, then vanished, she felt a rush of all those feelings she thought she had successfully quashed. All those feelings that had had her fantasizing about working up the nerve to suggest they get a cup of coffee or something sometime.

Then you'd find out what it's really like to have him laughing at you.

No, she'd run from that idea, determined not only that she would never make that move, but that she'd never even think about such folly again.

So she'd just listened to him explain they were more of a custom provider, of beef and produce. His dad, he'd said, had the green thumb to end all green thumbs, and loved tinkering around with all kinds of plants to get the best possible yield, in both quantity and quality.

"We don't have the longest growing season, so what he's done is amazing," Greg had said, and there was no way to miss the love and pride in his voice. What it must be like, to have a father you loved so much…

It was a longer drive than she remembered from the gate to the house. But the building looked the same, a three-story block painted barn red, with a deck built out over the patio on the bottom level. And off to one side, some yards away, was a smaller building painted in the same color, which Greg had mentioned that day was the guest house where he lived.

"You want to come in?" he asked. "It'll only be a minute."

She hesitated, then said, "Yes, please." She did want to and was honest enough to admit it wasn't just that she didn't want to be alone just now, but also curiosity about where he lived.

"You're still in the guest house?" she asked, nodding toward the secondary structure as they slowed.

"Yeah." He gave her a sideways look. "I love my brothers, but all of us under one roof…not so much." Then he let out a compressed breath. "Although Max isn't around much anymore. He's usually with Della."

"Wendy mentioned recently…he really quit the FBI?"

He nodded as he pulled up to the shed that she guessed served as a garage. He didn't pull into it, probably because they'd be leaving again soon. "Says it ain't what it used to be, and the bureaucracy running it was wearing him down."

"I can imagine. Every year the IRS about kills me off—"

Her breath caught, audibly. Her eyes stung, and she couldn't even swallow past the sudden lump in her throat.

Greg turned off the engine and twisted in the driver's seat to look at her. "Funny, isn't it, how many of our common sayings are linked to death," he said in a steady tone that helped her steady herself.

"Too many," she managed to get out.

"Because it's the shadow that hangs over us all."

And that was an almost poetic philosophical observation that she never would have expected from the gruff, sometimes laconic cowboy.

Chapter 5

Dad came out of the barn before they were even out of the truck and headed toward them. Greg suspected he'd been listening for them.

"Is that your dad?"

He'd forgotten Briony had never met him. "Yes. I'll make it quick," he added as he walked that way, as if he sensed her nervousness.

"I'm fine," she said, and he wondered it was a real "fine" or one of those ones that meant the exact opposite. But then Dad was there, his gaze skipping from him to Briony and then back again.

"It's true?" he asked, his voice a little rough.

Greg nodded. His father swore. Then, in a very Buck-like move, he pulled them both into a powerful hug.

"I'm so sorry, both of you. I know how important they are to you."

For a moment Greg closed his eyes, taking in the comfort this man had always been there to offer. He sensed Briony's stiffness, and felt a pang that, like Wendy, she had grown up without this heartfelt kind of support he couldn't imagine living without.

When Buck let go, he looked at them both in turn again. "If there's anything you need, anything I or anybody on the ranch can do…"

"I know, Dad," Greg said.

"I'll see to your chores as long as necessary, so don't even think about it. And when you're ready, I'll make any calls that need making, if you want."

Greg heard Briony make a tiny sound, and guessed she hadn't even thought about that yet, that there were other people that were going to need to be notified.

"Thanks, Dad."

"You're heading for the kids?"

He nodded. "I just needed to pick something up first."

"All right. Bring them back here, if that seems best. We can keep them entertained until things settle."

Greg only nodded. He didn't think he could say another word about it. So instead, he shifted gears. "How's the foal?"

Buck smiled then. "Oh, he's gonna be a terror."

"Up on his feet?"

"Yep. Within an hour after, and he's already nursing like a champ. And curious. Very curious."

"Good. I'm glad."

"It's all thanks to you, son. Now, get what you need to do done. I'll keep the phone handy in case you need some help. Don't hesitate."

They were almost back to his place before, very quietly, Briony spoke.

"I get it now."

"Get what?"

"Why you're...you."

He turned his head to look at her. Who else would he be? He must have looked puzzled, because she spoke again, just as quietly. "I mean why you're so nice, so kind, and do things for people, even though you refuse to take any credit for it."

He blinked. That was a heck of a compliment. From someone who was usually so restrained she almost seemed frightened sometimes. Wendy said she was just shy, but he hadn't had much experience with that.

Then she glanced back toward the big barn, where his father was just going back inside. And he understood. No one raised by Buck Colton would be shy and uncertain. They'd know their value, their worth, from childhood. And he felt a sudden need to give his dad his due.

"He's the only reason any of us made it to adulthood relatively sane. Our worthless mother bailed on us when I was ten. My sister, Lizzy, was only three. But Dad stepped up. He made it clear from the day he told us she was gone that he was here for us, that he loved us, that he'd…die for us. And we all knew he meant it. I think even Lizzy knew it. Or she did by the time she was five and Dad took a rattlesnake bite for her."

Briony gasped, her green eyes widening. As if the very idea astounded her. And not for the first time Greg said a silent thanks that it had been that worthless woman who'd abandoned them, that she hadn't managed to drive Dad away with her faithless betrayal of vows she'd apparently never meant. Buck was their rock, and Greg couldn't— didn't want to—imagine their life without him.

"Your mother," she began.

"No," he said bluntly, taking the two steps to the porch in one stride. "I don't talk about her. She's cold, totally self-centered and not worth the effort."

He yanked the door open and held it for her. For a moment she didn't move, then she stepped inside. He followed, then went past her.

"I was just going to say that maybe her leaving was…the best thing that could have happened," Briony said.

He'd been headed for the desk that served as his office space but stopped now and turned around. That surprised him, coming from a woman who'd never known her mother at all. He would have thought she'd consider any mother better than none.

"I think it was," he said honestly.

It hit him then, somewhat belatedly, that she had lived the life Justin and Jane were facing now. A life without parents. They were so young—would they even have any memories of them? Justin, maybe, but Jane? He didn't know enough about kids' development to even guess.

"We've got to make sure they know." He said it under his breath, but Briony heard him.

"Know what?"

"Know Rick and Wendy. How much they love them. Loved them," he corrected to past tense, hating that one single letter could change their world.

"Yes. Above all, they need to know."

He gave a short nod, then turned and walked to his desk. He'd purposely put the thing in the small, fireproof box in the back of a bottom drawer, the box that held his own important documents, a picture of his mother from back when he'd thought she loved them, and a couple of other mementos—including a locket he'd bought for Jill when he'd thought they'd eventually be getting married. Before she'd told him life on a ranch was not for her, but if he'd move to the city with her, she'd think about it. He'd been, or had convinced himself he was, so in love with her that he'd actually considered it. Until he found out the city she meant was Los Angeles, and she had Hollywood dreams.

He'd kept the locket as a reminder. Some people just weren't cut out for ranch life, and it was foolish to think they might change.

Why he kept the picture, he wasn't quite sure.

He bent and yanked the drawer open. The heavy metal box slid forward, and he was able to just pick it up.

He pressed his left thumb—his right one didn't work because of the scar that slashed diagonally across it from that day as a kid when he'd gone to help his dad free a calf who'd gotten tangled in a thorny hawthorn bush—on the fingerprint reader, and the box latch released. He reached in and lifted everything on top, until he could grab the envelope on the very bottom. He hesitated, not wanting to do it, wanting to do anything else, to deny it was necessary, to relegate all of this to the realm of nightmare.

If wishes were horses…

He yanked it out, slapped the lid of the box shut and locked it, then slammed the drawer shut. He straightened up, staring at the envelope as if it held something horrific. He could feel it held something heavier than paper, and remembered thinking it must be a key or something when he'd first shoved it in here, over a year ago. After Jane had been born.

"The thing you never wanted to open," Briony said. He looked up to see her staring at it much as he was.

"My dad wrote a couple of these," he said.

Briony drew back slightly. "He did?"

He nodded. "To his family. When he was in the army. They recommended it whenever troops were headed into a combat zone. The army kept it, to be added to their effects if…it happened."

She was still staring at the envelope. "I suppose when you have kids, you have to think about things like that, even if you're not military or law enforcement."

"Yeah."

Silence spun out for a long moment. Finally, very gently, Briony asked, "Do you want me to open it?"

He looked up at her then, and their gazes locked. Pain spoke to pain, and it was as if a conduit had opened between them. He could feel her pain, and he saw in her green eyes, shiny with tears, that she felt his.

"Yes," he said roughly, "I do want you to open it. But… no."

It made no sense to him even as he said it, but Briony looked at him as if she understood completely.

With one of the greatest efforts of his life, he slid a finger under the envelope flap and peeled it open.

A key fell out. No identifying information, no tag, just a number stamped on what looked like brass. He assumed the explanation was on the single sheet of paper. The one he dreaded looking at.

Now's not the time to become a coward, Colton.

He looked down at the front of the envelope. Saw the familiar scrawl, his name on the front. Had a sudden flash of memory, of a night long ago spent here at the ranch house, him and Rick wrestling with a tough homework assignment. Well, tough for ten-year-olds, anyway. They were supposed to write a story. About anything they wanted, but it had to have a beginning, a middle and an end, and be at least three full handwritten—computers hadn't yet invaded elementary schools—pages. They'd wasted at least half an hour complaining about the assignment. It was stupid! Write about what? How were they supposed to just make it up? Three whole pages?

It was Dad who'd gotten them started. He'd listened to their complaints, then made a suggestion.

"Why don't you pick something you'd like to do, and write about what you think would happen to someone who did it?"

That had gotten them started. Greg vaguely remembered

his own story about a guy becoming a Major League Baseball player and how he'd hit the home run that won the World Series. But he remembered very clearly Rick's story. It had been much less grandiose, consisting mainly of one thing.

He ran away from home and went to live with his best friend's family.

He remembered seeing his father's face when he'd told him about Rick's short story. He'd looked incredibly sad.

"Next time you and your mother get into it," he'd said, "think of this. To some kids, this is paradise."

He'd tried. He really had. But his mom was so…flaky sometimes. No matter what they did, no matter what she had, it was never right or enough. Secretly, and a little guiltily, he'd admitted he much preferred his aunt Jenny, whom they all called Mama Jen. How twin sisters had turned out so differently he didn't know. He only knew Jen was warm, kind, generous and loving, and his mother was…that flake.

And about a month after they'd done that assignment, she was gone anyway. Out of their lives for good and with barely a word, even to Dad. Dad, who had kept them together, from him down to three-year-old Lizzy, who'd been so bewildered by the change it had taken Dad, him, Malcolm and Max to keep her anywhere near calm.

Little Justin and Jane had had a different start, with two loving parents who'd adored them both. But now both those parents were gone. Forever. And he'd lost his best friend.

He hadn't even realized how rapidly he was blinking, how close he was to breaking down like a blubbering fool, until Briony was there, putting a hand on his arm and squeezing gently. She knew this pain. She'd been as close to Wendy as he'd been to Rick, if not closer. He remembered thinking once how amazing it was that either of the two women were functional, given they'd grown up in much worse circumstances than either him or Rick.

They might never have gone along with Rick and Wendy's efforts to match them up, but right now they were sharing this great, ripping pain, and that made him grateful for the support.

And at last he did it, slid the single page out of the envelope. A page covered with that familiar scrawl.

Dear Greg,
Well, hell. You weren't supposed to be reading this, unless maybe before my funeral years from now. But here you are, so I gotta think the worst has happened. I'm doing this by hand so there's no question about who wrote it. There's a list of stuff on the back of this, details and such. But now...

First things first: Thanks for being my friend. You know my life was a little wild growing up, and with your mother you can relate. But you were always there for me, and I hope I was for you. I need you to thank your dad for me as well. He was as close to a real father as I ever got, and compared to mine he's a saint. But you know that. Hanging out with you, at school, at the ranch, wherever, was the only taste I ever had of normal. And that was thanks to you and your dad. If I've been the slightest bit of a good dad to my kids, it's because of you.

I know I don't have to ask, but if you're reading this and I'm gone, look out for Wendy. She'll be devastated, and this is the last thing she deserves after her rotten life. (Quite a little nest of the wounded we've developed, isn't it?) When the time seems right, tell her I tried so hard to make sure nothing like this ever happened to her. Guess I didn't try hard enough, because here you are. But you of all people know how careful I was, because I knew I had to stay alive and healthy for my family.

My family. Yeah, there's the big one. The biggest ask. See to them, will you, Greg? I know it's a hell of a burden to dump on you, but you're the only one I know who's both strong enough and generous enough to do it. And I know you will, but that doesn't mean I'm not sorry about it. But you know the bottom line:

No Way In Absolute Hell is my father to get anywhere near my kids. Period.

I don't think I can say any more without getting ridiculously schmaltzy, so I won't. Just know I never had a brother except you, and I used to wish endlessly it was by blood.

I loved you, bro.

Rick

Greg knew he was swaying on his feet but couldn't seem to help it. He could barely breathe, nor swallow past the huge lump in his throat. He felt the trickle down his cheek and couldn't even muster the energy to swipe at his eyes. He was going to stand here wobbling and crying, and he couldn't do a damned thing about it.

And then Briony grabbed him, hugged him fiercely. She didn't say anything, just held on, so tightly he doubted he could have broken free.

He didn't even try.

Chapter 6

Briony knew one thing Greg didn't about the letter he held. It had been Wendy who'd told Rick to write it. Just in case.

"You and I, we talk so much you already know everything," she'd said when she'd told her about it. "But guys… they're different."

"That they are," Briony had agreed, rather wryly.

"Next to Rick, Greg's the best man I've ever known. I wish you two would—"

She'd cut her friend off there, not wanting to get on that merry-go-round again. Greg wasn't interested in her, and she understood why. He was so gruff and she so shy, they could probably spend an entire evening together without saying a word. But then, most of her evenings were spent in silence, as she was engrossed in her main passion, reading. It had been an escape for her when she'd so badly needed one as a child, and the kindest adult she'd known while in foster care had been the librarian down the block.

But that didn't matter now. Nothing mattered except that the letter he'd just read had nearly put this strong, steady man on his knees. She could only guess at what he must be feeling inside to let so much show on the outside. And for him to let her hold him like this, even hug her back, as if he was grateful for the human touch. Maybe he was.

It probably wouldn't matter who it was; right now he just needed some human contact. For that matter, so did she. As far as pain and grief went, they were in this together.

She didn't know how long they'd been standing there when Greg finally moved again. Let go of her and turned the page over to look at the list Rick had mentioned. Briony read it with him.

1. The key's to our safe deposit box. Our will is there, along with the kids' birth records and our own documents. You're on the access list. The name of our attorney who drew up the will is there, too. She's good, and smart, if there are any questions.
2. The insurance policy is in the deposit box, too. It's pretty big, and should cover anything the kids need, up to and including college if they want to go.
3. Bank account info is on either of our laptops, in a password protected file labeled "Trust No One." The password is the last name of your and my favorite teacher mixed with the name of your dog at the same time, the cattle dog, alternating letters, and bracketed with the year we graduated high school split into two parts.
4. I know I said it in the letter, but I'll repeat it here. Do whatever you have to but keep my father away from the kids.

"His father's really that bad?" she asked. Wendy had told her Rick had no contact with him at all, but said even she didn't know all the details, only that he hated the man and was better off without him in his life. It was peculiar to her, to think that someone might actually be better off without a parent, and now she'd thought it twice. She'd spent so many years thinking her life would have been so different if either of hers had wanted her.

"Rick always said he was a grifter, as crooked as the Kickapoo River."

She blinked. "The what?"

He looked away from the paper for the first time. "It's a river in Wisconsin."

"A crooked one?"

"Very. And Rick just liked the name."

She smiled, although her eyes were stinging again. "That sounds like him. Did you know he was the one who wanted both the kids' names to start with the same letter?"

He drew back slightly, giving her a quizzical look. "No. Why?"

"He thought it would help remind them they were connected, and to always be there for each other."

Slowly, he nodded. And repeated her words. "That sounds like him."

A shout from outside, someone yelling to someone about an open gate, snapped her out of the sweet but painful thoughts. She glanced at the clock that sat on his desk, an old-fashioned analog version. It fit the eclectic furnishings that looked as if they'd been chosen for function over form, with no real concern about matching pieces or style. It suited him, she'd thought when they'd first come in. Of course Greg would care more about how well something served its purpose than what it looked like while doing it.

It was nearly 7:00 a.m.

"We should go to them," she said. "Be there when they wake up."

"If they aren't by now, with all the fuss and phone calls," he said, but he was already moving.

She followed him back through the living area of the

house. Noticed what she'd missed in the rush on the way in, a bookshelf on the far wall that was crammed full, including some books lying sideways atop the rows on the shelves. Rick had once teased Greg about reading but she'd thought it was a joke, meaning he didn't. Obviously it was not.

It was silly, and she knew even as it happened that it was probably an escape mechanism her mind was using to avoid thinking about the reality to come, but an image formed that was so vivid it took her breath away for an entirely different reason. It was a revised version of the thought she'd had earlier, of indulging her passion for the written word. This time, an image of her in her favorite reading chair, and in the chair opposite…Greg, as deep into a book as she was.

She shook it off and picked up her pace. He was already at the door.

Back in his truck, they were out to the state route before she broached the subject that was now beating at her.

"How on earth do you explain this to kids so young?"

"I don't know. I'd say we should talk to somebody and find out, but that would really be stalling."

She thought for a moment. Then said, "Maybe we shouldn't immediately tell them. I mean, they're used to us being around, maybe we can just be there, take care of them like it's nothing unusual, then during that time maybe research or talk to someone about how to go about it."

There was silence as a big rig passed them going the other way, the headlights lighting up the cab of the truck. Lighting up Greg, showing her once more just how good-looking he was. As if she'd ever forgotten. She also saw that his right hand was resting on his leg, curled into a tight fist.

A white-knuckled fist.

After the cargo truck had safely passed them, he looked at her. "That's a good idea."

She felt pleased all out of proportion to the words. Because they came from him.

Danger zone!

She'd once sworn to herself she wouldn't be caught alone with him, because she needed the buffer of Rick and Wendy, or at least one of them, so she wouldn't do or say anything stupid.

One more thing lost in the tragedy of tonight. A small, minor thing compared to the rest, but still, another weight. For her, anyway.

I loved you, bro.

The last line of Rick's letter rang in her head. The past tense sliced at her painfully.

She and Wendy had said it often, almost every time they parted. *Love you, girl.* With a hug. And sometimes they'd done as Rick had done, calling each other sister because that's how it felt.

From what little she knew about guys, that's not something they said to each other, except under extreme duress. Like now. She could only imagine how it must feel to him to see it in writing, when it could well be the first time it had ever been said.

They lapsed back into silence. Briony noticed his still-clenched fist, now bouncing on his leg, as if he were trying to punch himself. It hurt just to look at. And before she thought, before she could talk herself out of it, she reached out and wrapped her fingers around that fist.

He froze. His fingers were still curled tight against his palm, but the hitting himself stopped. He didn't pull his hand free. He didn't look at her. In fact, she had the strangest feeling he was purposely not looking at her. Her innate uncertainty rose in her, and she wondered if he was imagining someone else holding his hand. She knew he'd gone out with the owner of a coffee shop in town couple of times a while back. And Wendy had told her of some years-ago love where they'd come close to making it permanent, but it hadn't worked out.

"Rick says she expected him to leave the ranch and go with her to some big city," Wendy had said.

Briony remembered laughing out loud at that, at the idea of Greg ever leaving the Colton Ranch. Even she knew better than that. And the idea of Greg Colton trapped in a world of concrete, asphalt and high-rises was almost laughable. No, he was a man of the outdoors and open spaces and always would be.

She thought of the story he'd told her about last night, and the abnormal delivery of the foal. No city boy would have been able to deal with that. And the fact that it was him they'd run to when it happened spoke volumes about his standing at the ranch.

"Sometime soon you should take the kids to the ranch like your father said. Show them the new baby. I bet they'd like that. Especially Justin—he's so aware of animals now, and he's fascinated by them."

It was a moment before he answered, and she wondered what he was thinking. As usual. The only thing she was sure of was that he hadn't yet pulled his hand free of hers.

"Including spiders?" Greg said, his tone a little too neutral. "Like you, that day at the lake?"

She gaped at him. "I can't believe you remember that!"

She saw his mouth quirk at one corner. "It was...unforgettable."

It certainly was for her. She knew she would never forget the time when, on a picnic with Rick and Wendy and at the time baby Justin, Greg had reached out to touch her hair. Her heart had leaped; he'd never made a gesture like that before, as if he…cared. She'd held her breath, trying frantically to decide what to do.

But a moment later, dangling from a silken thread in front of her eyes, was that spider. That he'd clearly just plucked from her hair.

"And humiliating. I shrieked like a banshee."

"You did. And it was just a garden spider. They're actually kind of pretty, with the stripes."

"Did you actually use *pretty* and *spider* in the same sentence?"

"I've become a lot more tolerant of them lately. Had an ant invasion a year or so ago. Real tiny ones. I got tired of having to clean them out two or three times a day. Didn't want to use poison, because Pacer—my brother Malcolm's dog—likes to come in and inspect every corner. Then a spider showed up, and I decided to give him a shot. Two weeks later, pfft. No more ants."

Funnily, what struck her most was his concern about his brother's dog. Not that it surprised her; she knew he was that way about all animals. Apparently even spiders.

"Is that his search-and-rescue dog?" she asked.

He nodded. "And he's the perfect combination. He's got the tenacity and the protectiveness of a German shepherd, and the nose of the hound that's his other half."

She hesitated a moment before asking, not wanting to bring the subject of death front and center again. But then she realized it still was right there, even if they weren't talking about it. In fact, she was fairly certain all this normal-sounding chatter was in fact trying to put a buffer of sorts between them and the reality they hadn't processed yet. So she went ahead.

"How is he doing, after…his fiancée died?"

Greg's jaw tensed slightly. "About how you'd expect. And being Malcolm, he blames himself."

"But…he went into the lake after her, didn't he?"

"Not fast enough, according to him."

She sighed. These Colton men certainly carried heavy loads and added to those burdens by taking on responsibilities that weren't really necessary or theirs.

She managed not to look back over her shoulder at that lake. And lapsed into silence, sorry now she'd asked. Especially since he'd pulled his hand free of hers and put it back on the wheel.

Greg drove on, steadily, smoothly. Interestingly, she often got a bit carsick when she wasn't the driver, but not with him. He was that smooth. When he started tapping his finger on the steering wheel she wondered if he was still thinking about his brother, or if he was back to their chaos. Then he startled her.

"I bet Justin would like fishing spiders."

She blinked. "He would?"

"Sure he would. How could a kid possibly not like a spider that can walk on water?"

She stared at him, certain he must be joking. "Walk on water?"

"And dive under the water, too. I read all about them after I saw my first one as a kid, at a pond on the ranch. They've got hairs on their legs that don't get wet, so when they—"

He broke off suddenly. She saw his hands had tightened on the steering wheel as he stared out the windshield. She looked the same direction, away from him, only then realizing how intently she'd been watching him.

Then she saw where they were. Approaching the turn to the street Rick and Wendy lived on.

And they couldn't put this off any longer.

Chapter 7

"Unca Greg! Aunt Briny!"

Somehow the pronunciation that had always made him smile—Justin had always dropped the *L*, and found the *I* and *O* combination hard to pronounce—made his eyes sting yet again. The first time it had happened Briony had laughingly told them all she didn't mind sounding like a salty old sailor. Greg remembered the day she'd said it, and how they'd all laughed. He'd wondered then about how she was so at ease with them and yet so quiet and shy around anybody else.

And now the whole world was different.

Justin's face lit up and he scrambled down from his chair—the higher one with the ladder side he and Rick had built for the boy so he could sit at the big table after he'd graduated from the high chair his little sister was now sitting in—and ran toward them. Greg tried his best for a smile as he bent down to the boy, who threw his arms around his knees. He picked him up and hugged Justin back, his throat once more so tight he could barely breathe.

He was aware of Mrs. Matson, the older woman who lived two houses down, watching them all, and could see the sheen of tears in her warm brown eyes. Her own kids were teenagers now, and she'd insisted she was glad to help Rick and Wendy out with the little ones, since she so missed that stage.

Justin leaned out from where Greg held him against his side, reaching with one little hand toward Briony's face. She took the proffered hand and kissed it with a loud smacking sound that made Justin giggle and Greg smile even through the pain.

A sudden burst of noise came from the table, a babble of sounds and coos and a couple of almost intelligible syllables, punctuated by a couple of solid blows to the tray of the high chair. A glance told him Jane had already wearied of being ignored by the new arrivals.

"I'll get her," Briony said, and went to lift the tiny girl into her arms before the recently introduced sippy cup went flying. They'd deduced she was By-By and he was Geg, also a fairly recent development.

First people she's "named" after Wendy and me. You should feel honored.

He'd laughed when Rick said it, at Jane's one-year birthday party a couple of months ago, and he had bowed to the baby in his friend's arms with an elaborate flourish. Jane had giggled delightedly at him, and he'd felt an unexpected sense of…well, honor.

And now, here they were, and…Rick and Wendy weren't.

It seemed both more impossible and more real at the same time, here now with the kids in their arms. It wasn't that this was unusual; he'd often ended up playing with Justin, easier for him than entertaining Jane, which Briony appeared to have a knack for, probably because she had no problem getting silly with the baby talk. Not that she talked baby talk per se, she used perfect English, but did it in that baby talk tone that seemed to delight the tiny girl.

His usual approach with Justin was to ask him questions. He'd pretend ignorance, point to something he knew the boy knew and ask what it was. Justin was thrilled to be able to teach this adult something.

"'S'a bird!" he would trill when Greg pointed at a robin.

The same response came that day on a picnic near the lake with the Krafts when he had pointed at a bald eagle overhead. Greg had felt compelled to add, "A very special bird."

"Why?" Justin demanded.

He remembered that day in particular, because after his explanation to the boy about power and grace and national symbols, he'd looked up to see Briony smiling at him warmly.

And when Justin had run off to play catch—as much as a four-year-old could—with Dad, Wendy had plopped down beside him.

"You forgot to mention they mate for life," she said teasingly.

"Like you and Rick?" Briony had asked.

"Exactly," she'd answered.

And there it was again, grabbing him by the throat until he thought he might pass out from the lack of oxygen.

Because Rick and Wendy had indeed mated for life. A life that had been cut short far too early.

"Unca Greg?" Justin said, snapping him out of the reverie, but not the pain. "Are you sad?"

He didn't want to lie to the boy. He might not know how to deal with this, but he was pretty sure that was not the way to start out.

"I am," he admitted. "But we'll talk about that later, okay?"

"'Kay," the boy said, and went back to his favorite subject, that someday soon they were going to get a dog.

Greg knew Rick had been talking to Sebastian Cross about maybe taking on any pups he got in at Crosswinds Training that looked like they'd be more suited to the family pet job than search-and-rescue, but as far as he knew talk was as far as it had gone.

"You could—" He had to stop, swallow and try again. "You could come see my brother's dog, Pacer, at the ranch."

The boy had been to the ranch before, but it had always been when Malcolm and Pacer had been off working.

"Is that the looking dog?" Justin asked.

It took him a moment. "The search-and-rescue dog, yes."

"He finds lost people," Justin said.

"You got it. He does, along with my brother."

That idea seemed to intrigue the boy, and he began to pepper Greg with questions, interrupted only when Briony came over with Jane in her arms.

"Hi, Aunt Briny," the boy said.

"Jane insisted on saying hello to Uncle Greg."

"Geg," Jane corrected immediately, sounding pretty insistent for a fourteen-month-old.

To his surprise Briony laughed. He could hear the strain in it, though, and realized she was working as hard as he was to put on a united, normal front, until they figured out what to do, how to tell these two innocent, happy, loving souls that their world as they knew it had come to an end.

After a few more minutes of chatter and interaction, they put the kids back down at the table to finish their breakfast. And finally, reluctantly, they drew back into the kitchen to talk to Mrs. Matson.

"It's really true?" she whispered, as if she were still holding out hope.

Greg closed his eyes for a brief moment, opened them again and realized he'd answered her without saying a word.

The tears overflowed, and the kindly woman turned away so the children would not see.

"I've told them nothing," she whispered. "They think they're coming home this morning. But I have to get home soon… You'll stay with them?"

"Of course," Briony said instantly. "Thank you for taking care of them."

Mrs. Matson nodded, then glanced at the table, where Justin was zooming his spoonful of cereal around like an airplane, while Jane started banging her own thankfully empty spoon against the sippy cup. "I just can't believe it. But Rick and Wendy trusted you so completely, I know you'll see to them properly."

"We will," Greg said, his voice still gruff. He would have tried to clear his throat except he knew it wouldn't do any good. He was afraid that lump was going to be there for a while.

After she'd gone Greg and Briony stood there looking at each other. They glanced at the children, then looked back at each other. Greg had never felt so lost. When his mother had abandoned them, he'd felt mostly anger. Maybe because he was the oldest and it fell upon him to help with his younger siblings.

Plus, he'd always known there was something…off with his mother. He had just been too young to realize what it was. He knew from hearing his classmates at school complain about their own mothers that what they'd experienced at home bore little similarity to what he had. He'd had a loving, understanding, patient parent, but it had been Dad.

He felt the sudden urge to call the man, ask for help, but it was a bit too humiliating to do it this soon. There would be enough time when they got some sort of sense of…anything.

But right now, here with Briony, godfather to godmother, he felt like he had to admit it. "I don't have a clue about this."

She drew back slightly, and there was an edge in her voice when she said, "You think I do?"

He knew she meant how she'd grown up. And she was right. At least he'd *had* one loving, involved parent, which was one more than she'd ever had.

"I didn't say that," he pointed out.

"Sorry," she muttered. "A little touchy."

"And exhausted, if you feel anything like I do."

"You have more reason," she said, and her tone had shifted to something much gentler. "You've done nothing but deal with emergencies all night."

He let out a compressed breath. "I have a feeling I should be thankful right now that I'm too tired to...feel much."

"We should both be thankful," she agreed. And yet she had to swipe at her eyes again, indicating she was indeed still feeling. He resisted the urge to reach out and help her wipe the tears away, although he wasn't quite sure why. They were in this together, and they had to handle it together, didn't they? Because he didn't think either one of them could handle it alone.

But he didn't want her to get upset with him again, so he thought about the words before he said, tentatively, "I think we're really going to have to pull together on this. Neither one of us knows much about this, but together, maybe we know enough to get by. At least until things are settled."

"Settled?"

"Meaning we have a chance to get and read the will. Knowing Rick, he spelled out exactly what he and Wendy want to happen."

She nodded, slowly. "I'm sure they did. And just so you

know now, they did ask me to be the financial executor, for the…life insurance for the kids."

He nodded, not in the least surprised. She was not only a trusted friend but an accountant, after all—Wendy had told him that after growing up in chaos Briony liked numbers because they were predictable—so it only made sense, and with her history he could understand that. He was glad she'd told him now. And wondered if Wendy had said anything else to her, about…those kinds of plans. Rick hadn't gone much beyond "I know you'll be there for them." Which was, of course, true. He'd do whatever he could to help.

Briony looked back over at the kids, where Justin was now just about to launch a spoonful of his cereal at his sister. Greg saw it in the same moment and swooped in to stave off the impending mess. Not knowing what else to do he grabbed the spoon from the boy, zoomed it around a bit as Justin had been doing, then popped the bland, too-liquid-for-his-taste cereal into his own mouth. And managed not to grimace at the blandness of it.

"Yum!" Briony said, loudly.

And suddenly both kids were giggling. He found himself grinning at them. Briony got another spoon from the drawer where the kids' smaller utensils were, and handed it to Justin.

"Nicely done," she said, glancing at Greg.

"Crisis number one averted," he said with an eye roll.

He could only imagine how many more there would be before the weekend was over.

He didn't want to imagine what would come after that.

Chapter 8

"I can officially state I have never been more exhausted in my life," Briony said as she collapsed onto the couch. "And it's only eight o'clock."

"At least they're both in bed," Greg muttered as he dropped down onto the next cushion. She saw him start to put his feet up on the coffee table, then stop.

"They wouldn't mind," she said quietly. "Rick puts his feet up there all the time." It was the first time she'd been able to get the name out without choking up, which she suspected could be attributed more to exhaustion than acceptance.

"It wasn't that," Greg said, sounding almost as weary as she felt. "I'm afraid if I get too comfortable, I'll fall asleep right here."

She appreciated the admission that he was as tired as she was. Although since he was used to a lot more physical labor than she was, it had to be the stress wearing on him as it was her. Plus, she suddenly remembered, he'd been up half the night anyway, helping that mare.

So he's spending his whole weekend—did ranchers even have weekends?—helping babies in trouble...

That didn't surprise her. Rick had always said Greg was the most solid guy he knew. That from age ten, when their mother had abandoned them, he'd helped his father see to the younger Coltons, even if he was only two years older than the next one, his brother Malcolm. He'd been especially good with—and protective of—the littlest, his sister, Lizzy, who had been a year younger than Justin was now.

She'd always wondered what it must have been like, to have a big brother who stood with you. Or a father like Buck Colton, who stepped up and then some when necessary. But at least she'd had Wendy, and they—

They weren't *they* anymore. It was just her. Alone. Wendy was gone, forever. The friend, the sister of the heart who had helped her survive, was gone. She was on her own, from here on, however long her own life might be.

And how selfish can you be, worried about that when Rick and Wendy are dead and their children—your godchildren—are orphans?

But in that, at least, she wasn't alone. Not completely. The man sitting a couple of feet away was in this with her, was her fellow godparent, and as Rick had often said, a friend so rock solid you could build a fortress on him. She'd known it was true. It was probably why she'd developed that silly little crush on him. Well, that and those big warm brown eyes and that wide flashing smile and the occasional great laugh. Never mind the rest of him, that tall, strong, powerful rest of him, honed to near perfection by the hard work of ranching.

But she was past that now. She'd gotten the message quickly when Greg kept chuckling at Rick and Wendy's efforts to match them up. He wasn't interested, and that was totally understandable. She was a painfully shy, boring accountant, and he was...Greg Colton.

"I used to think Wendy was joking when she talked about doing a load of laundry every day." Greg's tone was rather sour, and when she glanced at him, she saw he was staring at the pile they'd accumulated near the entrance to the hallway that led to the bedrooms and the laundry room.

"I'm just thankful they aren't using cloth diapers," she said. "That pile would be twice as big."

His eyes widened, as if the thought had never occurred to him. "And three times as smelly."

She let out a short chuckle. "That, too. Although I'm not sure they even still make cloth diapers."

"They do," he answered, and at her surprised look he shrugged. "Dad uses them to polish his car."

That made sense; they were probably perfect for the task. And then, because she couldn't seem to resist asking questions about him when the chance to do so without seeming pushy arose, she asked, "But you don't for your truck?"

He looked, surprisingly, a little embarrassed. "I did, when it was new. But it's a work truck, and how it runs is more important than how it looks."

"It looks fine," she hastened to say. "I just wondered when you find the time to keep it as clean as it is, with all you do at the ranch."

"Sometimes I just hose it down to get the big chunks off," he said, in the tone of a rueful admission. "And try to keep the inside decent."

"I noticed."

She had; the cab of the big pickup had had things in it, like a toolbox and a couple of other things she didn't recognize, but it also had a small trash holder that held the usual detritus she'd seen strewn about in other vehicles. She remembered thinking once that it showed that he cared more about what he lived in than what the outside world thought of what he lived in. She'd liked that idea. But back then she'd still been working on that crush…

He got up rather abruptly, and she had the feeling he'd

issued himself an order. He headed for the pile of dirty clothes, bibs and towels, swept them up in one motion, and headed into the hallway. By the time she got to her feet she heard the sounds from the laundry room. It was clear he had no problem tackling the job. She was curious about how he went about it so followed him.

Face it, you're curious about everything he does.

You're curious about him.

Which seemed odd, given how long she'd known him. But that was as Rick's best friend, and all their interaction had centered on that. She had, she realized with some surprise, spent very little time alone with him, despite Rick and Wendy's machinations.

Because you're a coward. And you know he doesn't want that anyway, and never has. Stop thinking about it!

And again she felt a horrible upswell of guilt, dwelling on herself at a time like this.

You have to think about yourself, Bri. Nobody else has in your life, ever.

You have!

Because you're my sister.

She teared up again at the remembered exchange, the first time Wendy had used that word to describe them. Sisters. She fought it back, knowing that the best thing she could do for that sister now was to see to her beloved children. She took in a deep breath and spoke as normally as she could.

"Want some help sorting that?"

He turned his head from where he was tossing things into the washing machine. "I gave up on sorting things long ago." He went back to the task, but added, "Except red. If there's something red, I pull it out."

And suddenly she was smiling, and more amazingly,

meaning it. "Spoken like someone who's wound up with pink underwear."

His head snapped around again. Then, slowly, an answering smile curved his mouth. For the briefest moment that dimple flashed, and it made her own smile widen. "Yeah," he said, sounding sheepish. For a long, silent moment, he held her gaze. Then, quietly, he spoke. "We'll get through this, somehow."

She only nodded, afraid that anything she might say would be far too colored by that "we."

Then, suddenly, he moved, and to her shock pulled her into another hug. A supportive hug like the others, she warned herself, even as she thrilled to the feel of his arms around her, his tall, strong body so close.

"We will," he insisted. "We'll do it for them, because… because…"

Words rose unbidden to her lips. "They were a gift to us both."

His arms tightened, and she thought she heard him whisper, "Yes." As if she'd found the words he couldn't.

And that was how this was going to have to work, each of them doing what the other couldn't at that particular moment. And together, they would get it all done.

They had to.

But she still savored the feel of this a bit more personally than she probably should have.

Chapter 9

"You survived the day, then." His father's voice coming through his earbud didn't sound relieved, but as if he'd only heard what he'd expected.

"So I hear. Not totally convinced, myself." Greg answered his father with an echo of the man's own knack for grim humor. "I don't know how you did it alone, with four of us."

"You can do a lot more than you think you can when there's no choice and there are people you love at stake."

Greg's throat tightened a little. It was becoming a familiar reaction to…well, just about everything. "Thanks, Dad."

"Just a little fatherly advice."

"I wasn't thanking you for the advice. I was thanking you for following it, all those years ago."

There was a moment of silence, which Greg counted as big points scored. It wasn't often his father was left speechless. So before Dad could dissemble or deny, he went on.

"How are things there? How's the new colt?"

"Already poking his nose in everywhere. Perfectly normal. You got it done, Greg. And in time."

He felt that burst of pride and accomplishment only his father's approval could spark in him. But he knew thanking the man again would just get brushed off.

"I'm sorry you're having to pick up the slack."

"Don't worry about it. What you have to do right now is more important. We'll still be here when you get back."

He didn't know how long he'd been standing there after the call ended, staring out the kitchen window at the Krafts' spacious backyard—notable for the various play outlets—when Briony's soft voice from close by almost made him jump.

"Everything all right at home?"

"Yeah," he said. "I was just…thanking my dad. For being there. For always being there."

"Good."

It was all she said, but her tone was utterly sincere. "I'm sorry…that you don't have a dad to thank. Or a mom."

She shrugged. "Given they dumped me in a dark alley at midnight when I was six, I was probably better off."

He stared at her. "They…what?"

She nodded, as casually as if she'd just confirmed her eyes were green. "I don't remember a lot about my time with them, just lots of fights. And when they weren't fighting it was because they were drugged up, although I didn't realize that until I was older."

He swore under his breath. How had he never known this? He'd known Wendy's folks had died in a freak storm when she'd been the same age, because Rick had told him shortly after he'd met her. That she'd come out so amazing was a tribute to her strength, Rick had always said. But while he'd known Wendy and Briony had met in the foster care system, he'd never known how Briony had ended up there beyond that she'd been abandoned.

"Just as well," she said with a shrug. "From what little I know about them, they probably would have sold me to some sex trafficker if they got desperate enough for drug money."

He was gaping at her now. He'd thought he'd had problems as a kid? Dad would have killed anyone who tried to hurt any of his children. And while his mother had apparently gone full cultist with that evil group that had recently been discovered around town, at least she'd never threatened any of them. She'd just…vanished, leaving them with their father. Their loving father, who would protect them unto death.

"How," he asked wonderingly, "do you not begrudge any and everyone who's had even a slightly normal life?"

"And what, exactly, would that accomplish?" she asked with another dismissive shrug. "Besides, normal can turn into abnormal at any moment. You know that firsthand."

He shook his head slowly. "My mother behaved irrationally. But Dad didn't. He was a rock. And still is."

Briony nodded. "I can see that clearly, now that I've met him. You were lucky there."

"Beyond lucky," he agreed, more fervently now than ever. But as he studied her, noticing not for the first time how her hair gleamed redder in the direct light, and how that with her bright green eyes made her look as if she'd be at home in the hills of Ireland, he inwardly chided himself. "How did I not know this about you? We've known each other since…since…"

"Rick and Wendy hooked up, yes." She gave him a wry look. "It's not like I tell everyone. In fact, Wendy's the only one who knows the whole truth."

He heard her tiny, sharp intake of breath. He saw her lips tremble in the moment before she spoke again, and he knew what was coming.

"*Knew* the whole truth. She's the only one who knew…"

She was visibly trembling. And once more, because he could no more turn his back on her in pain like this than he could have let that foal die, he hugged her yet again.

"I'm sorry," she said, brokenly. "I don't mean for you to have to hold me up all the time, it's just—"

"Shh. Don't apologize. The world's upside-down right now. Our world, at least. And…" He hesitated, but then realized she deserved the truth even if it was a bit uncomfortable for him to admit. "It helps me, too. To know I'm not the only one feeling like this."

She didn't respond, but she moved, her arms coming around him to hug him back. Once again. And after a long silence, she finally did speak again, low and clearly heartfelt.

"They'd want this, wouldn't they? Want us to help each other, be there for each other?"

He thought of Rick, the prankster he'd been as a kid—and the trouble it had gotten them into—and Wendy, who would have backed Rick in anything he tried, and suddenly he was smiling.

"Honey," he said, putting on his best exaggerated drawl, "they probably planned it this way."

He felt her go stock-still, and his mind took off, afraid he'd offended her, that it was far too soon to even try to joke, although he hadn't meant it as a joke but only an acknowledgment of who their dearest friends had been, a couple happy and complete in each other, who wanted the same for their best friends.

But then he felt an odd little jerk from her, almost like a twitch. He looked down, past that thick fall of auburn hair that looked like it would be warm to the touch, and realized that twitch had been a short but definite laugh.

"Yes," she said. "Yes, they would have."

And that easily the mood changed; they went from desperate clinging to mutual support. Her trembling had stopped, and his own mind had calmed, as if it were a horse settling into a steady lope after clearing a big fence.

It was several minutes before he noticed he was feeling a different kind of warmth. A physical kind he hadn't felt in a while. Quite a while. When he realized what it was, he almost jerked away. Instead, with an effort, he let go slowly, and took a half step back, leaning against the front of the sink as if that's what he'd intended to do. And he decided from the way she quickly turned to face the window over the sink that she was glad he'd let go. Maybe she'd somehow sensed that little change and wanted away from him before it got embarrassing. After all, she'd made it pretty clear she thought the idea of them…together was a no-go from the get.

She kept staring out the window. He wasn't sure what she was looking at, out in the yard, since it was nearly too dark to see anything. Yet she seemed focused on…something.

"Spot a moose wandering in or something?"

Her head snapped around. "They've never had a moose here. Have they?"

She sounded worried, and he felt bad. "Sorry, trying for a joke. No, they've never had a moose down here. One out on the road once, but not near the houses out here."

"Oh. Okay. Good. Because knowing Justin, he'd be so curious he'd toddle on over to check it out, and that might not go well." He caught the lighter tone, thought maybe she was trying to make up for missing his joke. Or maybe not. But right now a lighter tone was exactly what he needed, so he went with it.

"A thousand pounds of moose and thirty-five pounds of kid? Nah, no problem there."

She smiled, and it seemed once again they'd beaten back the tide of tension and pain. For now.

"Actually," she said, "I was looking at the…structure out there. Playhouse?"

"We called it a fort," he said. "Rick designed all the

climbing stuff for Justin, but Wendy made us redo the inside so it could be a playhouse for Jane, too." His mouth quirked as she stared at him. "Or the opposite, if that's the way it worked out."

"You and Rick built that?"

He nodded, puzzled at her reaction. "Last year. Although sometimes I think it was more for us, just to do it, since Jane is way too young and Justin is just now getting big enough to be interested."

She gave a slight shake of her head. "You know if you ever wanted something other than ranch work, you could make a living just doing that for families with little kids."

He laughed. "Kids these days are too glued to their screens. Not everybody's as tough on that as Rick and Wendy are." He realized he'd made the same mistake she'd just made, with the present tense. But he didn't make himself correct it and bring it back up front for both of them again. "But I'll never want something other than ranch work."

"You never get…tired of it?"

"I get tired, often. But not in the way you mean. It's my life, and I wouldn't have it any other way. Because for all the times when I've collapsed in exhaustion after a long hard day, there are other times, other things, like bringing that little colt into the world, that make it worth it."

She was looking at him rather strangely now. But not the way city people often did, boggled at the idea of voluntarily giving up taxis on every corner, in front of the Starbucks on the same corners. After all, she'd lived here in Owl Creek for years, at least since Rick and Wendy had been here, and it was hardly a big city. No, it was more in the way someone looked as they contemplated a life unlike their own, but not…despised.

He wasn't sure why that mattered to him, but it did.

Chapter 10

Briony came half-awake slowly, not certain why, not even opening her eyes. Nor was she sure why she felt so comfy and warm. Cozy, almost. As if someone were holding her close, protecting her as she never had been in her life. She sleepily wished that were true, and it was too sweet for her to even mind that the first image that floated through her lethargic brain was Greg.

She kept her eyes closed, wanting to drift back into that wonderful sleep, into that dream built on memories of the best times in her life, times like when she and Wendy had sneaked out to see a movie and gotten away with it, to when she had graduated with her accounting degree and Wendy had thrown her a party, and when—

This time she woke up with a start. To reality. Wendy. And Wendy's baby girl, whose cry had been what had awakened her this time.

"I'll get her."

The low, rough voice came from so close it made her almost squeak, "What?"

"You did it the last two times."

And so she found herself suddenly feeling both stunned and abandoned. Because apparently that cozy warmth, that sense of being held, safely, had not only been real, it had really been Greg. Greg, who had just wiggled out from be-hind her and gotten to his feet—sock-clad feet, she noticed, rather inanely—to head toward Jane's bedroom.

The couch. She was on the couch. And Greg had been behind her, indeed holding her steadfastly in place, and providing that wonderful warmth with the heat of his body.

That lovely, strong, work-toughened body…

The last thing she remembered was them sitting on this couch—on separate cushions—after the third and thank-fully successful attempt to get Justin to sleep. Justin, who was starting to realize just how long his mom and dad had been gone. The questions they had managed to stall were beginning, and she knew that soon there would be no stall-ing, no stopping, that they would have to tell the boy a truth he wasn't even old enough to fully understand. That they were never, ever coming home.

She yawned, stretched and tried not to think of how good it had felt to simply lie here with Greg's arms around her, even though she hadn't consciously realized that's what it was. Had she?

It didn't matter. Nothing mattered except getting through this. There was no room for feeling awkward, as she so often did around him. No time for being flustered, or wor-rying about what he thought of her. They had to work to-gether to get through this, and that meant setting aside everything else. For the kids' sake. For Rick and Wendy, who had trusted them both enough to make them the god-parents of their precious children.

Greg came back into the room, the toddler in his arms. And he was yawning, too. "Didn't they say she was sleep-ing through the night quite a while ago?"

She got to her feet. "Yes. Months ago. Does she need to be changed?"

He shook his head. "I checked." He'd surprised her with that, not being at all hesitant to deal with such things. But this was the guy who'd played obstetrician to a horse just last night, she reminded herself. She wouldn't be surprised if Greg Colton could handle just about anything.

"She shouldn't be hungry yet," Briony said, her brow furrowing as once more she tried to remember all the baby-raising milestones Wendy had so often excitedly told her about.

"It's quiet back there, and I didn't hear anything that might have woken her up," he said.

"Do you suppose she…somehow she…" she began, then let the words she didn't want to say trail away.

"That she senses something's very wrong? I wouldn't be surprised. She's a clever little widget."

Briony had to blink rapidly yet again as he used Rick's common phrase when referring to his baby girl. Fortunately, Greg was busy trying to calm the unsettled child and didn't see.

Jane quieted a bit as Greg sat down once more, although she was still fussy and, as Rick had always put it, squirmy.

"You suppose she's hungry?" he asked.

"Could be. I seem to remember Wendy saying something about trying to get her to sleep later, with no luck."

"Then maybe—" He broke off at a sound from the direction of the hallway. Then he looked back at her, his expression wearily wry. "Was that the sound of another pair of feet hitting the floor?"

"Afraid so," she said. "You hang on to her—she's calmer now—and I'll go get Justin."

As she tried to settle Justin, telling him his sister was going back to bed, too; it was the middle of the night—well, in child scheduling—she heard Greg's cell phone ringtone.

Moments later he appeared in the doorway, one arm holding Jane, the other hand holding the phone up to his ear.

"Where?" A pause, during which he put the now seemingly resigned Jane back to bed. "Got it. On my way."

On his way? He was leaving?

He ended the call and slid the phone back into his pocket. He nodded toward the door, then looked at Justin. "See you in the morning, buddy."

When they were back in the living room, she turned to face him. "On your way?"

He nodded. "That was Chase." He grimaced. "Late-night calls from him are never good news. My brother Max is already on the way, but he needs more backup."

"Backup?"

"Sorry to leave you with this, but hopefully I'll be back here before they even wake up." She didn't know what to say, so said nothing, just stared at him. "What?" he asked.

"You're just leaving?"

"Briony, he needs help. I'll explain it all when I get back, but right now somebody's in trouble so I've got to go."

And then he was gone, headed for his truck. She walked over to the front window, watching him run down the driveway to where it was parked behind Wendy's car with the car seats. He was obviously in a hurry.

Somebody's in trouble so I've got to go.

She had the feeling she'd just seen the Colton family motto. For the good ones, anyway, and Greg was definitely one of those. Rushing to assist when called.

Rushing, but still taking a moment to pull his rifle she'd noticed earlier from the rack in the truck. And she wondered just what kind of trouble he was heading out to deal with.

And suddenly she had a new thing to worry about. And wondered if it would ever stop.

* * *

Greg yawned widely as he practically staggered into Rick and Wendy's house. He wanted nothing more than to crash on that couch again——

His thoughts broke off with a jolt as he remembered how he'd crashed on that couch just hours ago. With Briony snuggled up next to him and his arms around her. It had been… unsettlingly comfortable. Warm. Nice. Okay, more than nice. A lot more.

Belatedly he realized she was there on that couch and was now sitting up sleepily.

"Sorry I woke you," he said. "I didn't know you were there."

She stifled a yawn. "I meant to wait up."

Greg blinked. "Why?"

She stared at him. "Why? You have to ask why?"

"I'm not a mind reader, Briony. If there's a problem, say so."

She stood up, slowly. "I watched you leave," she said, over-enunciating every word, "*after* you checked that rifle of yours. What was I supposed to think except that you were headed somewhere you might have to use it? Is that explanation enough?"

To his own surprise, he found himself smiling. Not at what she'd said, but at the fact that she'd stood up to him and said it. If nothing else she was teaching him that shy didn't necessarily mean weak.

"Chase's new lady——" he said the words with no doubt that they were now true "——got herself in a bit of trouble, asking questions about Rick and Wendy's crash. He needed some help getting her out of it."

"Oh." Her expression changed. "Is she all right?"

He nodded. "Chase wasn't about to let her get hurt." He

didn't feel it necessary to expand on the fact that he and his cousin had in fact gone in guns blazing, in a firefight that had ended with the man who had grabbed Sloan turning his gun on himself. He didn't understand that mindset and was glad of it.

"Did she…find out anything?" Briony asked.

He hesitated, but she needed to know. To be aware. "They don't think the crash was an accident."

Her eyes widened. "What? You mean somebody might have hit them on purpose?"

"It's a definite probability. He and Sloan found a suspect. She's a tech wiz and found a big money transfer to the driver of a vehicle that matches the evidence."

Briony went paler than he would have thought possible. "Is he…?"

"He was taken into custody." He left it at that for now. She didn't need to know, yet, that the man suspected of running Rick and Wendy off the road had in turn been killed while in a jail cell. Before he could talk. This was enough bad news for one dose. Besides, a lot of this was supposition, and he didn't want to put her through the additional pain if it might not be necessary.

She sat back down on the couch as if her legs wouldn't hold her upright any longer. Her next words, stammered out almost helplessly, solidified his decision. "But why? Why would somebody…want them…want that?"

She looked as if she'd already had more dumped on her than she could bear, so he didn't mention that that money transfer had come from an account associated with the Ever After Church, and thus Rick's father.

"They're still digging into that. I promise, when they have the whole story, you'll know as soon as I do."

She buried her face in her hands and looked so broken

sitting there he couldn't stop himself from sitting beside her and putting an arm around her. She moved, and he was afraid he'd made a mistake, but then she leaned into him.

When her head finally came up, he spoke quietly. "Look, I'm really sorry I woke you up. Why don't you go to bed and get some sleep before we have to get up and start again?"

She gave him a long, haunted look, but nodded.

He tried not to think too much about the fact that she'd tried to wait up for him.

And even less about the fact that she'd been worried about him.

Chapter 11

Greg stifled a yawn as the bank VP—Owl Creek didn't run to the big-name banks with tons of staff—pulled up the list for the relatively few safe-deposit boxes they had.

"Your ID, please?" he asked as he typed in Rick's name.

He handed him his driver's license. He glanced at it, went back to the screen, then his gaze snapped back to the license, eyes wide now. "Colton?"

"Yes."

Greg wondered why the pointed reaction. It was true, Colton was a very well-known name in town, but it didn't usually elicit a reaction like that. Lately there had been more dodging his gaze, as the truth had trickled out about his family drama. So why here, now, from this person? Had his uncle Robert bought this building along with all the others he'd acquired over the years?

"Related to Mr. Robert Colton?"

"My uncle," he said, guessing now he'd been right and wondering what was coming next. Some comment about Robert's double life, his cheating, his illegitimate children? Greg still hadn't completely wrapped his mind around the fact that he had two new half siblings. Half cousins? Both? He was too tired at the moment to wrestle with that. Besides, right now the most important thing was doing what Rick and Wendy had wanted.

"He was helpful to this bank," was all the man said. Then, with a suddenly warmer, kinder look, he added, "My condolences on the Krafts. They were lovely people."

When he went back to work at his keyboard, Greg felt bad that he'd suspected worse of the guy. "All right, you're here on the list, you have full access. If you'll follow me?"

He started toward the back of the bank, stopped at a rather heavy-looking door, and pressed a finger to the very modern-looking scanner lock. Greg followed him into a room about the size of the foaling stall he'd spent a lot of Friday—had it really only been two days?—night in. A few moments later he was alone in the room, surrounded by walls containing other boxes, with the box he held the key to on the table before him.

He didn't want to do it. Didn't want to open it, because somehow that would cement the reality of all this, a reality he still did not want to face. He'd never thought of himself as a coward, although he knew he wasn't the kind of hero his brother Max was, or even more so his war-scarred cousin Wade. But right now, he felt like the worst kind of coward, shying away like a skittish horse from simply opening a box.

But he had to do it. And soon. Briony was sitting outside with the kids in Wendy's car—they'd had to bring it because it was the only one they had with the proper child seats—and he knew it had to be horrible for her to be sitting in the car she'd ridden in so many times with her best friend. Not to mention that now Jane was so often wailing "Mama" for the woman who would normally be in that car with them, and Justin was asking more and more questions about where his parents were.

But Greg was the one on the access list for the safe-deposit box, so he had to be the one to go inside. And now that he was here, he couldn't even seem to put the damn key in the lock.

He sucked in a deep breath and made himself do it. The key turned easily, with an audible click when the lock was disengaged. It took another deep breath before he could lift the lid.

What are you going to do with it all?

Briony's question, asked as they were on the way here, echoed in his head now.

Run for the attorney?

Something he'd never thought he'd say. But even he had heard the helpless note in his own voice. It had taken him a moment to get a grip before he could look at her and say what he knew needed to be said.

We'll go together. That's how we have to do this, together. As Rick and Wendy wanted us to.

Her eyes had widened slightly, but she nodded. Decisively. And so here they were.

...do this together.

His own words rang in his ears now, and on impulse he grabbed all the papers in the box, plucked out the business card for the attorney and stuffed the rest into the large manila envelope the banker had kindly provided. He closed the box again and pushed it back into the empty slot on the wall of matching boxes. He slid the key back into his pocket—the man had told him the box was paid to the end of the year—and left the little room.

Moments later he was in the driver's seat again. And the irony of the phrase indicating he was in control made him laugh bitterly. The sound seemed to register even with the kids, because they fell silent.

"Is it bad?" Briony asked anxiously.

Greg shook his head ruefully. "Just feeling sorry for myself."

"You have reason," she said, and the idea that she, too, might be feeling sorry for him stung even more. "I mean, this on top of what's happened with your family already?"

"Right," he said with a grimace.

She was right. In the last six months his powerful and until then respected uncle had died. The respect had been badly damaged by the discovery of his affair with Greg's own mother, producing the two kids she had apparently decided were worth raising herself, unlike him and his own siblings. Then of all things bodies started turning up, serial killings likely connected to some mysterious cult masquerading as a church, and now...did Briony even know the last thing?

He gave her a sideways look that she apparently misinterpreted, because she immediately said, "I'm sorry, it's none of my business, I shouldn't have said—"

She stopped when he held up a hand.

"It's not that. I was just wondering if you'd even heard the latest in my family soap opera."

"The latest?"

He hesitated, but only for a moment. Things had changed. They'd spent the weekend flailing their way through unfamiliar territory for them both. To the point of exhaustion.

To the point of you sleeping with her in your arms, and it feeling so good you didn't want to wake up.

He shoved that unwelcome truth aside, and said flatly, "That my mother, she of the two kids with my uncle, is probably part of the Ever After Church. Cult. Whatever."

She stared at him, lips parted in shock. She hadn't known, then. She let out an audible sound, almost a cough of air.

"Yeah," he said, his tone sour now. "Charming, ain't it all?"

It was a moment before she spoke. "I never in my life thought I might one day be glad not to have a family."

"Family," Justin suddenly said. Both kids had been so quiet—so uncustomarily quiet—it startled Greg. And it also started the Mama wail from Jane, and they were back in the middle of it. "When is Daddy coming?" Justin demanded.

Briony and Greg looked at each other. They knew they could not put it off much longer.

"We'll talk about that soon," Briony said to them in a soothing tone. Then to Greg, "We need to look at this stuff—" she indicated the envelope "—before we go to the lawyer. Sort it, at least."

"Yes, we—"

"Now!" the boy demanded. Jane's wail became louder.

Greg gave Briony an almost desperate look. "Are you above bribing them with evil food? The fast-food place up the block?"

"Not a bit," she said.

It worked well enough that, sitting there in the car as the kids both played with and ate the rare treat of fries and ice cream, they were able to at least sort the papers. Greg set the attorney's business card—she was in Conners, he noted—on the dash as they went through the various IDs and records, the insurance papers, and at last, held together by a binder clip, what appeared to be the will. Greg hesitated, staring at the thing.

Then he looked at Briony. "Should we look now?"

"I wouldn't have a hope of understanding the legalese that's probably in there," she said. "I've never even seen a will."

"I read my dad's. He made me, so I'd know." He grimaced.

"Sometimes being the oldest sucks. But maybe we should look, so when we see the lawyer we'll at least have a clue?"

"Good point," she said.

On that, he turned the cover page. To his surprise there was what appeared to be a one-page digest of the pages that followed, signed by the attorney on the card and both Rick and Wendy. Seeing their names there, in Rick's inimitable scrawl and Wendy's tidy, feminine hand, made his eyes blur yet again, and he wondered if it would ever end. He blinked three times, until the typewritten first page cleared enough to read.

He never got past the first paragraph. He read it three times. Then looked up at Briony. He could guess what he must look like by her reaction, wide-eyed and wary.

"What is it?"

He swallowed, because he had to before he could even think about speaking.

"I…we…" He tried again. "They made us their guardians. Legal guardians. Permanently."

He saw her gaze shoot to the back seat, then back to his face. Saw she understood.

Rick and Wendy had left their children, and all legal and financial authority over them, to Greg Colton and Briony Adams.

Chapter 12

The woman who had come out from behind the big desk and invited them to sit on the couch in her seating area seemed to be studying them both. Attorney Tanya Carlson wasn't what Briony had expected. She'd formed an image in her mind of a quick, sharp, probably dressed to the nines with spike heels shark-type of lawyer. Instead, they'd found a motherly woman, older, clad in a businesslike dress, clearly expensive but in no way flashy. Her makeup was subtle, and she wore no jewelry except a pair of black pearl earrings and a simple gold wedding ring. Her hair was dark, touched with gray that framed her face.

But she had the eyes of a younger person, sharp, quick and a bright, light blue. Eyes that Briony suspected didn't miss much. And eyes that right now were looking at them with a warmth and sympathy she couldn't doubt was genuine. Although Briony had already guessed that, because the woman had cleared her schedule this morning to see them.

"I'm so very sorry. I quite liked the Krafts and admired their dedication to each other and their children."

"They were that." Greg's voice still held that rough timbre, as if he had as big a lump in his throat as she did. Every step they took on this painful path made it more real, more impossible to deny, that Rick and Wendy were really, truly gone.

For a moment there was silence. It seemed odd to her, and she realized it was the absence of the inevitable kid noise she'd almost gotten used to. The attorney's assistant had taken the kids into an adjoining room.

"She's very good with them. Since I deal a lot with family law, it seemed wise to have someone on hand who had the knack. And the playroom is well stocked with toys to distract all ages," the lawyer had assured them.

That had eased Briony's worry about more than just the kids being occupied. Clearly the woman had thought of all the possibilities, which was probably why Wendy had said she was utterly trustworthy.

The woman held her own copy of the document she'd written up and processed for Rick and Wendy. After confirming they were both dealing with the same version of the will, she leaned back in her chair opposite them as she tapped the cover of the document with her forefinger.

"At the time this was written, Rick was adamantly clear the children had never met his father, and he had never even laid eyes on them. To your knowledge, is that still true?"

"Yes," they said in unison, and both with the same certainty in their voice.

They exchanged glances, and Greg gave her that slightly crooked smile she knew so well. She looked away before the memory of the hours spent sleeping peacefully in his arms glowed in her eyes so brightly even he could see it.

"He never wanted them to meet," she said.

"Rick had nothing to do with him," Greg added, "and didn't want the children to have any contact at all. He made that even more clear in the letter he…left with me."

"He did write the letter?" she asked. "Wendy said he was going to, and I recommended he keep it updated."

Greg nodded as he got out the letter Rick had left him. He hesitated, tapping the edge of the envelope against his palm.

"I know it's very personal," Mrs. Carlson said gently. "But I do need to see it."

Greg took a deep breath, nodded and handed it over. "He said no way in hell was his father to get anywhere near the kids."

"That is what he said to me as well." She scanned the letter, her mouth tightening in a way that told Briony she'd meant what she'd said about being truly sorry. "And that was why they officially appointed you as legal and financial guardians to the children." Looking at Greg, she went on. "They said you and your family would be the perfect safety net—" she shifted her gaze to Briony "—and you would be more than capable of handling the financial end, to see that they had everything they needed. You're an accountant, they said?"

Briony nodded. "I have my own business, back in Owl Creek."

"All right." She folded her hands together and looked at them both. "Whenever someone other than a parent is tasked with guardianship, there has to be a formal appointment. I don't foresee any problem with that—Rick and Wendy made their wishes quite clear in both legal and personal documents. Now I know you must have many concerns, so let's go through them."

"We haven't even told the kids yet," Briony said, sounding as shaky as she felt just now.

"I can give you the name of a specialist here in town who deals in this type of thing. But I can say from my own experience, don't expect them to react the way you have. They won't feel the same emotions as you do, because they don't really get what death means. Or forever."

"My dad said just don't lie to them," Greg put in. "Or try to make it easier by saying stuff like they've gone to a better place. Just give them the truth and lots of time to process it."

The woman smiled. "Your father sounds like a very wise man."

Briony was looking at Greg in that moment and saw his smile at the compliment to his father. She felt an old, tired ache inside that she had never known such a thing. But Justin and Jane would. Greg would be like a father to them, and he'd obviously had a great example in his own.

She looked back to the lawyer, afraid she was going to start crying again. The woman was leaning back in her chair again, considering them both. "Are you two… involved?"

Briony blinked and drew back, uncertain what the woman meant. But apparently Greg wasn't.

"If you mean with each other…no." His mouth quirked. "Not that Rick and Wendy didn't keep trying to make that happen."

"I believe Wendy mentioned at some point her belief that you two were perfect for each other, just too stubborn to see it."

If the lawyer was waiting for a startled reaction, she didn't get it. Because Wendy had said that to their faces, and more than once. And Greg had always laughed it off, as had she. *After you saw Greg laughing. Because deep down, you wanted him not to?*

"Too bad," the attorney said, and that did get her a startled look, from both of them. "I just mean that if you were a couple, preferably married, it would make it that much harder for anyone, such as Rick's father, to contest your guardianship."

Briony's breath caught, and she saw Greg's eyes widen.

"He could contest this?" he asked, nodding at the will. "Even when they were so clear he's to have nothing to do with the kids?"

"He is, as far as I know, their only blood relative. That gives him standing. Enough to start a legal action, if he's so inclined. Not saying he'd win, but…"

"I wonder if he even knows," Briony said quietly.

"Fortunately," Mrs. Carlson said, "I'm under no legal obligation to make sure he knows."

"Are we?" Greg asks.

"Do you know how to reach him?"

"No," he answered, then glanced at Briony. She shook her head.

"And you two are the only ones on their emergency contact list?"

"Yes."

"Then I'd say we just proceed. The Krafts made their wishes quite clear, and that should hold up in court if necessary. As far as the police are concerned, they've done their due diligence by notifying you both. But he'll likely hear about it in the news, unless he's a hermit."

"Hardly," Greg said, his tone quite sour. "A hermit can't bilk others out of their money."

She nodded, as if that opinion were no surprise to her. So Rick must have been open with her about his father.

"We'll deal with that if and when it arises. So, I think we're down to one more basic question," the attorney said. She looked from Briony to Greg and back, then addressed them both. "You're willing to take this on? Both of you? Raising two children not your own?"

Briony wondered if Greg had thought about it that way. She honestly hadn't, not about the long term, anyway. She'd been too focused on just getting through the weekend. Opening that door would have left her looking at a long, complicated vista, at a time when it was all she could do to put one foot in front of the other.

Both of you...

That was the one thing that floated to the surface amid the chaos in her mind at the moment. Rick and Wendy had chosen them. Not just her, not just Greg, but both of them together, to raise the children who were the most precious things in their lives. They'd chosen them both, and clearly had expected them to work together to get the job done. And it was Wendy, who had saved her so many times, asking... how could she ever say no? Even if she didn't know the first thing about how a normal kid should be brought up?

But Greg did. Even with his terrible mother, he knew better than she did, because he'd had his father. And siblings. And an aunt he'd told her was more like a mother to him than his own had ever been. It was more than she had ever had. Surely between the two of them they could do this?

And how are you going to feel about all the time together that's going to mean?

She didn't know. She just knew the most important thing right now was that Justin and Jane get her very best, such as it was. It might be hard on her—them—but nothing could match the tragedy those two little ones in the other room were going to have to face, and very soon.

She looked up to find Greg looking at her. As if he were waiting to see what she would say. Did he doubt her, doubt that she'd agree to what her best friend had wanted? Or did he simply doubt she was up to it? She couldn't blame him for that; he knew enough of her history to know she knew very little about parenting, good, bad or otherwise.

She turned her gaze back to the woman in the chair. "I

owe Wendy my life. I will spend it taking care of the children she loved."

Mrs. Carlson nodded, then looked at Greg, who shrugged. "Rick trusted me to do this. I will do it."

Briony felt a little shiver of sensation, because she knew deep down inside that vow, like any other he'd make, was golden. She wasn't alone in this.

She wasn't alone.

Chapter 13

"There are funeral instructions in here."

Greg hit the brakes just before he pulled out onto the street and shot a glance at Briony. "There are?"

She nodded. "It's all…planned. Arrangements made, for back in Owl Creek." She looked up at him. "I had no idea. They were only in their thirties. Who does that in their thirties?"

Greg glanced over his shoulder at the back seat, where Jane appeared to finally be napping and Justin was looking out the side window, seemingly entranced by two people on horseback strolling through town.

"People who have them to think about," he said quietly.

Briony looked at the kids, took in a slow, audible breath and nodded. She slid the papers she'd been looking at back into the envelope and closed her eyes for a moment.

"We need to…get that task we talked about done," he began as he drove Wendy's car out onto the main road.

"The…telling?"

"Yes. I think we should go to the ranch. Dad'll be there to help. And there'll be distractions, like those horses over there."

"And the new arrival?"

He hadn't gotten that far, but nodded. "Yeah. Good idea."

She smiled, although it was a bit wobbly. "I'd like to meet that one myself."

"I'll introduce you," he said, trying to keep his tone light. He didn't want Jane waking up or Justin to start with his questions again. *Where is Mommy? Is Daddy there, too? I want them to come home.*

"So do I," he muttered to himself.

But it wasn't going to happen. He and Briony were on their own, in deep, deep water.

Eventually Justin recognized that they weren't going home. "Where we going, Unca Greg?"

"My house," he answered. "That all right with you?"

The boy perked up instantly. "The ranch?"

"Yep."

"Yay!"

It felt so odd, to hear such a cheerful sound from the boy. The boy whose world they were about to blow up. But he didn't have time to dwell on it because her brother's excited yelp had awakened Jane, who immediately started wailing again. To his surprise Justin tried to calm her, telling her eagerly they were going to see horses and cows soon, and to his even greater surprise it seemed to work. In the rearview mirror Greg could see her staring at her brother but couldn't tell if she was amused or simply puzzled by his excitement.

"Horsey?" Jane said.

"Yes," Justin crowed. "Horseys, an' cows, too."

Jane smiled.

Belatedly Greg realized he should probably let Dad know they were coming, with the kids. He still had his earpiece in and hadn't tried to connect his phone to the car's system, so waited until they were clear of town and pulled over to make the call. He explained quickly but a little vaguely, since Justin was paying attention.

"We'll get them through it, son. Hang in," Dad said. It centered him just to hear his father's steady, calm voice.

As they pulled in through the ranch gate, Justin was almost jumping around—as much as he could in the booster seat he'd recently graduated to—in excitement. Jane was giggling, either at what she was seeing out the window or how her big brother was acting.

When they got to the main house, Dad was outside, waving. And beside him stood a slim woman with short, dark blond hair barely touched with some gray at the temples, dressed in trim-fitting jeans and a blue sweater Greg knew matched her pretty eyes.

"As you can see," Dad said as they pulled to a halt and got out of the car, "I called in the varsity."

"You did indeed," Greg said, pulling his loving aunt into a warm hug before turning to Briony. "This is Jenny Colton, Mama Jen to us, and the only reason any of us are still sane."

"Amen to that," Dad said, heartfelt. Greg looked back at his father, but the man's gaze was fixed on Jen, and he thought how well they seemed to fit together. And not for the first time he had the thought that his father had married the wrong sister. And not just because he'd named his beloved mare after her favorite flower.

As usual, Jen charmed both children within seconds. As a nurse, she had the same knack with patients, inspiring an instinctive—and well-deserved—trust. Justin smiled at her shyly and took her outstretched hand, and Jane allowed her to pick her up and cuddle without complaint.

"While you grown-ups deal with the grown-up stuff, we'll go inside and get some lunch, okay?" she said cheerfully. Justin hesitated, looking back over his shoulder, not at Greg or Briony but at the corral across the way where a couple of horses were looking on curiously.

"We'll go look around in a few minutes, after you eat something," Greg said.

"'Kay," the boy said, looking reassured.

That left him and Briony with his father, who looked at them both consideringly. "Rough morning?" he asked sympathetically.

"You could say that," Greg answered, feeling suddenly weary.

"Where do things stand?" He explained about the funeral plans first, maybe to put off the big hit. "Smart guy," Dad said with a nod. "And responsible. So it all doesn't fall on someone else."

"Yeah." He glanced at Briony, who nodded. He looked back. "Dad?" He saw his father's gaze narrow, and knew he had his complete attention. "They left Briony and me full guardianship of the kids."

If he was shocked, it didn't show. "Not surprising." Dad smiled, and in that smile was all the love he'd always known from this man. "I'd pick you, too."

The protest he'd suppressed broke from him. "But I don't know anything about being a parent!"

"I would say," Briony interjected softly, looking at his father, not him, "you know a lot more than you think you do. You've had a great example."

For one of the very few times in his life, Greg saw his father blush. He could have hugged Briony just for that.

In the end, they took the kids into the barn to see the newborn. Even little Jane was intrigued, watching the colt peeking out from behind his mother as Briony held her up to see.

"Horsey?" she asked, as if puzzled by the newborn's size.

Greg picked up Justin so he could look into the stall, too. "He's little," Justin said.

"Yes. He was just born a couple of days ago," Greg said.

"Do you know what that means?" Briony asked.

"You mean borned like Jane was?" the boy asked.

"Yes," Briony answered. "Not there, and then all of a sudden there."

"I 'member."

Greg was thinking this might be a way into the painful subject, and wondering if that might have been Briony's plan, saying that in the way she had. "Do you remember how she wasn't there, before she was born?" he asked.

The boy looked puzzled. "Before Mommy and Daddy made her?"

Greg couldn't stop himself from glancing at Briony, who looked a bit disconcerted herself. "Yes," he finally answered. "That's what happens before you're born, and… after you die. You're just not there."

The boy's brow furrowed. "Daddy says everybody dies someday, when they're real old, or they get real sick."

So even in this, Rick had laid the groundwork. *Damn, I'm going to miss you, buddy.*

He tried to go on, but his throat was too tight. But Briony stepped in, saying gently, "Yes. Or if they have a really bad accident."

And there it was.

"Oh." The brow furrowed deeper. "Jimmy did that. He lived on our street. He tried to climb on the roof. He fell. He went away and never came back."

"That's what it means to die," Briony said gently. "The never-come-back part."

Greg took in a deep breath, then made the dive. "Your

mom and dad had an accident, Justin. A really bad one. That's why they're not here."

"You mean…like Jimmy?"

"Yes, only in their car. It crashed."

"Where are they?"

Don't lie to them. Or try to make it easier by saying stuff like they've gone to a better place. Just give them the truth and lots of time to process it.

His father's wise words echoed in his mind, and he braced himself. "They're dead, Justin. They died in that crash." It was the hardest thing he'd ever had to say, beyond even confirming to his younger siblings that their mother had abandoned them.

"Mommy and Daddy?"

"Yes. I'm so sorry, Justin," Briony said, hugging Jane as she held her, even though what they were talking of clearly didn't register with the fourteen-month-old.

"Oh." The furrowed brow lasted a few moments longer. Then the boy looked back at the newborn colt. "Can I pet him?"

In that disconcerting moment Greg was very glad Tanya Carlson had said what she had, that the children wouldn't feel the same emotions because they don't really understand what death means. Or forever.

But they would learn. Sadly, they would learn.

Chapter 14

"I find singing generally helps calm them down if they get restless during diaper changes," Jen Colton said as she briskly went about that very task.

Briony gave the woman Greg had introduced so lovingly a wry smile. "Not my singing, trust me. I love music, but got the vocal cords of a crow, I'm afraid."

Jen laughed. "Well, make Greg do it then. He has a marvelous voice."

She blinked. "He does?"

The older woman nodded. "We used to think he'd end up a country music star."

Briony knew she was staring but couldn't help it. She'd had no idea the man could sing.

Jen went on cheerfully. "But he had no interest in that whatsoever. He wanted to stay here on the ranch. This is the life he loves."

After learning what had happened with her husband and her own sister, the long affair that had resulted in two children, and the fact that it had taken Robert Colton's death to bring it all to light, Briony thought it more than a little amazing that Jen held it together so well.

Better than I would.

"I…gathered that," she said after a moment. "And he and his father seem very close."

"Buck?" The woman's eyes lit up, and just as she had when she'd first seen them together, Briony suspected Greg wasn't the only family member close to his father. "Yes. He's close to all his children. They love and respect him, because he gives them the same."

Unlike your husband?

She was finding herself unusually fascinated with the dynamics of this big family. She told herself it was because she had no family at all, so naturally she was curious about one this big and complicated.

When Jen was finished with Jane, they put her down for her 3:00 p.m. nap—Wendy had made sure Mrs. Matson had the schedule and she passed it along—in the portable Pack 'n Play they'd found in Wendy's trunk and Greg had quickly figured out. Then they went back into the big living area of the main house, with its open beams and two-story ceiling Briony found uplifting somehow. She remembered Greg mentioning once that his mother hated living in it because it had once been an actual barn, but Briony found it quite charming.

The pool out back was nice, but she found the surrounding garden even more beautiful, and remembered what Greg had told her, that it was all his father's doing. That he liked to try different plants and had a knack for getting things that normally wouldn't thrive here to do just that.

Greg and his father were in an apparently deep conversation, while Justin was playing with what appeared to be a set of toy horses and cowboys on the floor over beside the front window, out of earshot. She thought again of how Rick and Wendy had limited screen time, wondered if the boy was used to toys that required his own imagination in these days of video games seeming to rule playtime. No wonder he seemed so easily engrossed.

"—as Jen," Greg's dad was saying. "I'd trust her judgment more than anyone's on this."

"Careful," Jen said with a smile as they walked over to the pair, "it'll go to my head."

"Not a chance," Buck said, with a warmth that was unmistakable.

Briony sneaked a look at Greg as he watched this exchange, and by his expression she wondered if he'd had the same thought she'd had about these two. If so, it must seem odd, thinking that about his father and his mother's sister. Not that his mother had any place in this, after what she'd done.

Again, it struck Briony that it was strange that she, who once had wanted a mother, any mother, more than anything in the world, would think such a thing. But even though she'd only met him a few hours ago, she'd apparently already decided Buck Colton deserved much better. As did Greg.

"—funeral."

She snapped out of her reflections and tuned back into the conversation. "The funeral?"

Jen gave her an understanding smile. "As their guardians, it will be up to you if they go, of course."

"Not an easy decision, when they're so young," Greg's dad said.

The kids, she realized. They were talking about the kids going to the funeral. Or not going.

She looked at Greg. "Do you think they should?"

He let out an audible breath. "I don't know. I keep going back and forth between thinking it would be horrible for them now, to thinking it would be horrible for them later if they don't."

"You mean when they're old enough to understand, will they be sorry if they weren't there?" Briony asked.

He nodded. "Even if they don't remember much, will knowing they were there be important?" He gave a slight shake of his head, as if to try to clear it. Then he looked at his father and aunt. "Dad? Mama Jen? What do you think?"

Briony noticed that his father deferred easily to the woman beside him. It was easy to see why; the woman radiated compassion. And as a nurse, she'd had a lot more experience than they had dealing with this kind of thing.

"I think Justin at least should be given a choice. Maybe explain to him this is how we say goodbye, and that it's painful and people will probably be very sad and even cry, but it's also how we show how much we loved them. But he could do his own kind of remembrance at home, if he thinks it would be too scary."

"Reality bites at four," Greg muttered.

"Yes," his father said. "But better that than him always waiting for them to come back."

"Yes," Jen agreed. "And be prepared, they'll be asking you for a long time yet when their parents will come home. Don't sugarcoat it, or they'll misinterpret it or put their own spin on it that could be worse for them than the simple truth."

Briony stared at the three people standing there, marveling at what she was seeing. Simple, solid, unwavering support. An odd emotion flooded her, a sort of longing she hadn't felt since childhood, when she had wondered what it must be like to have a real family.

"Briony? You okay?" Greg sounded worried.

"I'm okay. I just…" She couldn't find the words, so simply said, "I admire you all."

Both his father and aunt looked a little startled but smiled. "Here's an idea," Buck said. "Why don't we come to the funeral, and we'll wrangle the kids? Jen, you can handle Jane, and I'll take Justin, and if they get upset or too restless, we can take them away from it all, so they don't disturb anything or go ballistic on you."

Greg's aunt gave his father an absolutely beautiful smile. "That's perfect, Buck. That way they'll have been there, but not traumatized."

To Briony it seemed the perfect solution. And Greg looked so relieved she was certain he felt the same way.

That, however, did not make explaining it as best they could to the kids any easier. Jane's requests for Mama were almost constant now, and Justin, as Jen had warned, asked more than once when his parents were coming back. The stress of each time having to try to explain the concept of never to a four-year-old was taking a toll already.

The only thing that seemed to distract the kids was visiting the barn and seeing the new colt, so they spent a lot of the afternoon there.

"I was thinking," Greg's dad said now, as they relaxed a little as the children watched the newborn, "we'd name him Wick."

Greg gave his father a quizzical look. "You mean like the movie guy?"

"No," he answered.

Briony sucked in a breath as it hit her, and her eyes widened as she stared at this rather incredible man Greg was lucky enough to have as a father. "Wendy and Rick," she whispered. "Wick."

Buck Colton gave her a smile so warm she didn't know how to feel. And again, that longing for something that could never be, to have grown up with a father like this in her life, flooded her.

"Exactly," he said approvingly.

She looked at Greg, who was smiling now, too. "What I said about him? I understated it."

"Yes," Greg agreed, carefully not looking at the man, "you did. He's even more amazing than you said."

"Okay, it's getting thick in here," his father said, sounding embarrassed.

"Hush," Jen said. "They're right, after all."

For a moment Buck Colton closed his eyes, as if he were afraid of what they'd see there. Or perhaps he was tearing up and didn't want them to notice. Jen reached out, grasped his arm and squeezed. He opened his eyes and looked at her, and for an instant Briony saw the kind of longing she'd once felt for the man's son, before she'd intentionally shut it down, knowing the feeling wasn't returned. But glancing at Jen's face told her that was not the case here. And she wondered what was keeping them apart, other than the chaos that had descended on the family this year.

Buck and Jen were true to their word about helping the children through the funeral a couple of days later, not to mention helping them in between as well. Briony thanked them profusely after the ceremony, knowing none of them would have gotten through it without them. She'd been a little surprised at the number of people who had turned out. There were some who had worked with Rick or Wendy, and even several of the Coltons she'd never met who had shown up simply because Rick had been Greg's best friend. Another example of the kind of family tie she'd never known.

It had been wrenching, heartbreaking, and she'd nearly lost it completely when Greg got up and spoke so clearly from the heart about what his best friend had meant to him. She'd had to fight her own nearly overwhelming shyness to stammer through her declaration of her love for her oldest and best friend, the person who had saved her as a child and been her rock ever since.

Everything after they'd left the small cemetery was a blur to her. And it broke her heart all over again when little Justin ran into the house looking for his parents, even after having just come from their funeral. This was going to be a long, hard haul, and she truly didn't know if she was up to it. But she had to be, for Wendy. She stumbled through the motions, grateful all that was left to do was get the kids down for their afternoon nap, which even Justin, although at the stage of saying he didn't need naps anymore, seemed willing to do today.

When they were settled, Greg came out of Justin's room and dropped down on the couch beside her, although not so close it made her nervous in that way only he did.

"I'm glad that's over," he said with a weary shake of his head.

"Me, too. You spoke beautifully, by the way."

"So did you."

She gave a short laugh. "Hardly. I could barely get five words in a row out."

"It only showed how much you loved Wendy." She managed a smile at that, although it was none too steady. And she was utterly unprepared for his next words. "So, when should we make the move?"

She stifled a yawn before saying, "What?"

"The kids, out to the ranch."

Briony gaped at him. "What?" she repeated, wide-awake now.

"I'll have to rearrange things at my place, but they can stay in the big house until that's done. Dad'll help, and Mama Jen said she would, too. And—"

"Just hold on a minute," Briony interrupted. "What are you talking about?"

He looked puzzled. "The kids. Dad already said it's okay, and a good idea, and you've said you can work from anywhere, so we just need to—"

"You need," Briony said rather fiercely, "to just be quiet for a minute and explain where you got the idea they were going anywhere."

She realized the contradiction after she'd said it but didn't care. He blinked but didn't point out the impossibility of what she'd asked.

"You saw them there," he said, sounding puzzled. "It's obviously the best place for them to be."

"The best place for them to be is here, in their home. Where everything's familiar. They've had enough upheaval in their lives already."

She was a little surprised at herself and how firmly she'd said those words. But she felt strongly about where the kids belonged, and she had to admit it irked her that he'd apparently made this decision without even asking her.

"But at the ranch, they'd have lots of people around, and the animals as distraction and—"

"No."

She said it so flatly he stopped dead. Then, slowly, almost cautiously, he said, "Wouldn't it be harder for them where they're used to…their parents always being there?"

She had to admit, she hadn't thought of it quite like that. But she wasn't going to shirk her part of seeing to her best friend's children by letting Greg handle everything. Rick and Wendy had chosen and trusted them—both of them—and she took that very, very seriously. She would be in this 24/7, just as Wendy had been.

And there was no way she could live on that ranch, entertaining though it might be. Not among all those strangers, even if they did seem kind and well-intentioned. She just couldn't do it.

"If they stayed on the ranch, it would be like they'd not only lost their parents but been sent away from their home."

Greg looked thoughtful and then, surprisingly, echoed her own earlier thought. "I didn't think about it like that." He grimaced. "Guess I need to remember how confused Lizzy was. She was only three when the mother left."

She didn't miss the intonation. *The* mother. So in truth, he did have a more similar experience, that of having then losing, rather than her own of never really having at all. And she was impressed that he'd thought that way. Rick had always said he'd never been a hardnose.

He had, however, made a heck of an assumption about this. And that was something she had to conquer her shyness to confront. It was that important. Still, it took her a moment to be able to say what she needed to say evenly.

"You might also want to remember that Rick and Wendy left the kids to both of us, before you start making decisions without even consulting me."

He looked startled. "But… I saw you, watching them, when they were having so much fun with the animals, especially Wick—" she saw the flash of combined pain and approval at his father's choice of a name cross his face "—and you were smiling at them, so I guess I assumed you'd want them to have that all the time."

"I was glad they were happy, for the moment. But that doesn't change their reality. And that's the biggest change there could be for them. I don't want them to have to deal with leaving the place where they were happy at the same time."

"So…you're going to move into the house with them?"

She hadn't stated it so concretely even in her mind, but she nodded. "I couldn't live there, on your ranch, anyway."

He blinked. "Why not? You said you could work from anywhere, and there's plenty of room in the big house, if you don't want to stay in mine."

"I couldn't. I won't."

"Speaking of making decisions without consulting the other party..." he muttered.

He did have a point. Was he going to argue with her? Her mind began to race. She wasn't sure she could stand up to a determined Greg Colton, and she couldn't deny there would be advantages for the kids to be at the ranch, but she could not be, and she also knew she was right about too much change at once. Knew firsthand.

And then there was the simple fact that never had the differences between them been so starkly apparent. And she was very glad she'd hidden her response to him, written it off as foolish wishful thinking. Why Rick and Wendy had ever thought they could be together was beyond her. They couldn't even agree on what to do.

But now they had to.

Chapter 15

Greg rammed a hand through his hair, curling his fingers to give it a tug, hoping the small protest from his scalp would be enough to help him focus on what would be best, not what he wanted. He'd been taken aback by Briony's reaction, and her resistance to what seemed to him the obvious solution. It was a good life, ranch life, especially for kids. It had kept him and his siblings going after their mother's desertion.

He was also surprised by Briony's almost fierce stance. Ever since he'd known her, Briony Adams had been a shy, retiring sort who went along to get along. Yet now here she was, standing her ground, glaring at him.

"Look, I can't commute from here to the ranch every day, not and get done what needs to be done."

"You wouldn't be with the kids all day anyway, even if they were there," she pointed out. "You have work to do."

"But I'd be there every morning, and I could check on them during the day, between chores. And you could be there—"

"I couldn't." He thought he saw her tense up, as if she were suppressing a shiver. "I couldn't live there, with all those strangers."

"But they wouldn't be strangers, they'd be my family—"

"They would be strangers to me."

Was this part of that innate shyness Wendy had told him about, or something more? Was she afraid of something about the ranch? Or was the thought of being among people she didn't know that terrifying?

Summoning up the patience he'd learned dealing with recalcitrant or frightened animals, he managed to keep the bite to a minimum.

"So you're going to move in and be here 24/7, while I… what, visit now and then? They chose me as a legal guardian, not a surrogate uncle."

"They chose me, too. And I know in my heart Wendy would want them to stay here, in this home they provided for them."

"How can you be so certain?" he asked.

"I just know how I felt every time I got comfortable in a foster home, only to be pulled out and dumped somewhere else to start all over again."

Greg felt a sudden chill. He'd been so focused on the kids, on Rick and Wendy's death—and the stunning idea that it hadn't been an accident—that he hadn't even thought about the fact that she knew a lot more about being orphaned than he did.

He sagged back on the couch, rubbing at his tired eyes. Life had gotten too damned complicated. Bad enough they'd uncovered an apparent serial killer, that some weird cult that had sprung up was connected—hell, his mother was now connected to that cult—but now Rick and Wendy were dead. Probably murdered by a member of that same cult, or someone hired by them, if what Chase's Sloan, the computer genius, had discovered was true. And because of that, overnight here he was, in essence a father to two very young children.

He'd never thought of his life as carefree, not with his

mother abandoning them all those years ago. He'd always felt like he had to step up and help his younger siblings, on top of the undeniably hard work it took to keep the ranch going, considering what they were trying to produce on a fairly small ranch, compared to the bigger commercial concerns.

But suddenly it seemed that way, when compared to hers. Because he'd ever and always had that rock, his father. And his home. Even with all the work, the ranch had been home. Had been a bastion of stability amid the chaos of the mother's desertion. Had been the center, the core of his life. Even when he'd moved out of the big house, it hadn't been far, only the short distance to the guest house. Briony had never had any of that; she'd been forever adrift by comparison. And now the only stable thing in that life, her dearest friend, was gone.

Like this house was for Justin and Jane.

"Please, Greg." She whispered it, and it sent a little frisson of…something through him. "For now, at least. Later, when they've had time to…adjust, maybe it'll be different."

His eyes snapped open, and he met her gaze. Saw the pleading in it, atop all the hurt and sadness. And suddenly denying her, arguing with her, felt a little too much like kicking one of those frightened animals he'd thought of.

"All right," he finally said. "I won't fight you on this… now. But later, we'll reassess."

She looked so relieved he felt his own tension ease a bit. He tried to get his weary brain to think logistically.

"I'll be here as much as I can. We could trade off on weekends, so the kids always have at least one of us and the other can relax a little."

"Relax? Is that what you do on the weekends at the ranch?"

He drew back slightly, staring at her. "Not exactly, no."

He caught the tiniest twitch at one corner of her mouth— funny, he'd never noticed the perfect shape of it before, natural, real—and realized she was teasing him. That she knew perfectly well relaxing and ranching rarely went together. He felt an odd sense of...something, that she had felt confident enough to do that. Or maybe it was simply because she'd won.

He'd clearly made the right decision for her, agreeing the kids could stay here.

He just wasn't sure it was right for the kids.

But maybe she was correct about how this should all happen. If she moved in here, worked from here, she'd always be easily accessible. She'd be there if the kids needed something, or if something happened. And she was taking this on without hesitation, for Wendy.

He drew in a deep breath. Then, with a slow nod, he said, "Rick and Wendy chose both of us, and I won't break that trust. I meant what I said, that I'll be here as much as I can. And if I'm not here and you need a break or help, you call me and I'll work it out."

She nodded. "We need to do this together. Like they wanted."

Her breath caught again, he guessed on the past tense, since he was having the same problem even in his thoughts. "We will," he agreed. "It'll take some time to work it all out, but we'll do it."

"With the least possible upset for the kids. Their lives have already been shattered."

"So we'll pick up the pieces and put it all back together as best we can. It won't be the same for them, ever, but it'll be a lot better than what you and Wendy had."

She gave him a startled look then, as if she hadn't expected the comparison. *Well, it took you long enough to get there, no wonder...*

"I know I'm...odd. About not wanting to be around strangers, but—"

"I get it. At least, I think I do. I just hadn't put it in context before, how you feel now with how you grew up." And he'd never wondered before if she'd been born shy, or if it had been hammered into her by her life and circumstances.

"Thank you, for understanding."

He studied her for a long, silent moment. Almost decided not to say what he wanted to, but then realized that with the kids and everything else, he might never get the chance.

"How long do they get to win, Briony?"

She frowned. "What? Who?"

"All those people who failed you."

The frown deepened. "What do you mean?"

"Don't you ever wonder if you'd be different, about new people I mean, if you'd had a more...normal childhood?"

She drew back sharply. "Like yours, you mean?"

He gave a half shrug. "Sure, my mother was a bi—was what she was, but Dad was solid, strong and always there for all of us. He taught us not just about life and work and values, but about being true to ourselves. And about not letting his poor choice of a wife determine who we became."

She was staring at him now. He didn't usually vomit things out like this, but it seemed important at this moment, so he kept going.

"If you'd had someone like him in your life, maybe everything would have been different. Maybe you'd even be different. But our job now is to make sure Justin and Jane have that. So you may be right about keeping them here, but I'm right about what else they need."

"I didn't argue with that," she pointed out.

"Just making sure we're on the same page."

"We are. If that page reads 'the kids come first.'"

He studied her for a moment, and it hit him what kind of nerve it had taken for normally quiet, shy, withdrawn Briony to stand up to him as she had over this. And that told him all he needed to know. That she meant exactly what she'd said.

The kids come first.

Chapter 16

Briony could see that Greg was tired. Yet he still showed up at the house every day, as he'd promised. Sometimes it was in the evenings, when she could see how worn out he was after a hard day's work on the ranch. Sometimes, when he had a break, he'd show up earlier. Often, he brought food with him, sometimes a toy for Justin or some bright, colorful thing to intrigue Jane. And once, in a gesture that nearly brought tears to eyes she'd thought cried out, he'd brought her a bouquet of flowers. Chrysanthemums, she thought. Not that it mattered, just that he'd done it made her feel… something. Or a lot of somethings.

She herself felt exhausted after only a week. She'd known Wendy worked hard taking care of the kids, even though she joked about it and called it a joyous kind of work. But trying to keep up with the kids and her own work seemed impossible. And this morning as she dragged herself out of the fold-out bed in the den—there was no way she was sleeping in the only other open bed in the house, Rick and Wendy's—she began to wonder if she'd made a huge mistake in insisting they stay here. Began to see the advantage of having other people around as distraction, even if it made her uncomfortable.

Some cold water splashed on her face helped to wake her up, then she headed for a quick shower. She got out and dried off just in time to hear Jane's first wail of the day. As she threw on her robe—she'd made a trip to her condo and packed a couple of bags the second day, while Greg handled the kids—she braced herself for Justin waking up next. With her luck he'd be full of more questions about his parents. Each time it scraped that already raw and bleeding spot in her heart, and she had to remind herself that was because she knew what death—and never—really meant. The children didn't.

And then there was that hammer blow that had made what she'd thought was the absolute worst even more horrible. That it hadn't been an accident at all.

Her phone chimed an incoming text notification. She rubbed at her eyes before picking it up and trying to read.

Greg. And it was from ten minutes ago, when she'd been in the shower.

On my way with reinforcements.

Reinforcements?

She was too tired to figure out what he meant, and too busy dealing with Jane, who'd decided that it was time she did more than just toddle two steps and then hit the floor for a fast crawl. The girl was trying to walk across the entire room and falling too often for Briony's comfort. Then there was Justin, who insisted on dressing himself and emerged wearing an inside-out T-shirt and shorts. In Idaho. In October.

She'd gotten him changed into long pants at least, and to the table for breakfast. Then she picked up Jane and settled her into the high chair. The first thing the child did was look around for something, anything probably, to drop on the floor. She seemed to have a fascination with watching things fall.

A memory struck, and she found herself smiling despite it all as the image of Jane doing just that, dropping a grape from her seat in the high chair and watching it fall to the floor and bounce.

"Okay, Newton," Greg had said to the child as he'd bent to pick up the small fruit. "Want to drop two now, to see that they both hit at the same time?"

Briony had laughed, the first time in what seemed like forever. "Don't give her any ideas."

She was still smiling at the recollection when there was a knock on the front door. Greg was good about that. Even though he had a key as she did, since she was living here full-time, he always knocked rather than just come barging in.

"Daddy?" Justin yelped as his head turned toward the sound.

"No, Justin," she said wearily. "Daddy's not coming back."

She went to the door and pulled it open to Greg. And his reinforcements. She gaped at the sight of Greg's dad and his aunt, who were holding bags of who knew what, and big smiles.

"I…hello. What…?"

She could tell she sounded as befuddled as she felt as she backed aside to let them in.

"The cavalry is here," Jen said. "And we're armed. Toys, snacks and a picnic lunch for later."

She was sure she was gaping now.

"Enough to keep them out of your hair for a few hours, at least," Greg's father said, with an understanding grin.

"Because you both need some rest," Jen said firmly.

Jane, who had started babbling a string of sounds the moment she saw Jen, was now holding her arms out, asking to be lifted out of the chair.

"I'd better get her," Briony said, "or she'll start drumming on that tray and you won't be able to hear yourself think."

"I'll get her," Jen said. Within a moment she had the tiny girl cooing in her arms.

Greg smiled as he shook his head in wonder. "She's a miracle worker."

"You'll get no argument from me," his father said, before bending to greet Justin, who was looking up at him with the utmost interest.

Briony and Greg exchanged a glance, and she saw that he was thinking what she was, that there was more than just friendship here. Or at least, there could be, if they'd allow it.

"We'll be off. Won't be back until dinnertime," Buck said.

"Which we'll bring with us," Jen added.

"So you two," Buck added almost sternly, "get to bed."

He seemed to realize instantly what that sounded like, and his eyes widened. Jen saved him from further embarrassment by laughing charmingly and saying, "How you choose to follow that order is up to you. Bye!"

And then they were gone, the four of them, leaving her with Greg in a suddenly quiet house. She stole a glance at him. He was looking at the door his father and aunt had just left through, looking bemused.

"They're…quite something," she said, desperate to fend off any jokes about what his father had said.

"Yes. Both of them."

"Apart and…together."

He looked at her then, one corner of his mouth quirking. "Yes. And I kind of like them together."

She smiled at that. "Do you think they…would ever…?"

"I can only hope," he said.

"And your brothers, and sister?"

"Pretty sure they feel the same."

She lowered her gaze. "It must be…interesting. All that family, I mean."

"That's one word for it," he said dryly. Then, in an entirely different tone, he added quietly, "I wish it was something you'd known."

She didn't know what to say, knew he'd meant it kindly, but it was a useless wish. As she knew too well, having wished it for so long herself. She started to turn away, to go back and clean up the breakfast mess. Greg turned at the same moment and they collided. She tensed, intending to immediately pull away, but couldn't seem to move. Memories of the hours on the couch, with his arms surrounding her, holding her safely, flooded her with remembered warmth.

In the moment she wished she had the nerve to hug him, he put his arms around her.

"We're going to make it through this. We have to, for the kids."

She was savoring the feel of this and was a little late to speak. "I know," she finally got out.

…you two get to bed.

She was glad he couldn't see her face. Embarrassed that the reason he couldn't was that it was buried against his chest. Yet he didn't pull away, didn't end the embrace.

And she didn't know how to feel about that.

Or about the fact that, when he finally let go and told her to go get some sleep, she wanted to ask him to take his father's words literally.

Chapter 17

Greg sat for a moment, his head resting on the steering wheel of his truck. It was gut-wrenching, every time. Justin had clearly bonded with him, judging not by the toddler's—was he still a toddler at four and growing fast?—glee whenever he arrived, but by his heartbroken sobs whenever Greg had to leave. But leave he had to, to go back to his other life. The only life he'd ever wanted. Or so he'd thought.

When they were all together under Rick and Wendy's roof, it felt…oddly right. He and Briony had figured out some things, how to deal with the kids' fussing and occasional tantrums, how to distract them, even how to make them laugh. Justin, for instance, was a builder in progress. Or maybe an artist of sorts, given the last thing he'd constructed with his snap-together blocks looked pretty much like a castle. And he'd swear Jane was a budding physicist at least, as she continued to drop things from her high chair and watch intently as they fell to the floor. She seemed to be more intrigued by the things that bounced, which unfortunately included her plastic sippy cup, resulting in more messes to clean up than he could remember just now.

But it was still always tension-inducing, for him at least. He was much more comfortable when he took them back to the ranch, which he was going to do tomorrow because Briony had a big account she had to finish some work for, and she couldn't afford to be late. He'd wondered if that was why Jane seemed more drawn to Briony, if it wasn't just a female to female thing, but brains that worked alike, with numbers and such.

That thought recurred to him early the next morning, as he was pushing hard to finish the absolutely necessary work so he could get over to the house and pick up the kids. And on impulse he gathered up a few things and stuffed them into his jacket pocket before he left.

He got there in the middle of breakfast, which, to his surprise, Briony had expanded enough to feed him, too. Since it was pancakes, who was he to say no? Justin chattered away delightedly from the moment he arrived, only once veering into the questions that had no answers he could understand.

When they'd finished, he helped Briony clean up while Justin ran to his room to get dressed, but when she went to lift Jane out of the high chair he asked her to wait a minute. He went over to where his jacket hung on the rack by the front door and reached into the big pocket. Then he came back and pulled out one of the chairs so he could sit eye to eye with the girl who had officially, Briony had said, earned the name of toddler now, since she'd gotten to where she could walk several feet before plopping. And Greg had been quick to realize that their reaction to those plops determined whether the landing resulted in tears or laughter.

But now she was looking at him curiously. "Geg," she said, and he rolled his eyes at her. She giggled.

He put the things he'd gathered this morning on the tray. The child's eyes widened as she looked at all the round objects.

"Okay, Newton, go for it," he said.

When Jane looked uncertain, he reached out and took the

one that would have the most extreme reaction, the Ping-Pong ball. He held it out to the side, where she always did when she dropped things. He made sure she was looking, leaning to the side, before he dropped it.

She squealed with obvious delight as the ball bounced nearly halfway back up, then shorter bounces as it headed away. He went for the almost perfectly round stone next, which merely hit, bounced once, and stayed. Jane looked perplexed then. Then the golf ball, which bounced maybe half as high as the Ping-Pong ball had and rolled only half as far.

Jane was ahead of him then, grabbing the wooden ball he'd made himself this morning, dropping it and watching intently. It bounced a couple of times, then rolled, but crookedly. Then she was at the marble, which bounced twice, then rolled the farthest of all.

The little girl squealed again, her hands clapping together, then stretching out, reaching toward the floor.

Greg gathered all the round things and put them back on the tray. Immediately Jane began dropping them, one by one, watching them until they stopped moving before she went to the next.

"Wow, she has patience. I figured she'd want to drop them all at once," he said, speaking obviously to Briony but still looking at Jane.

When he got no answer, although Briony was standing right there, he glanced at her. She was staring at him, the oddest expression on her face.

"What?"

"You thought of this?"

"Yeah, this morning. I just grabbed whatever I could think of—well, except the wooden one, I had to sand that down from a wood chunk—because I thought she might think it was fun."

"You were obviously right. She's having more fun with those than any of her fancy toys."

He smiled at that, feeling inordinately pleased. "Small victory, but right now I'll take 'em where I can get 'em."

She looked as if she was about to say something, seemed to think better of it, and said only, "Thank you for taking them today, so I can finish this job."

"You're the one doing most of the grunt work."

"At my own insistence," she said, sounding as if she almost regretted it. "But you're the one having to drive here and back all the time."

He shrugged. "No choice. My work can't be done from anywhere else."

Again, she looked as if she was about to say something, and again stopped. But by then Justin had come back, dressed, Greg noticed, in his little jeans with his shirt buttoned up, albeit off by one button. He'd pulled on lace-up boots, although the laces were untied and flopping on the floor. The boy stuck one foot out, clearly expecting Greg to tie it for him. Glad the boy hadn't stepped on one and taken a header, he quickly tied both laces snugly. The shirt he let be, figuring it wouldn't matter at the ranch.

Even as he thought it Briony bent down to fix the shirt.

"You started one button too low," she said as the boy watched her.

"Oh," Justin said.

He looked up at Greg, who shrugged yet again and said, "I would have mentioned it if we were going somewhere where anybody cared."

Briony froze for an instant, then finished the rebuttoning. When she straightened up her face was flushed.

"I suppose you think I'm being too fussy. Too controlling."

He shrugged once more, this time only one shoulder. "I figure it's just your organizing brain."

"It doesn't…bother you?"

"Why would it?"

"It does some."

She said it in a way that had him thinking it wasn't just some, but many. "Maybe it doesn't bother me because I know how you grew up. It's no wonder you wanted to control what little you could."

She stared at him. "Did Wendy tell you that?"

He looked at her, puzzled. "No. I just guessed. If I'm way off, I—"

"No. You're exactly on. It was the one thing I could control, the only thing. Where and how the few things I owned were placed."

"Makes sense."

"But hard to live with for some people. The whole 'a place for everything and everything in its place' thing."

He grinned at her suddenly, and for some reason her eyes widened. "I should turn you loose on our tack room. It could use some organizing."

It was a moment before she said, "I'd be happy to, except I don't know anything about…tack? That's the horse stuff, right? Saddles, bridles?"

"I'll bet you could learn it in ten minutes, and have it organized in an hour. Rick told me you did the garage." Since she seemed a bit sensitive about it, he made sure his tone was light, teasing. "He told me you interviewed him for twenty minutes, then whipped it into shape perfectly."

She actually blushed. "I needed to know what he used most, and what things were usually used together. Then I went from there."

"See, that's the kind of thing we need. The hands tend to just toss things when they're done and tear the place up when they can't find something."

"Are we goin'?" Justin's rather plaintive question cut off the discussion.

"Right now, buddy," Greg said, picking the boy up easily.

A small scramble ensued as they gathered the things needed for even a short trip with Jane, then the child herself. And soon he was pulling out of the driveway, once more in Wendy's car with the car seats. They'd agreed that's what they'd do for now, whoever had the kids used her car, at least until they figured out what they were going to do long-term.

Long-term.

As in from now on.

He still hadn't quite wrapped his mind around that.

Chapter 18

Once they were gone, the house seemed almost preternaturally quiet. Briony had thought she'd relish a pause in the chaos, but instead she stood in the living room as if at sea. She knew she needed to work, but for a moment all she could do was stand there. Stand there and think about that moment that had momentarily taken her breath away.

That grin of Greg's had lost none of its impact since the first time she'd seen it, when Rick and Wendy had decided it was time their best friends met. They'd prepared a picnic at the lake for them all.

Rick had cracked a joke about something; she'd been too far away to hear what. But that grin had seared across the space between them like some heat-seeking—and dispensing—missile, aimed at her. Their gazes had locked, just for a moment, but that had been enough. She'd stood there, immobilized, long enough that Wendy had noticed.

"Beyond cute, isn't he? And, I happen to know, he's quite unattached at the moment."

It had taken a moment for her friend's point to register. When it had, she'd stared at Wendy in shock. There was no way she would even think about trying to get involved with a guy as good-looking as this one was.

"Hey, come on," Wendy had teased, "you know you have

a weakness for the studly cowboy type, and that's Greg Colton down to the bone."

"Colton? Is he one of…" That would make it even more ridiculous.

"Those Coltons, that own half or more of Owl Creek? Yes, he's related to them, but he's one of the ranching Coltons, so don't hold it against him."

Wendy had seized upon the immediate response Briony hadn't been able to hide, and thus began the efforts to get her and Greg together. Efforts had been ineffective and sometimes even messy, because Briony froze up every time she was near the guy. Even after Rick and Wendy were married, she was still a wreck around Greg, because she really did think him the most appealing man she'd met in a long time. She had developed a bit of a crush on him starting that day at the picnic, but the combination of his looks and the fact that he was a Colton put him way out of her league, and she knew it.

She'd buried her reaction deep and hoped Greg had never noticed. She thought she'd been successful, because more than once she'd heard him refer to her as "Wendy's best friend" to others. And that's what she was to him. Not even really his friend, just a friend of his best friend's wife.

And that was for the best. She had no doubt about that, no matter that occasionally a silly, useless longing would rise in her, needing to be quashed all over again.

That they were now inextricably tied together, for the foreseeable future and beyond, didn't change that. They would do what had to be done for the kids, and they were working hard at getting along to do it, but it would never be any more than that.

No matter that sometimes she wished it could be different.

* * *

Greg thought it had been a good day overall. Justin seemed to have had a great time, and Jane was still fascinated by Wick. They'd spent a lot of time with the colt, and Greg thought when the kids were a little older, he'd explain about his name. Although he suspected Justin would understand even now.

He got a text from Briony earlier than he'd expected, saying she was done and he could bring them home whenever he wanted. He texted back that they were making cookies with Mama Jen at the moment, and they'd be on their way when those were done. And although she didn't ask, he sent another message saying they'd bring some with them, because those snickerdoodles were unmatched in human history.

She sent back a GIF of a redheaded girl gobbling up a cookie, which made him literally laugh out loud. He sent back the appropriate laughing emoji, and was still smiling as he shoved his phone back into his pocket.

"That's something I haven't heard in a while," Jen had said, sounding pleased as she watched Justin carefully spoon cookie dough onto a baking sheet, while she held Jane up to watch. "And I've missed it."

He realized she was right, it seemed like forever since he'd really, genuinely laughed. He pulled the phone back out and showed her the cookie girl.

She smiled. "She seems really nice, Greg."

"She is."

"You said she and Wendy grew up in similar circumstances?"

He nodded. "They managed to stay friends, even getting bounced around in the foster system."

"That took some genuine effort."

"Yes." He grimaced. "I just wish sometimes she wasn't so…" He tried again. "She takes shy to new levels."

"Yet she stood her ground about keeping these two in their home."

"Yeah. Surprised the he—" he glanced at the kids, just as Jane reached down and stuck her finger in one of the globs of cookie dough on the sheet "—heck out of me."

"Sounds like she can be strong, but has maybe had to hide it?"

He'd never thought about it in quite that way. He turned and hugged her, making Jane giggle.

"You know, I never would have made it without you, Mama Jen."

"I love you. All of you. I feel like you're all mine."

"Trust me, we know. What you did for us, on top of raising your own family…you're amazing. We all wished, repeatedly, that *you* had been our mother, not…"

"My sister?" Jen said quietly.

"Yeah."

It wasn't until the last batch of cookies was in the oven, Jane was plopped within view on the couch and Justin sent off to gather all his things before heading home, that Greg broached a touchy subject.

"She's really connected to that…church," he said, shaking his head in disbelief. He didn't even mention the distinct possibility the so-called Ever After Church was connected to the bodies they'd been finding, and to Rick and Wendy's deaths.

"So it seems." Jen grimaced. "Not that I believe for one second that she's found religion. No, there's money in this somewhere, somehow. That's what she cares about." She sighed. "I shouldn't talk to you that way about your mother."

"Truthfully, you mean?" he asked. "You've got every right. She's your sister. And your twin to boot."

"Only on the outside, I hope."

"Actually, not so much anymore," he said. "I mean, I haven't talked to her, but I saw her when she showed up in town after Uncle Robert's money, and she looks… Well, let's just say her true character shows."

"I'm going to take that as a compliment."

"It was meant as one. But it's also the truth."

They both nearly jumped when a deep, almost rough voice came from behind them. "What she's become has changed her on the outside, and you're still as beautiful as ever, inside and out."

Greg saw color rise in Jen's cheeks as his father came and gave her an enveloping hug. And held it, long enough to have Greg studying them, wondering yet again if maybe…

He was still thinking about that on the drive back to the house. Jane was asleep in her car seat, but Justin was still going strong. The boy had been chattering away, which, given his reticence and near-total silence when things had first caved in on him, Greg took as a good sign. But then he'd lapsed into silence, long enough that Greg looked over to see if he, too, had dozed off after a long, busy day at the ranch.

Finally, in a low, almost tiny voice, the child asked, "Are they mad at me? 'Cuz I got mad at Mommy that time? 'Zat why they don't come home?"

Greg's gut instantly knotted. He was a little shocked at both the fierceness of his reaction and the power of it. He was in a good spot, so he pulled over onto the shoulder, put the car in Park and turned to face the boy.

"Listen to me, Justin. It is not your fault, not in any way. Sometimes bad things happen, and there's no explanation.

It doesn't mean it's anyone's fault. And your parents…" He hesitated, but remembered the advice they'd gotten and went ahead. "They're dead, and that means forever, but they loved you more than anything in the world, and you must always remember that."

"Then why did they go away?"

He searched desperately for the right words. "They didn't go away because they wanted to, Justin. A bad person did something bad or stupid and killed them." His stomach roiled anew at the probability it had been intentional, that they'd been targeted. "It wasn't their fault, either. But it especially isn't yours."

"Oh."

The boy seemed to calm a little. Somehow he'd found the right words.

He thought of all the questions that remained, hanging over them all, and just wished to hell they'd find the right answers.

Chapter 19

She had to admit it, she was exhausted.

Briony undid what she'd been trying to do—a simple braiding of her hair, which she usually did at night to keep it out of her way while trying to sleep, and from looking like a rat had nested in it in the morning—and rubbed at her eyes. She wondered how she could be so tired after mere days. And tried not to think about the years ahead that were going to be like this, wondering how Wendy had done it so seemingly effortlessly.

I have Rick by my side, and he works as hard as I do with the kids. It makes it easy.

Funny that she should remember those particular words now, while Greg was putting Justin to bed, just down the hall from the bathroom. Because even though he wasn't living here, he did work hard with the kids. Very hard. And he made sure it wasn't always just her, even though she could see in his eyes the weariness he tried to hide, proving that he was as exhausted as she was.

Probably more, if you're honest. He's the one driving back and forth every day. And staying until Justin goes to sleep so they could avoid the burst of tears that always came if he saw Greg leaving.

She brushed her hair once more, thinking of what Greg had told her, about what Justin had asked him. That the boy thought it could be in any way his fault seemed so awful to her she couldn't imagine dealing with it. But Greg had, and had apparently done it so well the boy's questions had actually eased up for a while.

She wondered how anyone survived being a single parent, with no one to share the job with.

She heard his voice, since she'd left the bathroom door open while she tried to do what was usually simple, although he was speaking so quietly she couldn't make out any words. Almost involuntarily she stepped out into the hallway, as if drawn by an irresistible force.

He wasn't speaking. He was singing.

He has a marvelous voice.

His aunt's words flashed through her mind. And now she knew they were true. Because the low, deep voice she was hearing, singing some sort of cowboy song she guessed was old and traditional, was indeed marvelous. It gave her shivers of a delicious kind she'd never known before.

She listened until he stopped, savoring the sound of him. Then she went back to wrestling with her oddly uncooperative hair even as she thought maybe she should put it off until she was actually ready to go to bed herself. Although as tired as she was, that could well be the moment Greg walked out the door.

Or not, she amended, as a memory shot through her mind.

...you two get to bed.

He had never even commented on his father's words, jokingly or otherwise. It was probably just her silly heart, still harboring vestiges of that long-ago—or so she'd thought—crush she'd had on him, that made it keep going through her mind. Which apparently made her fingers nonfunctional as she had to once more untangle her hair to try again.

"Want me to do that?"

She gave a little start. She'd been so lost in her thoughts—yet again—that she hadn't realized he'd stopped at the open door.

"Do…what?" she managed to get out. Barely.

"Braid it for you."

She just stared at him, not sure if she was more stunned by the offer or the ease with which he'd said it. He must be joking. Surely he was joking.

"You… Braid my hair?" she asked finally when he didn't speak.

He gave that one-shouldered shrug she was coming to know. "I braid horse's manes and tails, can't be that much different."

And so, moments later she found herself standing with Greg so very close behind her, sorting her hair into three long tails with obviously efficiency. She felt pressure growing inside her, rapidly. She should say something. Shouldn't she? She couldn't just stand there and…and…

Enjoy the feel of his fingers in your hair? Her breath caught, and her thoughts veered. *Please, don't let him look up and see me in the mirror, see me blushing like a schoolgirl around the campus hero…*

"You have a wonderful voice," she said abruptly.

Those deft fingers—would they be that good at…other things?—paused. "So I've been told. Never used it on a kid before. Seems to calm the cattle, so I thought it was worth a shot."

She could just picture him riding alongside some big herd, keeping them calm with that voice. If it did to them a fraction of what it had to her, his worry wouldn't be them stampeding away, but more trampling him trying to get closer.

"Do you know where you got the red hair?"

She blinked at the unexpected question. "Not out of a box, if that's what you mean."

He leaned to one side slightly, to meet her eyes in the mirror, and he was clearly confused.

"I just meant if you knew if either of your bio parents had it."

"Oh." And there came the damned blush again.

He went back to work on her hair for a moment before saying, "I didn't mean to embarrass you."

She gestured at her flaming cheeks in disgust. "It comes with the hair. And no, I don't know. I don't know anything about either of them, except they were worthless. If I ever knew anything else, I've erased it from my memory completely."

He'd apparently reached the end, because he reached around to pick up the elastic band she'd laid on the counter next to the sink. It brought him even closer, and his heat warmed her. In more ways than one.

As he worked the band around the end of the braid, he said, "So you got the hair, but not the fiery temper that comes with it, according to all the stereotypes." When she couldn't think of a thing to say to that, he went on in a very soft tone, "Or maybe you just only aim it at yourself?"

She stared in shock at those warm brown eyes in the mirror as he spoke words she'd heard before.

"Yeah," he said, "Wendy told me that once." His mouth quirked. "You didn't think I was Mr. Sensitive and figured it out on my own, did you?"

She felt almost relieved, which in turn almost made her laugh. She did manage to smile back at his reflection.

"She…worried about you," he said. Briony wondered if the hesitation had been because he'd been about to use the present tense, as if her beloved friend were still here. "She said you didn't stand up for yourself enough."

She decided to borrow his one-sided shrug for an answer. And immediately realized why he did it; it made things so much easier than trying to find the words for something she couldn't express.

"But you stood up for what you thought best for the kids."

"That was…different."

"So Wendy was right. You'll do it for others, but not for yourself."

She let out a long, sighing breath as her dear friend's oft-repeated statement made her eyes sting. "Wendy was usually right."

She felt the slight touch as he released her braid—which felt perfect, not too loose, not too tight—and it brushed her back. But then he leaned in closer and put his arms around her, giving her more of that warmth. That sweet warmth. That warmth that was almost enough to ease the ache.

That warmth that was more than enough to cause an entirely different kind of ache.

Every well-trained, self-protective instinct she had screamed at her to pull away. Instead, like the fool she knew she was, she leaned into it, seeking more and more of that luscious heat only he had ever seemed to cause in her.

"Both our lives got turned upside down, didn't they?" he said.

"Yes," she said, trying to make it sound like an answer to his question and not her own inner wish.

"All we can do is what we're doing. See to the kids."

And that quickly—and kindly, she had to admit—he quashed all those urges and longings, reminding her why he was here, and that he was holding her in support, not…

desire. She pulled her emotions back, as she'd had to so many times in her life.

"Yes. And we will," she said, glad to hear her voice sounded calm and steady.

It wasn't until he'd gone, after a final peek into their bedrooms to check on both children, that she thought to go back into the bathroom, grab the hand mirror she'd found in the top drawer of the vanity and look at the braiding he'd done.

It was, of course, perfect.

Chapter 20

Greg knew something was bothering Briony within minutes after arriving at the house. And that it was something more than Jane's wailing "Mamamama" over and over again, inconsolably. But every time he tried to ask her what was wrong, something—or a very short someone—would interrupt, until he was feeling as frazzled as she was acting. How did people *do* this?

He'd already had a long, hard day. A big tree had gone down and taken a chunk of the main pasture fence with it. He and a crew of three men needed several hours to get the tree removed and the fence repaired. He'd have liked nothing better than a long, hot shower and an early bedtime. Instead, he took a quick, wake-up-cold shower, dressed again in clean clothes and headed for his truck.

Dad had caught him just before he pulled out.

"Something else go wrong?" he'd asked wearily.

Buck leaned on the driver's door. "No. Just wanted to acknowledge something very right."

"Well, that'll be nice for a change. What?"

"You."

Greg blinked. "Me?"

"I'm very proud of you, son. You're handling this like a man, doing what needs to be done."

He couldn't speak past the tightening of his throat. Barely got out, "Thanks, Dad." He swallowed, then managed to say more steadily, "I had a great example."

He'd thought about that exchange all the way over to the house. That he indeed had always had a great example, the man who had taught him more about life and how to deal with its ups and downs than anyone else could have.

Briony had never had an example like that in her life. Yet she was also rising to the challenge, and proud as he was of his dad's approval, Greg found that much more amazing.

Which was why her current state of obvious worry was nagging at him.

But he still had to wait until, at last, both kids were tucked in and asleep. Jane had apparently exhausted herself from the constant wailing, and Justin had fallen asleep on the couch during the kids' movie he'd insisted he had to watch. Again, Briony had said, adding that he'd seen it three times already this week.

Briony, who was still wearing her hair in the braid he'd impulsively done last night. He wasn't sure how that made him feel, only that it did make him feel…something.

And now here they were, collapsed themselves on the living room couch, the television now muted as the cartoon characters played out their story. Greg tried to think of a tactful way to ask, finally decided he was way too tired to be delicate about it and just asked.

"What's bothering you? You've been on edge all evening."

"That's not enough?" she said wryly, nodding toward the now-quiet children's rooms.

"More than, but…this seems like something else."

She let out an audible breath. "Don't write off that Mr. Sensitive title just yet, then." Then, looking as if it were a tremendous effort, she sat up straight. "It may be nothing, but…"

"What? Tell me."

She drew in a deep breath before saying, still hesitant, "I think someone's watching us."

His brow furrowed. "Watching?"

"I've seen the same black car parked in different spots for the last couple of days. Always with a man sitting in it. And it's never been here before that. And then when I took the kids to the park this morning…it was there, too. With the same man in it."

Greg was upright too, now. All the tension and speculation about how and why Rick and Wendy had died, which he tried to smother around the kids, came roaring back full strength. "I assume you didn't recognize him?"

She shook her head. "No. Or the car."

She leaned far over, stretching to reach the end table, he guessed for the phone that sat there. The action made her shirt ride up and bare some skin above the waist of the knit pants she had on. He'd never really noticed until these past few days that she had a very nice shape, long legs, nice hips, trim waist, and breasts that were nicely rounded and full enough that he couldn't quite believe he hadn't taken note before now.

Of course, she didn't exactly dress to attract. The opposite, Wendy had always said. *The less attention she draws, the happier she is*, she'd said, and she hadn't sounded happy about it. *Even if the right man comes along, she'll never believe it. Or let him get close to her.*

In an odd, incongruous thought, he realized he was close to her. So he guessed that meant he wasn't the right man. But he already knew that. Had always known that. Hadn't he?

She had grabbed her phone now, and straightened back

up. She tapped at the screen a couple of times while she said, "I got a couple of pictures, but not from very close, so you can't really see him."

She held out the phone to him. He took it, telling himself it hadn't been intentional that he'd brushed over her fingers, it had been unavoidable. The tingle it had caused was weird, though.

He focused on the screen.

It was a fairly nondescript black car, not unlike a dozen he could think of owned by people he did know. But even though the image of the man in the driver's seat was distorted a bit by the car's window glass, he was fairly certain he didn't know this guy.

"See? You can't really see him that well, so it was probably a waste of time even trying—"

"Hush, Briony. It was not a waste of time. Not by a long shot."

"You know him?" She sounded utterly startled.

"No."

"But—"

"It wasn't a waste of time, because you got the license number on the car in this second shot."

"Oh."

"Send it to my phone."

She did so, but with a worried look. "But...he hasn't really done anything, except hang around. Hasn't broken any laws, I mean."

Yet.

The warning rang in Greg's head, and no matter how much he told himself he was probably overreacting, it wouldn't go away. Chase telling him Rick and Wendy's crash hadn't been an accident had been seared into his memory as if with acid, and he couldn't just put it out of his mind. And now this guy hanging around Rick and Wendy's house?

"Maybe I'm just being paranoid," Briony said.

"Careful," he corrected, starting to hate her self-doubt. "You're being careful. Just like you're supposed to be."

He grabbed his own phone. Checked that the image had arrived and was clear. Then he called up his cousin Fletcher's number. He knew Chase would have told his brother what was going on, given that Fletch was now a local cop, having transferred to Owl Creek from Boise PD a while back.

"Greg?" Fletcher answered. "We were just talking about you."

That detoured his racing thoughts. "You were?"

Fletch laughed. "Yeah. I'm at the bookstore, and Frannie was saying she needed to call you and let you know that book you wanted came in. By Alexis…detoke something?"

"De Tocqueville. Okay."

"Interesting reading taste you got there, coz."

"Tell her I'll be in to pick it up."

"I will. Now, what's up? I'm assuming you didn't just call to chat."

"I need to send you a photo, and for you to tell me if the guy or the car looks familiar."

His cousin's tone changed instantly, and Greg knew he was now talking to Fletcher Colton the cop. "Send it."

He forwarded the image Briony had sent him.

"Hmm." His cousin's tone was thoughtful, and Greg knew he'd registered something. "Let me call you back in a couple."

He didn't even say goodbye, but Greg knew that was because Fletcher was already on to the next step.

"What?" Briony asked, starting to look a little anxious.

"He's checking on something. He'll call back."

"The car?" Her expression cleared suddenly. "Is he the cousin who's an Owl Creek cop?"

He nodded. "Detective. And he reacted like something was familiar about either the car or the guy."

He saw fear dawning in her eyes and almost wished he hadn't said it. She'd been concerned before, but not afraid until he'd planted the idea this unknown man might be familiar to the local police.

"Maybe it's nothing," he said. "Maybe he's…house hunting or something."

"Do you really think that?"

Greg met her gaze. Odd, before all this had happened, when he happened to think of her, like when Rick or Wendy had mentioned her, he'd thought of her red hair. Now he wondered how he could have thought of anything except these big green eyes.

And looking into them now, he couldn't bring himself to lie. "No."

Less than ten minutes later, he was, to his disquiet, proven right. Fletcher called back, and still in cop mode, didn't waste any time on niceties. The moment Greg heard that inflection in his voice, he put the call on speaker, both so Briony could hear and so he didn't have to tell her after.

"He's a PI from Conners," Fletcher said. "He and the car looked familiar because his photo went around the department here when he got in a scuffle with some guy he was tailing in a divorce case."

"Damn," Greg muttered.

"You're not having some fling with a married woman, are you, coz?"

He assumed that was a joke, since if he had a list of

things he'd never do, that was definitely on it. "No," he said flatly.

"Sorry, man," Fletcher said hastily, like a man who'd just remembered there was a personal reason that joke would fall flat. Greg let it pass; after all, Fletcher had been hit by that just as he had. And it didn't matter just now that his mother had had a long affair with Fletcher's father.

"Forget it, man. We all agreed they're irrelevant to us."

"Yeah." Fletcher cleared his throat, then said, "You got a problem I can help with?"

"Not unless you can find out why this guy has been hanging around Rick and Wendy's house. Where the kids are." *And Briony.*

Even as he thought it, she spoke. "Is," she corrected as she stared out the front window. "He's back."

Greg crossed the room in two long strides, looked out the window and quickly spotted the black vehicle across the street.

"He's back," he confirmed to Fletcher. "Across the street and about three houses east."

"I'm close. Why don't I come over there and badge him and see what he says?"

"He hasn't done anything but hang around," Greg warned.

"But my brother says that car crash wasn't an accident."

"No. It wasn't."

"He also said the guy they think caused it was conveniently murdered while in custody."

"Yeah."

"Reason enough," Fletcher said easily. "You stay put, and I'll just stop by and find out what one of Conners's less than finest is up to."

"Thanks, coz."

He ended the call and for a moment just stood there, thinking, turning over possibilities in his mind. Then he realized Briony was staring at him and turned to look at her. He couldn't even define the expression on her face. Some combination of bemusement and…longing?

"What?" he finally asked.

"That's what it's like?"

He frowned slightly, puzzled. "What what is like?"

"To have family. You just call, and they jump to help?"

He felt a knot tightening in his gut again. "Mine does, mostly. But don't forget, we have a couple of prime ass—" he broke it off, changing mid-sentence "—jerks, too. So maybe you were lucky, in one way. You didn't have any of those to deal with."

"Not sure that outweighs what you were just able to do," she said quietly, and he felt a jab of rueful regret.

"Sorry," he muttered. "I know I don't really get it, but—"

He stopped abruptly when she reached out and put just her fingertips against his chest. He wasn't sure he could have kept talking after that anyway.

"You get it more than I ever would have expected."

He wanted to hug her again, to hold her, reassure her that everything would be all right. Except that would be a lie— he couldn't be sure everything would. And strange things, puzzling things, happened when he hugged her, held her. Things he never would have expected.

So instead, he lifted a hand and put it over hers on his chest, curling his fingers around hers, holding them there against him. That was the only thing that kept him from pacing the floor while they waited. And although they stood that way for a long time, he still felt it was too short when she finally moved, pulling back her hand and looking away from him.

"Do you think it's something to do with the accident?" she asked, sounding anxious again.

"I think speculation at this point is useless," he answered. "We'll know soon. Fletch'll find out why he's here."

Even as he said it his cousin's car pulled up, halting beside the black sedan, carefully blocking it from leaving. Greg thought about grabbing his rifle from his truck and going over there, just in case Fletcher needed some backup, but things seemed calm enough.

Just because you got involved in one shoot-out doesn't make you an expert.

The memory made him grimace, although at least it had turned out well, with Chase's new lady safe and sound. That had made him feel good about what could have ended much worse.

When Fletcher arrived at the door a few minutes later, he didn't look happy. "I can't order him to leave. He's not violating anything. Yet. But I did get him to let slip who he's working for."

Greg sensed he wasn't going to like this. He glanced at Briony, who was clearly still anxious. "Who?" he asked.

Fletcher grimaced before saying flatly, "A Mr. Kraft."

Greg felt it like a punch to the gut. Rick's father.

The one person both Rick and Wendy had trusted them to keep away from the children.

Chapter 21

Once again Greg's father came through, immediately agreeing to take the kids while they headed to Conners, to the attorney's office.

"I'll call Jen, she'll come help." He'd smiled in a way Briony could only interpret as loving. "She's quite taken with those two. I think she misses having little ones around." A grin flashed, and Briony saw where Greg got his own devastatingly appealing beam. "And much to my surprise, so do I."

"I figured we would have cured you of that," Greg said, managing a smile despite the tension she could feel thrumming just beneath the surface.

"I might have felt that at the time, but it's different now. The responsibility is elsewhere, leaving us just the fun parts."

"You sound like a doting grandparent," Greg said, the smile less forced this time.

His father met his gaze and held it before saying quietly, "Well, they're yours now, aren't they? So I am."

They were in Greg's truck, leaving the car with the car seats at the ranch just in case, and on the road to Conners Briony said, a bit hesitantly, "Your dad is an incredible man."

"He is," Greg agreed. "He's the grandfather the kids need. Not that piece of—"

He cut himself off, and to her surprise Briony found that she liked the fact that he tried not to use rough language, at least around her. She'd already noticed it when he was around the kids and appreciated that he extended it to her. She'd grown up hearing some pretty crude things on a regular basis, and she didn't care for it, and especially didn't want the kids subjected to it as she had been.

"Yes, not that horrible excuse for a father Rick had." She gave him another sideways look. "Maybe you had a better point than I realized, when you talked about me not having had to deal with family like that."

He looked surprised. Whether it was because she'd acknowledged the possible accuracy or that she remembered what he'd said at all, she didn't know.

What she did know was the source of the tension that practically hummed in the truck's cab. The very idea of innocent little Justin and Jane ending up in the hands of the man Rick had so hated was beyond abhorrent to her, and she knew Greg felt the same way. And he, having been Rick's close friend for so long, probably knew even more about the evilness of the man than she did, having gotten her information filtered through Wendy.

When they arrived at the office in Conners, Greg declined the offer of coffee from the receptionist, but Briony accepted, as much to have something to do with her hands as anything. But it ended up untouched when they were ushered into the office right away and Tanya—she'd told them to just use her first name—got right to the point of the information she'd confirmed.

"Can he do that?" Briony knew she'd practically yelped it

at the attorney but couldn't contain her incredulity. "He could try to take custody of two children he's never even met?"

"I'm afraid a blood relative, especially a direct one like a grandfather, would have standing in a case," the woman said regretfully.

Greg, who had never even sat down and was still pacing the lawyer's office, covering the relatively large space quickly with those long-legged, powerful strides of his, stopped and turned to face the woman behind the desk.

"Despite Rick's insistence that his father get nowhere near them? Even though he specifically assigned guardianship to us to keep that from happening?" he demanded.

"He still has standing."

Briony was looking at Greg's face and saw his jaw tighten. "Look, I know who and what Rick's father is. And how much Rick wanted to keep his kids far, far away from him. They even considered moving out of state to get away from him."

"I understand," the lawyer began.

"I'm not sure you do," Greg countered, and Briony could hear the tension vibrating in his voice. "He's a founding member of that cult that calls itself a church."

Tanya drew back slightly. "That…Ever After thing?"

"Yes. The one that may be connected to those bodies they've been finding," Greg answered flatly. He hesitated, but after a moment went ahead. "And it hasn't been proven, but he may have been connected to the non-accident that killed Rick and Wendy."

That took the woman a moment to process, and in that moment Briony's accountant brain woke up. She asked Greg, "Do you think he's after the insurance money? For both kids together, it's not an insignificant amount."

"Oh, I'm sure he is," Greg said, sounding almost glacial now. "He'll hand it over to the bastard who runs the thing, and the kids to God knows who." His mouth twisted sourly. "Not that God has anything to do with that farce."

Briony felt an odd sense of appreciation for his anger, because she was feeling some of that herself. And she agreed completely with his assessment. She turned back to the attorney.

"What exactly does that mean, standing?" Briony asked.

"Boiled down to the essence, it means most courts would hear his case. Not that he would necessarily win, but—"

Her phone rang, and she held up a finger as she took the call. It was brief, and Briony could see by her expression when it ended that it was not good news.

"He's filed a plea," she said bluntly. "For full custody."

Greg swore, looking as if he wanted to punch something. Or more likely someone. If Winston Kraft were in the room now, she'd be willing to bet he'd be on the floor before he knew what had hit him. And she had to admit she liked the idea of that ranch-hewn power unleashed on the evil man Wendy had so often told her about, fear in her eyes and voice. Her friend knew too well what life would be like for Justin and Jane in the hands of someone like Rick's father. Or worse, simply handed over to that dangerous cult.

"What chance would he have of winning?" she asked.

"To a certain extent it depends on the judge, of course," the lawyer said. "That he's apparently well-off—" she held up a hand as both Greg and Briony started to speak "—I know, it's probably mostly cult money, bilked from unknowing members, but nevertheless, he's got money, and he's married, and that will matter. A married couple always has a better shot."

"He's on his third wife who's half his age," snapped Greg. "But it still counts?"

"All I can say is it would be a factor in his favor. Just as if, say, you two were married it would be a factor. A rather large one, in fact, given that third wife, and that he's so much older and the kids are so young. Plus, there's the fact that the kids are obviously quite familiar and comfortable with you two, while Winston Kraft has never even met them. The connection to the Ever After Church might play into it as well, depending again on the judge."

"You're saying we'd have a better chance of keeping the kids out of his clutches if we were married?" Greg's voice was flat, suddenly unemotional.

"That, plus Rick and Wendy's clearly stated wishes would definitely give you a much better chance." She looked from him to Briony, then back. Then she got to her feet, saying, "Excuse me, I'm going to see if we have a copy of Winston Kraft's filing yet. They were supposed to send it right over."

Briony had the feeling that wasn't the only reason the woman wanted to get out of the room. Greg was still on his feet, while she wasn't sure she'd ever be able to get out of this chair. She lowered her gaze, noticed the ripples in the surface of the full cup of coffee and set it down carefully before she managed to splash it all over.

When he finally sat in the chair beside hers, it was uncharacteristically heavily. His head was down, as if the weight of the world had descended on his shoulders. She understood. Her stomach was churning with growing nausea, and she was flooded with fears and feelings she hadn't had since her own miserable childhood.

It was a long, strained moment before he finally looked up at her and spoke.

"It would be the worst betrayal ever of Rick and Wendy to let that monster get away with this."

"Not to mention how awful it would be for Justin and Jane." Just the thought of those two precious beings she had loved before but utterly adored now in the hands of the man Wendy had told her about made the churning worse, and she had to fight it down.

"I won't let it happen," Greg said, his voice grimly firm.

"Nor will I. If I have to sell everything I own to pay to fight him, I will."

"There's a better…no, an easier…" His voice trailed off as if he couldn't find the right word. "A more effective way. As she—" he nodded toward the name plaque on the desk "—pointed out."

The ripple of shock that went through her as she realized what he was getting at managed to overwhelm the nausea. She stared at him, unable to put together a coherent sentence even in her mind, as if his struggle for the right word was infectious.

"Did you mean it?" There was a stress, an urgency in his voice that she'd never heard before, would never have expected to hear, not from strong, steady Greg Colton. "That you'd do whatever is necessary to keep them out of Winston Kraft's clutches?"

Knowing she was answering both that question and the one he hadn't yet asked, she took a deep breath, let it out slowly to calm herself and said simply, "Yes."

In the end he didn't ask a question at all. He simply said it.

"Then we have to get married."

Chapter 22

Greg knew it wasn't exactly a romantic proposal. But this wasn't a romance. It was a…business deal. No, it was a necessity. This was for Justin and Jane's sake, and if this was what it took to keep them out of the hands of the man Rick had so hated, what it took to keep his best friend's worst nightmare from coming true, then so be it. Besides, it wasn't like there was anyone in his life who was going to feel betrayed. He hadn't even been on a date in…almost a year. Hadn't even thought about it until he'd met Sloan, but his cousin Chase had laid claim, fiercely, before it had gone beyond just a thought. And Briony had said that she wasn't seeing anyone, either.

It would work. It had to. He and Briony had gotten along well enough since they'd pitched in together to see to the kids. Of course, most of the time he at least had been too tired to fight with her, but right now he couldn't remember much he'd felt like fighting about. The initial argument over where the kids should live had been the biggest battle. A battle, he suddenly realized, they were going to have to fight all over again.

Belatedly he realized she hadn't said a word. Maybe he'd made it a little too businesslike, a little too abrupt.

"Look," he said hastily, "I know that wasn't—"

"Yes."

He blinked. Was she acknowledging the coldness of the statement, or…agreeing with it? "Yes?"

"We have to get married."

For some inane reason all Greg could think of was how far removed from any scenario in which he would have expected to hear those words this was. It gave him a clue as to what she might be feeling.

"I know this isn't what either of us want," he began, stopping when she shook her head.

"It has to be done."

For a moment he just looked at her, seeing an unshakable determination in those green eyes that startled him. For all her quietness, all the shyness that generally made her retreat into herself, when the chips were down, Briony Adams didn't run.

"And soon," she added, proving his point.

He nodded. "I'll look into it. We need a judge, I guess."

"And a license." She nodded toward the nameplate on the desk. "She'll probably know what we need to do."

She was so calm it was almost unsettling. He would have expected her to be rattled, upset at the whole idea, or at the very least upset at this turn life had suddenly taken. But the only thing he could hear in her voice or see in her face was a steady determination.

And he wondered if he'd ever really known this woman at all.

Footsteps warned them Tanya was returning. When she was back at her desk, she studied them for a moment, and Greg got the strangest feeling she had guessed what had gone on while she'd been out of the room. Or maybe it wasn't strange. A good lawyer could probably read people well, and he remembered Rick saying she was one of the best lawyers in the state. It was why they'd chosen her.

He knew he'd need the best to go up against his father if necessary.

And now it was necessary.

"No copy yet, so they're dragging their feet. Whether that's because they're stalling or don't have confidence in their case, I have no way of knowing." Her mouth twisted slightly. "Or, from what Rick told me, he's possibly just being obstructionist."

"Something he's very good at," Greg agreed sourly. The urgency of the need to protect the kids made him set aside the niceties. "You meant what you said, that we'd have a better chance at keeping the children out of Winston's hands if we were married?"

"It would be a significant factor, I think."

He glanced at Briony. She nodded. He looked back at the attorney. "Then we will."

For a long moment the woman across from them just looked at them consideringly. And, he noticed, without much surprise. "I gathered from Rick and Wendy you two have known each other for some time?"

"Since shortly after they met," Briony said.

"And you both agree this is what you want to do?"

"It's what needs to be done," Greg said flatly.

"The children will need to feel you're truly together in this," she said warningly.

"We'll make it work. For the kids. He can't be allowed to get his hands on them."

"We're hoping you can tell us how to go about this," Briony said. "I'm guessing the sooner the better?"

"The more time you've been established before this goes to family court the better, yes." She tapped the pen she'd picked up on her desk a couple of times, then spoke quickly. "You'll need to apply for a license at the county recorder's office, over by the courthouse. There's no waiting period in Idaho, but you'll need someone with the legal ability to officiate." She thought for a moment, then went on. "I happen to know a retired judge who could handle that. You let me know when, and I'll give him a call."

Greg looked at Briony, searching her face, her eyes, for any sign of doubt or that she might be changing her mind now that they were talking details. Any sign that the reality of what she'd agreed to had struck and she wanted to back out. She seemed to realize what he was doing and held his gaze steadily. Then she looked back at the attorney.

"How about today?" she said.

He felt a little jolt. Today? Suddenly he was the one dealing with the reality of the decision they'd reached. But maybe it was a good thing. The less time they had to think about it, the less time the insanity of it all had to register.

"The kids are already safe with your dad, let's get it done," Briony said.

"I...yes. Sure." He shook off the remnants of his own shock—when had shy little Briony become so steadfast and determined?—and looked across the desk. "Can we do that?"

"I'll make the call to the judge. And hopefully the recorder's office won't be jammed. You have the necessary ID? Driver's licenses will do."

They both nodded.

Ten minutes later they were back in Greg's truck, the county offices their destination. Briony was staring out the side window, as if she didn't want him to be able to see her face.

"Second thoughts?" he asked as he started the engine, his voice sounding as rough as his gut was feeling.

"No." She said it firmly, but she still wouldn't look at him.

He opened his mouth to speak and realized he had no idea what to say, so shut it again. In this case, he had the feeling the less said the better.

It wasn't until they were on the main road headed south that something else hit him. "I'd better warn Dad."

"Which will shock him more, that you're getting married, or married to me?"

There was an almost bitter undertone to her voice that jabbed at him. "Actually," he said coolly, "I wanted to warn him about the PI hanging around."

She had the grace to sound embarrassed. "Oh. Sorry. That was self-centered of me."

He glanced at her, then went back to the road ahead. And nearly groaned aloud at the phrase his mind had chosen. "This isn't about us. It's about Justin and Jane, and keeping them safe."

"I know. I just…"

His mouth twisted wryly. "Not how you ever thought about getting married, huh?"

"Actually, I never thought much about getting married at all."

He blinked. Glanced at her. "I thought…" His voice trailed off, his at the moment chaotic mind warning him he could be stepping into quicksand.

"That all women spent half their time dreaming about it?" she asked sweetly. Too sweetly, telling him it was good that he'd stopped when he did. "I didn't. I didn't think I'd ever trust anyone enough."

Given her history, he could understand that. He waited while the car in front of them, a compact, trendy thing driven by a guy who looked terrified by the bigger utilitarian vehicles around him, decided what to do about the semi rig they'd just caught up to, then when they were finally clear of the backup the guy had caused, thought maybe he knew what to say.

"I'd never do anything to hurt you."

"I know that."

That surprised him, and he shot her another sideways glance. "You do?"

She shrugged and said, "Rick always said you were a straight arrow. He told me if I ever needed anything, and he or Wendy weren't around, I could go to you. That you'd help however you could because that's who you are."

And that quickly the harsh, bitter ache was back, tightening his gut and his throat and making his eyes sting.

"He was the best friend anyone could have," he said, not even caring that every bit of that blast of emotion echoed in his voice.

"As Wendy was for me."

"So we'll do this for them. And we'll keep their children safe." He said it in the tone of a vow more real than any other he'd make today.

"We will," Briony said, and her voice held the same certainty his own had.

They would make other vows today, but none were more important than that one.

Chapter 23

She was married.

Briony felt a little numb as she sat in the truck staring at the paper in her hand. She hadn't lied to Greg when she'd said she hadn't thought about it much. And just about the only times she had were when Wendy had brought it up, insisting that there were trustworthy men out there.

That Wendy's usual example, after her own beloved Rick, had been Greg seemed the highest of ironies now.

Look at Greg. He's not just honest and trustworthy, he's kind, hardworking, loyal, not to mention superhot...

Wendy had said it with utter sincerity. She hadn't been able to argue any of that, then or now. It was why back after they'd first met, she'd had to spend so much energy stifling that stupid yearning she felt every time she saw him. But she'd done it because she had to. Because it would never work out, and the very last thing she wanted was some silly crush of hers to affect the dearest thing in her life, her oldest and closest friendship, the only thing that had enabled her to survive her chaotic childhood. If Wendy, who even as a kid had been more outgoing, tough and self-admittedly stubborn than she, hadn't essentially taken her under her wing, Briony wasn't sure she would have made it at all.

And now, after maybe five minutes in a little alcove off

the judge's office, she was where Wendy had always wanted her. Married to Greg.

Married.

The word rang in her head until she wanted to put her hands over her ears to see if it would muffle it a little.

"This is a business arrangement, right?" she said, not looking at him.

"What?"

"We're clear on what it is, and isn't, what it will and won't be, right? Do we need to lay it out in so many words?"

There was a moment of silence before Greg answered, in a brusque, almost sharp tone. "Focus on the kids, not us. This isn't an accounting job."

She felt her cheeks flush with embarrassment and was glad she was turned away from him. "You're right," she said, her voice barely above a whisper. "Sorry."

There was another pause, but his voice had changed completely, become something soothing when he said, "You don't need to protect yourself in this, Briony. We both want the same thing, and we can work with that."

How did he know her so well, know that the hard-learned urge to self-protect had risen up in her anew? Or was she just that readable?

And it has nothing to do with the simple fact that you could so easily fall for him like a ton of bricks.

She sat in silence, not even seeing the buildings they were driving past. And a couple of blocks later, she was barely aware that he'd pulled over to the curb and parked along the main street of Conners.

"You coming in, or not?" Greg's voice cut through the buzz.

"What?" she asked.

He nodded toward the store they were in front of. She

looked. Blinked. A jewelry store. She turned her gaze back to him. Couldn't think of a thing to say.

"You heard what he said. If we want to present the right image, you need a ring."

Had she heard that? She vaguely remembered the retired judge, who had obviously been apprised of the situation—and had a strong personal opinion of the Ever After Church—had said something about the custody case, but she had been so dazed at the reality of the fact that she had just pledged herself to this man forever she hadn't really processed the details.

"What about you?" It was the only thing she could think of to say.

He grimaced. "A ring would only get in my way on the ranch."

For some reason she didn't stop to analyze that jabbed her into saying, a bit snappishly, "So I'm the only one who's supposed to declare myself to the world?"

"I didn't mean—"

"I thought the whole idea was a united front?"

"I know that, I—"

"Or at least the image of one?"

For a long moment he just stared at her. Then, with the slightest twitch of his mouth, he asked, "Who are you, and what have you done with quiet, shy, retiring Briony Adams?"

She realized he wasn't, as she'd expected, angry. He was amused. In fact, he sounded almost…pleased? She wasn't sure that didn't jab at her more. With an effort, she kept her voice cool.

"It's Briony Colton now, isn't it?"

This time he blinked. And she knew he hadn't processed that any more than she'd processed what the judge had said.

"I…yeah, it is." He lowered his gaze, but it almost instantly shot back to her face. "That is, if you want it to be."

"That united front, remember?"

He nodded slowly. "Okay." He took in and let out an audible breath. "Okay, two rings. As long as you understand that there are times I'll have to take it off."

"As long as it stays on until the kids are officially ours."

He nodded. And Briony was just thinking that Wendy had been right, he really was kind, and loyal and all the rest, when he blew up her train of thought completely by adding three words.

"Agreed, Mrs. Colton."

"You did what?"

Greg saw the shock in his father's face and felt an inward twinge. No, more than a twinge. If there was ever a person in his life he didn't want to disappoint, it was this one.

They'd found him in the big barn, scrubbing his hands after doing some cleanup. Greg didn't find the various scents of the barn, from fresh hay to manure, at all distasteful, but he was used to it. Briony was another matter, and he'd been a little wary. But she'd only watched for a moment and asked if that's what he'd been talking about. It had taken him a moment to realize she meant his comment about the ring getting in the way. When he'd nodded, she'd nodded in turn, as if she understood now. And the tension of those moments seemed to fade away, even as he found himself yet again running his thumb over the simple gold band that now graced his left ring finger. The band that matched hers, and that he'd seen her doing the same with, that frequent testing of something you're not used to.

But now he was facing an even bigger tension, as his father stared at him. "The lawyer and the judge agreed, it betters our chances of keeping the kids out of the hands of Rick's father," he explained. "Especially now that we know Rick's father is coming after them."

Buck looked from him to Briony. "And you're…okay with it?"

"I'm okay with anything that will help those children. They need us, and I…I need them."

Such wonder echoed in her voice that Greg felt a pang of longing as if he were feeling the emotions that were so clear in her voice and expression. In the distance he heard a child's laughter and recognized it as Justin's. He looked past Dad and saw Mama Jen at the far end of the barn, walking toward the foaling stall with Jane in her arms and Justin happily trotting alongside her.

"We'll win," he said firmly. "He won't get them."

His father, who had looked about to say something, now flickered a glance from him to Briony, then turned an ear toward the sound of the children. When he looked back at Greg, he said firmly, "Whatever you and the kids need."

It was only later, when Briony and Mama Jen were dealing with dinner and getting the kids ready, that Dad took him back outside on the front porch. Greg knew what was coming, had expected it, but that didn't mean he was looking forward to it.

"You really did this," Dad said, glancing at his left hand.

"Yes." He explained everything the lawyer and the judge had said.

His father listened, as he always did. Then, quietly, he said, "I know you have the kids' best interests at heart, but I have yours. So take it from someone who got married…in haste. It can hurt." Greg didn't know what to say to that. And Buck quickly added, "It was worth it, because it brought me you, but it wasn't for the right… I didn't…"

He stopped, ramming a hand through still-dark brown

hair that was gray only at the temples. His father, usually quick to smile and tell a corny joke, was rarely flustered, but clearly he was now. And the sight of this man who, Greg knew, loved his children more than his own life in such straits made him bring up something he'd known for years but they'd never talked about.

"I know you only married her because she got pregnant with me."

His father went very still. "You do?"

"I figured out she was already pregnant as soon as I put my birthday together with when you got married." He managed a slightly crooked smile. "Of course, that wasn't until Lizzy was born, so by then I figured it didn't matter." He grimaced then. "Boy was I wrong."

Because three years later the mother was gone. From them, anyway. And on her way to an affair with his father's own brother, resulting in the two half siblings they'd never known about until that brother had died.

"Greg, listen, I—"

"It's okay, Dad. It really doesn't matter, to me, anymore. I got the best out of that deal. Just think, what if she'd taken me with her?" He gave an exaggerated shudder. When he saw the slight smile curve his father's mouth, he went on. "And this is different, really, Dad. I mean, it's similar, we didn't get married because we're madly in love or anything, but it was the right thing to do."

Madly in love with Briony Adams. Now, there was a wild thought.

Briony Colton.

Even the silent mental correction rattled him. He wasn't nearly as calm on the inside as he was trying to appear on the outside. And his father was studying him so intently it was adding to his nerves.

"Tell me, son," he said, very quietly, "how do you feel now about being the reason your mother and I got married?"

"Like I said, I got the best end of that deal. I feel bad for you, all those years when you could have been with… the right sister."

Now he'd done it. His father gave him a startled look, glanced toward the house as if Mama Jen could have heard him, then looked out toward the barn with a totally disconcerted expression on his face. Did he really think nobody had noticed the way he looked at her? The way he changed around her, smiled more, laughed more?

"We're not talking about me," Dad said gruffly. "We're talking about you."

"We're talking mostly about those two little children in there," Greg corrected gently. "And we're going to see that they have the best life they can have, under the circumstances. Just as you did with us, building a loving home for us here on the ranch." He took a deep breath before continuing. "Which brings me to the biggest favor I have to ask."

"I told you, whatever you need. I meant it."

"Even having us all live here, on the ranch?"

To his surprise, his father lit up. "Especially that. It would be great to have you all here, and easier on you, too. Lots of people to help out."

"Including Mama Jen?" he asked, just to see his reaction.

"Don't poke that bear, Gregory," Dad warned.

He threw up his hands in surrender. "Okay, okay. I'll butt out. But just so you know, I'm all for it."

And he dropped it there before his astute father could point out that a guy who just got married not out of love but out of pure responsibility was in no position to opine on someone else who'd done the same thing.

Chapter 24

"Move in here?"

Briony was feeling suddenly exhausted, emotionally if not physically, and was in no mood to have this fight again.

"My place only has two bedrooms," Greg said, "but the kids can have one, you the other, and I can bunk in the main room. We can leave them here with Dad while we go back and get whatever you and they need from the house."

She summoned up what little reserve energy and resolve she had left to say firmly, "We resolved this, and you agreed it's best for the children to stay in the home they're used to."

He stared at her as if she'd made that up. "Briony," he said, almost gently, "they can't stay there now. He wants the kids—the money that comes with them, anyway—and he already knows where the house is, thanks to that PI."

She felt a sudden chill that she hadn't realized that. She'd been so swept up in everything else—getting married, among other things—that she hadn't really put together that the PI who had been outside the house had likely already reported to Rick's father where it was.

She felt a fierce ache as all her old uncertainties rose anew, telling her she wasn't smart enough, wasn't good enough to handle this, to see to the safety of Wendy's precious children, not if she couldn't even figure out something this obvious.

"They'll be safer here," Greg went on, "with my family. My brother Malcolm has his search dog who's also a good watchdog, my cousin Wade who works with us a lot is former Special Forces, and while my brother Max is with his new lady now more than he's here, he's still former FBI. And Dad will be fierce about protecting them, just like he was with us. Plus, the hands will help look out for them, and watch for trouble all over the ranch."

"I didn't… I should have realized…" She sounded as shaky as she felt. She must have looked it, too, because he reached out and grasped her shoulders. Strangely, it steadied her, not just on the outside, but the inside, too.

"Look," Greg said, "it's been hectic. A lot's happened, most of it ugly. Cut yourself some slack."

She let out a harsh little laugh. And her voice was shaking when she said, "I've worked so hard to…have control over my life, and now I see all I've done is make myself unable to handle change."

Only when he pulled her closer for another of his wonderful hugs did she realize how much she'd wanted it, wanted him to do it. And when he spoke, she could actually feel the rumble of that lovely deep voice as her ear was pressed against his chest.

"Hey," he said, "that's not true. You've changed your entire life for the kids, and you've done a great job of it. But now you're going to have help, lots of it. Just because they…" Her heart wrenched a little as he stumbled on the word, if only because it was proof it was still as painful to him as it was to her. He tried again, as she somehow knew Greg always would. "Just because they left them to us doesn't mean they expected us to do it alone. After all, they had us to help them. So now we've got Dad and my brothers and sister to help us."

It made so much sense when he put it that way. But she had to fight the innate shyness that rose up to protest the idea of being around so many people, all the time. "I don't handle lots of people well, I pull away. They'll think I don't like them."

He was silent for a moment, as if he were considering what to say. She'd always liked that about him, that he seemed to think before he spoke, rather than blurt out whatever popped into his head first.

"They'll think you're overwhelmed. Because they know I have been, since…that night."

That startled her. She pulled back and looked up at him, albeit carefully, since she didn't want him to pull away. "You? Overwhelmed?"

"Between the kids and the ranch, it's felt like I've been underwater, never getting close enough to the surface to breathe."

She felt a little stunned, not only at the admission, but that he'd made it. And to her. "I…but you're always so strong."

"As my Dad would say, that's not strong, that's stubborn. But sometimes stubborn's the only thing that gets you through."

That made her smile, at least as much as she could manage just now. "I like your Dad."

"He's the best," Greg said simply. "And I'm sorry you never had somebody like him to be there for you."

I've got that now…

It was a silly thought; he was here for the kids, not her. She knew that, but at the same time she had the feeling that if she truly needed help, he would be there. Hadn't he proven that already?

Before she said something irretrievably foolish, she

dived back to the original subject. "Your father… He's okay with this? With the kids, and me, moving in?"

She was sorry she had when he did let go of her, but not before he'd given her a last reassuring squeeze.

"My father," he said with a grin, that devastating Greg grin, "is delighted."

"What about—" she held up her left hand, with the gold band that felt startlingly heavy on her finger "—this?"

The grin faded, and he shrugged. "That, he's not so sure about. But he has his own reasons for being wary that don't have anything to do with…us."

Us. Her and him. Together. They really were an us now. An official us. And Briony didn't quite know how to deal with the feeling that gave her. The kids had kept her too busy and often too tired to worry about anything except what came next. And now all of a sudden here she was, looking at her life upended, her future completely changed, and with no idea how it all made her really feel.

But somewhere, buried down deep, there was a tiny part of her that was saying, "You're not alone anymore." And she couldn't deny she liked the sound of it.

But neither could she deny the knowledge that were it not for Rick and Wendy and their love for them, they wouldn't be here like this at all.

She guessed that meant the inveterate matchmakers had won in the end.

"Do I want to know what you just thought?"

Greg's quiet question snapped her out of the swirl in her mind. She looked up at him, one corner of her mouth lifting in a wry half smile. "Just that…Wendy and Rick would be laughing if they were here."

He blinked. "Laughing?"

"They finally got their way."

It took him a split second. But then she saw him rubbing his thumb on the ring, much as she often did. And his mouth quirked. "I guess they did."

When Dad called in the troops, he really called in the troops. The main area around the house was awash with people—siblings, cousins—and several dogs. And they'd all come prepared to get the job done, be it moving boxes or distracting the kids. The kids who were clearly enamored of Malcolm's search dog, Pacer, who was doing a beautiful job of keeping them entertained.

In the end, they had presented it to the kids as just staying here for a while, since at the moment that was true. Once the court case was decided, then they'd have more decisions to make, but for now, they made it sound like a vacation. Justin was thrilled with the idea, while Jane was more wary, although she was obviously quite taken with Mama Jen. But then, most kids were. Still, the little girl was fascinated with the animals and seemed quite willing to stay, with no wailing to go home. Yet, anyway.

They'd decided they would bring enough of the kids' things over to make it feel familiar, which required some things that had been occupying the space to be moved out to the barn for now. But there were a lot of strong Colton hands available, and it got done in short order. And eventually Greg found himself collapsed in one of the lawn chairs his brother Max had built, with Justin in his lap. The boy had unhesitatingly climbed up on his own, which he took as a good thing. That feeling was confirmed when he looked up to see his Mama Jen smiling at them both and nodding.

"We really gonna stay here, Unca Greg?"

"For a while. You okay with that?"

The boy nodded, looking around. "I like it."

"I think you just like the animals," he teased, and the boy grinned.

Greg supposed it was the total change of scene, perhaps letting the boy forget for a little while just how long it had been since his mother or father had held him, kissed him or tucked him in at night. He hadn't missed his own mother much at all, but that was different. Very, very different from having a loving, giving mother like Wendy had been.

After a dinner prepared to thank them, the helpful and no longer hungry crew departed. Greg did the cleanup, since Dad, Mama Jen and Briony had done most of the cooking. It was nearly dark, and he came out of the kitchen to find Jane asleep in Mama Jen's arms and Justin asleep in Dad's. He felt an upswell of emotion that nearly cut off his breath.

"I took a picture of them," Briony whispered beside him. He'd been so enraptured by what he was looking at he hadn't even heard her approach. "It's just so sweet."

"I…thank you," he managed to get out. Then, turning his head to meet her gaze, he added, "For the picture, and for reminding me how lucky I've been."

Something warm and yet slightly unsettling came into her eyes then. "I wish I'd been that lucky."

"Well, you are now," Greg said.

"Because I'm married to you?"

Greg pulled back with a start. "I didn't mean—"

"Relax, silly. I was just ribbing you."

He relaxed a little. Was glad she was able to joke, and his mouth twisted in a half smile, a little rueful. "This is a whole different kind of 'had to get married,' isn't it?"

"Every day a new adventure." She quoted Rick's oft-repeated saying with the same intonation he'd always used.

And Greg couldn't help himself—he laughed. But as he did, he felt the sting of moisture in his eyes yet again.

And wondered if it would ever stop.

Chapter 25

She'd teased him. She'd actually teased him. She'd never done that before, unless they'd been with Rick and Wendy and the joking had been going all around, usually at a picnic or barbecue at the lake. Only with the armor of her dear friends had she felt strong enough to join in the friendly mockery.

Briony felt that now familiar tightness in her chest, the fierce ache of missing that convivial connection, and the agony of knowing it would never, ever happen again.

They were on their way back to the house, and she was mentally going through what to bring now that there was much more empty space. Fortunately, Greg had had the presence of mind to ask the kids what toys they wanted, so she had a list. She was surprised at how short it was but guessed that Justin at least was so focused on the novelty of the ranch he wasn't thinking about other things. And Jane was simply unhappy at the moment, which Briony certainly understood.

Greg spent some time taking Jane's crib apart, but she was a little amazed at how quickly he got it done.

"I helped Rick put it together," he said when she made a comment about it. And the undertone in his voice told her he was feeling none too happy about this, undoing what he and his best friend had done.

She felt the same qualms as they gathered everything and got ready to leave the home Rick and Wendy had made for their family. But she couldn't argue the facts as Greg had presented them, and still felt a bit naive for not having realized them herself.

"Don't worry about it if you forget something," Greg said when at last they had everything they could think of. "I can come back if necessary."

She noticed he said *I*, not *we*. Just as he'd at first said to give him a list of what she'd wanted from the house, and he'd go get it. The idea of him pawing through her underwear and other things she'd moved to the house had made her uncomfortable enough that she'd insisted on coming along. Only—once again—later did it hit her that he might have been thinking of her safety, with that PI on the loose and Rick's conniving, unscrupulous father's intentions now declared.

But only on the way back to the ranch did it strike her that the man she'd been worried about going through her underwear, even just to pack it, was…her husband. She laughed at herself and nearly let it slip out as they drove through town.

When they reached the gate to the ranch, it really hit that, for now at least, this would be her home. This vast, expansive place was the kind of place she'd always wanted to live. The problem was, when she'd imagined it, it was so she could live with lots of room, away from other people. And now she was going to be in a guest house with three other people, more in the big house just yards away, and even more who worked here, coming and going.

As if to prove her point, three ranch workers crossed the driveway in front of them, all waving cheerfully. Another was washing down a piece of equipment she didn't recognize, and also waved as they passed.

"Not exactly your solitary life, is it?"

Greg's quiet comment startled her out of her reverie.

Why'd you become an accountant?

Because it's solitary. I wanted to work by myself, without a lot of people around.

They'd had that exchange about the third time Rick and Wendy had finagled a joint evening together. But it had been so long ago she was beyond stunned that he'd remembered it after all this time.

"No. No, it's not. But it's for the kids, so I'll adapt." *I hope.*

He pulled his truck to a stop in front of his place, turned it off, but didn't make a move to get out. She saw his jaw tighten slightly as he stared through the windshield at the tidy place that had become his home.

The home she and the kids were about to invade.

"It's not exactly your life anymore either, is it?" she said quietly. "Not your personal space, either."

"It's not that," he said, barely loud enough for her to hear. "It's just… I miss him. Them."

"He was your best friend just as Wendy was mine. The hole in both our lives is…immeasurable."

He turned his head to look at her then, and she knew she hadn't mistaken the sheen in his eyes. And it warmed her more than she ever would have thought to know she wasn't alone in this pain.

"Then we have to fill it with their children," he said, and she caught an undertone of determination in his deep voice.

She held his gaze steadily as she agreed. "They're the only thing that can do it."

For a moment neither of them said anything more. As

if everything that needed to be said had been. But then Greg reached out and took her hand, clasping it firmly, part handshake, part reassurance and part understanding. They were in this together because it was the only way it would get done.

And it had to be done.

With that, Briony and Greg Colton got out and went to get the children.

"Jane!"

Briony's startled exclamation kicked up Greg's adrenaline. It took him a moment to spot the child in the big room of the main house, but when he did, he let out a short laugh. "Well, doesn't that just figure."

He watched for a moment as the child toddled across the entire length of the great room, aided by hanging on to his brother's dog. Pacer walked carefully, slowly, as if he completely understood what his job was here, just as he did on a search-and-rescue mission. Jane was giggling with every step, any sign of the shyness around strangers he'd noticed before vanished now. She looked like a delighted little cherub, with her bright blond hair, big blue eyes and rosy cheeks. And Pacer was the perfect height to help her keep her balance as she moved into this new adventure.

He looked over at Malcolm. "Teaching Pacer another new skill, bro?"

His brother laughed. "Not me. They did this on their own. I just kept an eye on them."

Briony looked a little rattled, and Greg wasn't sure why. But then Jane looked up at her, smiled widely and crowed, "Bri, doggy!"

Briony's expression changed completely. He'd heard the phrase about someone melting, but he'd never thought about it much. He did now, because that's exactly what she looked like, as if she'd melted inside. He couldn't remember if Jane had ever really tried to use Briony's name before. By-By was as close as he'd ever heard her get.

"Unca Greg!"

He turned in time to see Justin headed for him at a run, arms upstretched, something clutched in his right hand. He turned, braced, because he'd learned what came next, a flying leap in his direction, leaving him the responsibility of catching the four-year-old. He managed it fairly neatly this time, unlike the first time when it had been like grabbing an unruly calf who had squirming refined down to an escape technique.

"Look!" he exclaimed excitedly. "Look what Mr. Buck made. Just for me!"

The child held out a small wood carving of a long-legged foal. Dad had a knack with a knife and wood, always had. In fact, he had a carving very similar to this on a shelf at home.

"It's Wick," the boy explained, his eyes gleaming with excitement as if the gift had been the latest, coolest video game or something.

"I can see that."

"Do you know where that name came from, Justin?" Briony asked as she reached out to put a gentle hand on the boy's arm.

Justin nodded. "My mommy and daddy. Mr. Buck told me."

"That makes this even more special, then, doesn't it?" she said softly.

The boy nodded. "I'm glad we came here," he said. "I like it."

"Good," Greg said. "Now get all your stuff that's here at

the big house, okay? We brought the things you asked for, so now we have to decide where to put it at my house."

The child's brow furrowed. "Your house is the one over there?" he asked, pointing in the right general direction.

"Yep."

"Good. It's close," he said, the furrow vanishing. "'Cuz Mr. Buck said I could come over anytime."

Still clutching the wooden horse as Greg put him down, the boy quickly started to do as asked, and gather up the few things that were here, including his jacket and a toy truck that looked as if it had lost out to the hand-carved horse.

"Your father is really something," Briony said, looking at Greg.

"He is," Greg said.

"And then some," Malcolm agreed from very close by.

Briony looked down quickly, and Greg saw that Pacer had gently nudged her knee. Beside the big shepherd mix, Jane stood holding her arms up to Briony. She bent and picked the little girl up.

"Okay, buddy," Malcolm said with a grin at his dog, "looks like you're off duty for the moment."

"Thank you for watching out for her with the dog," Briony said.

Malcolm blinked. "She's family now. And so are you."

Greg felt a little jolt. So that answered that. Dad had told him. He was glad; he didn't want to have to explain over and over again.

"By the way," Malcolm said, "Mama Jen's coming back over tomorrow afternoon and we're going to have a big barbecue, so everybody can meet Briony and the kids. Dad wanted a sit-down dinner, but Mama Jen thought it would be easier on you guys if we did a barbecue outside."

Greg noticed his brother's gaze flicker to Briony, who

had tensed immediately at his first words, but eased a bit as he finished. He wondered if Jen had singled her out as the reason for that. He'd told his aunt she was really shy, and a barbecue would give her more chance to escape, at least now and then. It would be like her to think of something like that.

"Probably a good idea," he said, picking his words carefully. "If we're asking them to keep watch, they should at least meet everyone."

He felt Briony relax. Which was weird, because he wasn't touching her or anything. He could just feel her tension fade away. He'd be willing to bet it was because he'd presented a logical, realistic and necessary reason for the gathering. Just as she had when he'd pointed out why they should stay here, she put the welfare of the kids ahead of her own nervousness.

But the main thing he was thinking as they gathered everything up and headed for his place was that as... interesting and sometimes unpleasant as his life had been, it couldn't have been anywhere close to hers.

Chapter 26

"He asked it again," Briony said wearily as she quietly closed the bedroom door on the sleeping children. Then she had a second thought and reopened it a little, thinking if they woke up in a strange place and were scared, it would be easier to hear them.

Greg looked at her from where he was, a little to her surprise, tidying up the debris from unpacking the kids' things to get to their pajamas while he'd put Jane's crib back together. Stuff had ended up a little strewn about, and she'd already had it in mind that she'd pick up everything before she even sat down, because she had the feeling once she did sit it would take a bulldozer to get her moving again. She was exhausted, and not just physically.

"When they're coming back?" Greg asked.

She nodded and saw a muscle jump at the side of that strong jaw. Funny how she noticed—and almost treasured—every sign that she wasn't alone in this quagmire. It was almost like she was…glad he was hurting, too, and that seemed perverse of her, or at the least cold.

Misery truly does love company.

"I kept to the script," she said when he didn't say anything.

"Good." He seemed to hesitate, then added, "I know it's hard."

"It is, but we have to think about how kids who have no idea about…death…might interpret platitudes," she said.

"Yeah." He grimaced. "You tell them they're in a better place, then they're liable to go looking for it."

Despite everything, she smiled a little at that. She'd always liked his sense of humor, and that had never changed.

A long moment of silence spun out between them before Greg, stretching in a way that seemed to emphasize the breadth of his shoulders, his chest, asked, "Are you as exhausted as I am?"

She had to fight down an unwanted reaction to the way he moved before she could say, fairly evenly, "If I sit down, I'll be asleep in thirty seconds."

"Sounds about right," he agreed, his tone wry.

"Much as I would like to, we have to talk first, don't we?"

He looked suddenly wary. "Talk? Like one of those capital *T* talks?"

She studied him for a moment. She really didn't know that much about his relationship history, other than a couple of times when Rick had teased him about a woman named Jill. Greg's reaction had been an eye roll and a promise to put Rick on the floor if he didn't drop it. But that had been spoken like a man who'd had too many of the kind of talks she knew he meant, those deep, emotional ones. The kind she knew people had—Wendy had assured her of that—but she'd never experienced because the few relationships she'd had never got that deep or lasted long enough.

Wendy had told her more than once that was her own fault, that she shied away from deep connections because she didn't trust them. Didn't trust other people. And she couldn't really deny that.

I know it's true, because I felt the same way, until I met

Rick. But he wouldn't budge, and eventually I realized he was for real.

Wendy had tried so hard to convince her there were people she could trust. How brutally cockeyed was it that it took Rick and Wendy dying to prove that to her? Because if nothing else, she knew she could trust Greg Colton when it came to the kids. He would do what was right. And she was pretty sure his father and his aunt fell into the same category. Judging by what she'd seen today, probably his siblings, too. They'd already been so much help—

"So, talk," Greg said, making her realize she'd been once more lost in her thoughts. When you were generally wary of people, that happened a lot.

"I just meant about how this is going to work. Logistically, I mean."

"Oh." She almost smiled at the sound of relief in his voice. Then, in a very businesslike tone, he said, "Well, there's only the one bathroom, so we'll have to figure that out. Are you a morning or evening shower person?"

"Morning, usually."

"Good. I'm evening, because working on the ranch all day can make a guy pretty grubby."

A sudden realization flashed through her mind, all those days when he'd come to the house from the ranch, and she'd noticed his hair was damp. He'd showered after his workday at the ranch and before heading to another few hours of working with the kids and giving her a break. Then, unexpectedly, an image of being here while he did just that, of standing maybe right here at the kitchen counter, listening to the water run in the bathroom just off the hallway entrance, imagining it running over that tall, strong body... that tall, strong, naked body...

She sucked in a long breath, trying to steady herself. She

thought she had buried this kind of reaction to him long ago, back when Greg had laughed at Rick and Wendy for trying to set them up together, telling them that just because they were the only two single people they knew that didn't mean they were a match. Because back then, even when she was agreeing with what he said, she was regretting the truth of it.

"—try to be quiet when I roll out in the morning," he was saying, and she tuned back in hastily.

"I don't want to kick you out of your bedroom. I can sleep out here. You're too tall to sleep on this couch."

To her surprise, he chuckled. "You're not exactly vertically challenged, lady. What are you, five nine or ten?"

"Nine," she said, surprised he'd gotten so close.

"So I've got three inches on you. Big deal. And that couch is almost eight feet long. I'll survive. At least until things settle down and we get Winston Kraft out of the kids' lives. Then we can reassess."

He was so…reasonable. And generous. And kind. And… trustworthy?

She gave in because she couldn't really counter anything he'd said. But after they'd both finally surrendered to that weariness, she wished she'd fought harder. He'd come in with her to grab some things, including clothes and a book from the nightstand—one of his many cousins ran the bookstore in town, she remembered—and had pointed out a couple of empty drawers in the chest beside the closet, where he also shoved his own things on hangers to one side, leaving her a nice empty spot that would more than accommodate what she had with her.

She tried not to think about whose space she was invading as she got into her preferred knit sleep pants and shirt. A moment later there was no way she couldn't think that she should have taken him up on the offer to change the sheets on the bed. But he'd said he'd only slept on them once since they'd been washed, so she'd said not to bother.

And now she was lying in a swath of cloth that smelled like him. Not that she couldn't smell the clean of the laundry soap, but there was more. Not just the scent of the bar of soap she'd seen in the shower, or the aftershave she'd seen in the bathroom cabinet, but that indefinable something that had said "Greg" to her from the first time she'd sat next to him at a table, on Rick and Wendy's first effort to get them together.

She tried to focus on the fact that she was finally going to get to sleep, and that she'd better do it before Jane woke up in the night and her wailing for her momma woke Justin, and they'd be in chaos again. That was more important than the fact that she was at last sleeping in Greg's bed.

Without Greg.

When she finally fell asleep, she dreamed about that pitiful wail. Stirred restlessly, not knowing what to do to comfort the distraught child. On some level her brain thought it was real, and she felt as if she were underwater and fighting to reach the surface. But by the time she did and opened her eyes, it was silent. So it had been just a dream.

When she woke again, the sky was slightly less dark, and she knew dawn was approaching. She felt a little more rested, despite the worrisome dreams. That in mind, she tiptoed quietly down the hall to peek into the room to check on the kids. She opened the door a couple of inches and peered in.

Jane was gone.

Jolted fully awake, Briony smothered a gasp and went through the doorway, thinking she had to just not be seeing right in the dim light. But there was no denying the crib was empty.

She whirled around to look at the twin bed against the opposite wall. Justin was there, sleeping apparently peacefully after his long, active day. She turned again, heading for the door, her heart hammering in her chest. Where was Jane? Had something happened to that poor baby? God, she had to wake Greg, tell him. Had Kraft somehow gotten to her? Found out they were here, gotten past all the barriers and broken in to steal her? But then why not Justin? Unless he was afraid the older child might make too much noise, might tip off—

She came to a halt three steps into the main room. And as the scene before her registered, she thought her heart physically jumped. Greg was there all right, stretched out on his back on the couch.

And a sleeping Jane was cradled carefully on his broad chest.

She had heard that wail; it had been real. His eyes opened, telling her he'd only been dozing, probably out of concern the baby might slip or fall to the floor if he went fully to sleep.

For a moment she just stood there, her gaze locked with his. Greg had done what Greg would always do, the right thing. Tears stung her eyes and then overflowed. And for the first time it wasn't for Rick and Wendy. It was because they couldn't have picked anyone better as guardian for their children than this man.

This man who was now her husband.

Chapter 27

Greg wanted to jump to his feet and go to Briony, but he couldn't without waking Jane. So he just looked at her. She seemed so…something. She seemed smaller somehow, dressed in a short T-shirt–style top and loose sleep pants. She was crying, as she had often since that awful night, and to be honest he'd had his own bouts with fighting back the flood of emotion that still battered at him at the thought of never seeing his best friend again.

But this seemed different somehow. And it wasn't just that she looked oddly relieved as she stared at him. Belatedly it struck him. She'd probably checked the other bedroom first and found Jane wasn't there.

Even as he thought it, she whispered, "I looked and she was gone. I was afraid…"

Her voice trailed away without completing the thought, but he could imagine what she was afraid of, what she probably imagined when she saw that empty crib. That somehow Kraft had gotten in here and grabbed the tiny girl now sleeping so soundly on his chest.

"Sorry," he whispered back. The child didn't seem to be stirring at their quiet exchange, so he went on. "I heard her and remembered Rick saying he used to do this until she went to sleep. I was about to get up and put her back."

She shook her head. "Don't apologize. You're both… beautiful."

He blinked. Felt an odd rush of heat. It took him a moment to realize he was both embarrassed and pleased by her words. And had no words of his own to answer that clearly heartfelt declaration.

Gingerly, he shifted on the couch, holding Jane close while swinging his legs down to get his feet on the floor. Once he was upright, he stopped, waiting, to be sure the tiny girl hadn't awakened. He carried her back to the bedroom and laid her gently down in the crib, Rick's laughing explanation of all the things he'd had to learn about babies running through his head. He tried to focus on that, but his mind wanted to dwell on the look in Briony's eyes when she'd called them beautiful. He knew she probably meant the moment, probably the sight of Jane sleeping so peacefully, but she'd said…both.

When she was settled, thankfully still sound asleep, he straightened and turned to look at Briony. There was a gleam in her lovely green eyes he'd never seen before.

Lovely green eyes?

They were lovely. Especially when they were focused on him like they were now. As if he was the only thing that mattered to her right now. And not just because of the kids.

He shied away from the fact that the idea pleased him. As if he liked the idea that he mattered to her beyond the situation they found themselves in. Which was…silly.

He'd wondered on occasion, after Wendy had told him that, how differently she might have turned out had her life been different. Would she have been the lively, vivacious woman her hair and eyes suggested? Or was that just his imagination, sparked by the occasional flashes of spirit he saw?

Like when she faced you down over where the kids should be?

He smiled inwardly at that thought. Because for all her shyness, when it came down to what she thought was the best for the kids, she'd gotten past her reticence and stood her ground. And he had a gut-deep kind of feeling that she always would. Which was a side of her he'd never seen or known even existed before.

Even as he thought it, he realized how unobservant he'd been. You didn't survive the kind of life she'd had and come out steady enough to build your own life and business as she had without having a pretty solid core. And who was he to criticize how she protected herself in her life? After all, as his father had once told him, his tactic of pretending he wasn't hurting inside didn't make it go away. At the time he'd thought it was just typical fatherly advice. Only later, when he'd grown up a bit more and understood what his mother had done, did he realize Dad had been speaking from firsthand experience.

All of this ran through his mind and somehow, he ended up saying, very gently, "It's still early. Why don't you try to get some more sleep?"

As if the suggestion had triggered it, she yawned. She quickly put her hand up to cover her mouth. The movement of her arm made her shirt ride up a little, and he got a glimpse of smooth, pale skin and the beginning of the curve of one hip. When the arm came down it shifted a breast just slightly. A nicely curved, full breast.

Whoa. Back off, Colton.

"I think I will," she said, "and you should, too."

Still reeling a bit at his unexpected reaction, he couldn't find any words to say. And as she turned to go back to the bedroom, he found himself noticing her nicely curved back-side, too. And it was like another kick to the gut.

She was almost to the hallway when she stopped and looked back. Caught him dead to rights, staring at her. But she didn't seem to notice. *Or care, more likely.*

"They knew what they were doing when they picked you," she said quietly.

Again, words failed him. And then she was gone. He had to fight the urge to go after her, to figure out what had just happened here. What had suddenly awakened him to the fact that she wasn't just Rick and Wendy's friend, she was someone he'd like to know better. That he was curious about what was going on behind those green eyes when she silently studied something. Or someone. Like him. Wanted to know what she was thinking, what made her so sure he was the right guy for the job of raising Justin and Jane.

Then of course there was that other pesky little detail. That after all this time he'd realized that while she might be quiet and shy, she was also a knockout. After all this time, his body had suddenly realized it and kicked to life so fiercely it had almost taken his breath away.

Great, Colton. Complicate things even more, why don't you?

Trying to shove it all out of his mind, he went back to the couch, hoping to grab a little more sleep before the long day ahead began. But when his head hit the pillow, he knew it was futile. Because all he could think about was that that pillow was from his bed. His bed, that Briony was now in, in those loose-knit pajamas that somehow made that slight reveal of skin and shape sexier than any blatant lacy nightwear.

He stared up at the ceiling, wondering how, in the space of just a few minutes, he'd gone from the slight and oddly gratifying pressure of baby Jane on his chest to the greater and very different pressure of Briony on his mind.

It wasn't until later, when he shifted position yet again, trying to find that elusive sleep, that it hit him that the woman he couldn't get out of his head was his wife.

And he groaned aloud at the ridiculous morass his life had become.

Chapter 28

Briony didn't think she would ever get that image of Greg and little Jane out of her mind. The big, strong man so gently cradling the tiny girl on his broad chest, and the baby—she knew Jane was a toddler age-wise, but in that moment, that image, she had looked so small she couldn't call her anything but a baby—sleeping so soundly, trusting utterly in the man who held her. As if she somehow knew she was safe there.

Anyone would be safe there.

Rick had always told her she could trust his best friend. And she'd believed it, or at least believed that Rick believed it. She'd just never expected to have to rely on that assessment.

But here she was, curled up in his bed while he slept, certainly less comfortably, on the couch a few yards away. There was only a closed door between them, but she knew it might as well be a steel barricade, because he would never take advantage of it. Even if it was his own house, his own bedroom, his own bed she'd taken over.

Her husband's bed.

She buried her face in the pillow to stifle the faint moan that escaped her. But the pillow still had that faint, clean scent of that soap in the bathroom, which made sense if he always showered in the evening. But that sent her mind careening into other areas, like again imagining him in that shower, imagining water sluicing down over that masculine body, sliding over the taut muscles of his chest, the tight curve of his backside, and...other parts.

This time there was nothing faint about her moan. Her attraction to the man broke free of the compartment she'd so carefully kept it in for years, billowing out like an erupting volcano's smoke.

The man she had just married. Tied herself to for life. That was the vow she'd made, even as she knew—as they both knew—this was more a business arrangement for the sake of the kids than anything.

They hadn't yet talked about what would come after. After they'd won the case and been given full custody of Justin and Jane. She wouldn't let herself think it would come out any other way, because the thought of those two innocents going to the likes of Rick's father was too horrific to even consider. They had to win. They would win. And she would do whatever she could, whatever she had to, to make that happen.

Including baring her soul and letting what she'd always felt show to the world. Or at least, the judge who would decide the case. She would look at Greg as if it were all true, as if she truly were his wife in more than just name. She would look at him with everything he'd made her feel last night showing. Given how powerful it had been, that ought to do it.

And if it made things more awkward between them afterward, once the kids were safely theirs, so be it.

In the meantime, she had this big gathering to get through tonight. She'd never been comfortable at large parties, and that's what it seemed this was going to be. At least it would be casual dress, and outside where everybody wouldn't be crammed into one room. Maybe she could even escape for a breather now and then. Surely nobody would miss her—this was for the kids after all, so everyone would know who they were protecting. They just needed to be able to recognize her, and over the years she'd found her hair alone was usually enough to accomplish that.

When the time finally came, even outside she was a little stunned at how many people there were. She'd known the Coltons were a big family, but she hadn't quite realized how big until she was confronted with most of them. And it hit her anew when she was introduced as not just the children's co-guardian, but as Greg's wife. She understood their shock, since there had been no lead-up to it, probably never even a mention of her.

They had to know Greg had married her only for the sake of the children, and they were probably feeling sorry for him. Yet there was no sign of that in any of them. Some were brusquer than others, some friendlier and more welcoming, but no one shunned her or looked at her as if they didn't want her here. Especially welcoming was his sister, Lizzy, a slim, pretty strawberry blonde who smilingly said she was glad to have another redhead in the family.

But most importantly, they were all wonderful with the kids. Particularly Greg's cousin Hannah, who had brought her precocious five-year-old daughter, Lucy, who immediately joined up with Justin and Jane to keep everyone entertained.

Greg's dad fired up the big grill and had everyone lined up for some of his amazing ribs and chicken. Mama Jen added her plethora of savory side dishes including garlic mashed potatoes—this was Idaho, after all—and, to Briony's surprise, her effort at a pumpkin custard pie with a whipped topping vanished quickly and earned her more than one accolade.

It was the kind of thing she'd never experienced in her life, and sometimes throughout the afternoon she had to remind herself that all these people, save the ranch hands who stopped in for their share of the fun and food, were related. She had so little experience with this kind of family, in both size and strong connection, she was a little bewildered by it. But they were all kind to her, and she got through it, only retreating for a breather twice during the three-hour affair.

And the next day, Sunday, was the peaceful, restful antidote she needed. The children were quiet, probably having shouted and whooped themselves out yesterday, and while it had become clear to her that the ranch workers never took a day off, even they were less harried than during the rest of the week. They spent time watching Wick frolic in the small corral next to the barn, and she would have sworn the little colt recognized the kids by the way he trotted over to the fence on those long, gangly legs to greet them.

And looking at the animal who already seemed to be growing reminded her of the story Buck had told her of the night he was born, including what Greg had left out, that he had likely saved the little guy's life by doing what was necessary at that dangerous moment.

"I have a feeling," she'd said, "that's what he always does."

Buck had given her an approving nod, which warmed her more than it should have coming from a man she'd only just recently met. "Then you know my son," he'd said, and the pride in the older man's voice nearly brought tears to her eyes.

After that, the time at the ranch both flew by and dragged, depending on what was happening. The slow part was having to wait, impatiently, for the custody hearing date. The attorney had promised to let them know the moment they had a date, and she jumped every time her phone rang, but it was always a client. Or Greg, checking in on her and the kids when he was out in some far corner of the ranch.

The time when she wasn't obsessing about the hearing seemed to pass in a rush. The kids were kept so busy, so occupied with this fascinating place and its various human and animal occupants, that they were tired enough to sleep soundly most nights. And Briony found the relief of no longer being the only one to look out for them amazing. Greg's aunt was so caring and generous with her time, and his father almost beyond belief with his patience and wise suggestions. Beyond her belief, anyway. She'd never known a man like Buck Colton before.

Except Greg. He had learned well from his father.

She almost felt guilty about how much easier her life was here, with all this help, especially when she watched how hard Greg worked both doing his ranch work and then coming home after a long day and expending even more effort with the kids. At least he wasn't having to drive to the other house every day. If she'd had any idea how truly hard he worked she would have given that more weight.

And it was clear he was always thinking about the children, because one day he'd take Justin with him when he was going someplace he knew the boy would like—he had a fascination with the forest and its creatures, and occasionally a calf would stray—and the next would take Jane with him, carefully held in a sling she never would have imagined him using, when he had to head toward a marshy area where the song sparrows that so fascinated her tended to gather and sing their chirping, trilling songs.

He was so kind, so loving and gentle with them...and

yet he was the man who'd gone racing toward a gunfight when his cousin Chase had needed him. She'd never known a man like that in her life. Until now, hadn't been fully convinced they existed.

And so she caught herself in the quiet evenings she relished, usually when they were ensconced on the couch, her checking figures on her laptop, him reading whatever book he had going—he clearly preferred print books, but beyond that seemed to have a bit of everything on the shelves on the far wall—glancing over at him. Often. And loving the image that seemed to imprint on her brain, that matched her earlier fanciful imaginings, his chiseled profile, his concentration, and the way his brow sometimes furrowed, or he smiled as if something on the page had amused him. Once she asked him what had made him smile, and he said only, "Nice turn of phrase."

So much for the stereotype of dumb cowboys…

She'd felt as if she wasn't doing her share, since the kids were so enraptured by the ranch and all its doings, even little Jane who had decided that playing in a big pile of clean straw was the greatest thing ever. So, at the risk of falling into a stereotype herself—and because he usually cooked more than she did—she took to the kitchen. She did a little investigation first, checking with the ever-helpful Buck, on what Greg's favorite foods were. For a moment he looked at her a little oddly, but then quickly gave her a helpful answer of "Beef's his favorite, other than that anything but brussels sprouts."

She wrinkled her nose at the very thought, making Buck laugh. It was only later that she realized that perhaps he'd been surprised that she didn't already know what Greg did and didn't like to eat. But when she put a savory beef stew that had turned out even better than she'd hoped on the table and called Greg to eat, and he'd raved over it between hefty spoonfuls, she suddenly understood the gratification you could get from cooking for someone who did so much for you. Someone special.

Your husband.

It still jolted her every time she thought it. But the jolt was overwhelmed by the warm feeling she got watching him eat what she'd made. That he didn't expect her to do it all only sweetened the feeling.

It was Monday evening when the phone call came. Greg put his book down to answer. She could tell by the way he went utterly still, his expression intense, that it was important. When he finished with "We'll be there," her heart took a little leap.

He put the phone down and looked at her. And Greg-like, he didn't make her wait. "That was Tanya. Some other case reached an agreement out of court, and the judge agreed to give us the spot on the calendar. Wednesday morning. So now we're in a rush and we need to be in her office tomorrow for prep."

For a long moment they just looked at each other. It was finally here, the moment when the rest of their lives, the kids' lives, would be decided. She'd been so anxious for it to be settled she'd thought she'd feel a blast of relief when they had a court date. Instead, she was suddenly trembling.

"Greg," she said urgently, "what if…what if we lose?"

"We won't," he said, sounding rock-solid determined.

"But if we did, the kids…if he gets them…" She couldn't get past the horror of the idea to finish the sentence.

"He won't," he said this time.

"You can't know that. He could buy off the judge, or—"

"He will not get his hands on them. Even if I have to take them and run to keep them safe, he will not."

Briony stared at him, stunned by his words. That he would do that, leave this place he loved, his home, his amazing family, give up his entire life to fulfill the vow his best friend had asked of him... She knew, now that she'd been here and seen his life here, what a sacrifice that would be. And yet he was clearly decided, determined. He would do it, for the children. He would do it for his best friend. He would do it because he'd promised. Because he was the kind of man she'd never known in her life, the kind who kept promises, who helped others, who didn't always put himself first but also stood his ground, the kind of man who would never, ever intentionally hurt anyone—unless it was to protect someone he'd made one of those vows to.

He made a vow to you.

Sure, it had been more of a legal agreement than a wedding, but still Briony knew that he would take it as seriously as any other vow he made.

And in that moment, as she sat staring at his man unlike any other she had ever known, Briony admitted the truth she had buried so deeply she'd hoped it would never surface. But it burst free now, and she was left to deal with the simple fact. She may have just had a crush all these years, but now she knew the man, the real man. Knew who and what he was. Which, she supposed, made this inevitable. Even though they'd never so much as kissed.

She had utterly fallen for Greg Colton.

Chapter 29

Something about the way Briony was looking at him made Greg…uneasy? Uncomfortable? Unsettled?

Maybe all of those.

Because she was looking at him as if he'd done something wonderful, something amazing, even though all he'd done was voice his determination to do exactly what she was doing, devoting everything to keeping Justin and Jane safe and as happy as possible under the circumstances. He didn't know why she was so…whatever she was.

What he did know was that he was suddenly flooded with the need to live up to that look in her eyes. To have earned it. To deserve it. And he didn't quite know when or how her approval had become so damned important to him.

Or why he'd been obsessing about the feel of her in his arms, when all he'd meant to do was offer some comfort, some support in this monumental job they'd been tasked with.

In a way, it had started the night she'd made that amazing beef stew. Other than Dad, and Mama Jen if she was here, he pretty much saw to his own meals, and admittedly they weren't always great. Too often he went with whatever was quickest and easiest because he was too tired after a long day to think about anything else. And that beef stew, with whatever combination of spices and flavorings she'd used, had been a wonder.

So you're some old-fashioned male, charmed by a woman cooking for you? Some chauvinist who likes his woman barefoot, pregnant and in the kitchen as the old saying—

He felt as if he'd been hit by a wrecking ball. Because he'd suddenly—and ridiculously—remembered she wasn't his woman.

She was his wife.

His wife, and he'd never done anything more than hug her.

"And if it comes to that," she said now, very softly yet somehow defiantly, "if the judge rules the wrong way...I'll be right there with you."

She'd go on the run with the kids, with him? The thought that if worse came to worst, he wouldn't be alone made his stomach do an odd little flip.

He told himself she'd only do it for the children, but... she was still looking at him, steadily, with that warming glow in her eyes. As he stared back at her, her lips suddenly parted, as if she'd needed to take a deeper breath. He knew the feeling. He was feeling it himself. And suddenly he wanted to do more than just hold her.

He wanted to kiss that mouth, to see if those lips were as soft and sweet as they looked. And that kick-in-the-gut feeling suddenly dropped lower, and his body woke up in a rush.

"Don't look at me like that," he said thickly.

Her head tilted slightly. "Like what?"

"Like you want—" He cut himself off sharply. "I think I'd better go for a walk."

She blinked. "Why?"

"Because right now I want to kiss you."

Her breath caught audibly, and bright color rose in her cheeks. "And that's…a problem?"

His own breath jammed up in his throat. "You saying it's not?"

"Maybe I'm just saying…I'm curious, too."

"You know what they say about curiosity."

"I am not," she said slowly, "a cat."

"And I," he said slowly, replacing the bookmark and closing his book slowly, methodically, as if concentrating on that would divert everything else that was rocketing through his brain and body, "need that walk."

He stood up. Something changed in her then; she seemed to collapse into herself. And it unexpectedly hit him what courage it had taken shy, quiet, unassuming Briony to be as…forward as she'd just been.

"Briony," he began, then stopped, not knowing what to say.

"Never mind." It was almost a whisper. "I'm too much of a coward for you anyway."

Coward. The woman who had done what she'd done, who had faced him down more than once, who had taken on a load she'd never expected to carry and done it without hesitation or complaint, and who had just now offered to give up what life of her own she had left to go on the run from Winston Kraft, a coward?

He sat back down, this time right next to her. "You are many things, Briony. A coward isn't one of them."

She looked up at him then, those lovely—really, how had he not noticed how gorgeous they were?—green eyes glistening. That urge he thought he'd quashed rose up again, more fiercely this time. Almost undeniable.

Her lips parted and she lowered her eyes, making him

wonder what those long, thick lashes would feel like against his skin.

And then it was undeniable. He was moving before he even realized it, leaning in, lifting her chin with a gentle finger, giving her every chance to retreat but hoping she would not.

She didn't.

Her lips were softer, warmer, more enticing than he could have imagined. He caught the scent he only now realized he'd always associated with her, a light, clean, almost sage-like fragrance. Instinctively he moved closer, cupped her face with his hands to deepen the kiss. He felt the drag of his own work-roughened skin against the silk of hers, and half expected her to pull away at the harshness of it. Instead, she lifted her arms to his shoulders, as if hanging on. As if she needed the contact.

As if her senses were swirling as wildly as his own were.

When he finally broke away, only because he had to breathe, he stared at her in something resembling both wonder and shock. Never, ever would he have expected that kissing quiet, shy Briony would send every nerve in his body into overdrive. And she was staring back at him with an expression he couldn't quite put a name to. Almost… resignation?

And then, so low he had to strain to hear it, she whispered, "I knew it."

"Knew what?"

"That it would be…like that."

His brain was still spinning enough that it took him a moment to come to the conclusion that this meant she'd thought about it. Before. Maybe even before just now? Rick had once hinted that he thought Briony had a bit of a crush on him, but he'd thought it was just part of their matchmaking scheme.

Now he wasn't so sure.

Nor did he have any idea how he could have missed the potential chemistry between them. Had Rick and Wendy's machinations made him blind to it? Or at the least, resistant to the idea? He didn't know. All he knew for sure was... he wanted more.

Lots more.

"Don't worry," she said, and his gaze snapped back to her in time to see the look that was now definitely resignation on her face.

"What?"

"I know that it's just...circumstances. That we've been forced together, that it's...convenient, that we're married in name only."

"Briony," he began, but stopped when she shook her head.

"I said don't worry. I won't cross that boundary again."

"As I recall," he said wryly, "I'm the one who started that kiss."

"Only after I practically begged you."

He raised a brow at her. "I missed that part."

"Greg, please..."

Sudden doubt assailed him. "Look, if it wasn't...if you don't want...all you have to say is no and it'll never happen again."

She stared at him, wide-eyed. "How could you ever think I wouldn't want...more? I thought you wouldn't. You've never been in the least interested, all those times when Wendy and Rick tried to set us up."

"I know. Maybe I was just being...stubborn."

For the first time since the kiss, he saw a glint in her eye that had become familiar by now. Usually seen right before she launched a volley at him. Which had surprised him no end, coming from she who was usually so quiet and almost withdrawn. Wendy had always said Briony had more spirit than she'd ever shown in front of him, and he knew now that was true.

And he knew he was right now when she said, in that light, teasing tone, "You mean you resisted being pushed? I don't believe it, not you."

"Yeah, yeah," he muttered, but couldn't stop his mouth from quirking upward at one corner. And he realized with a little shock that he liked it—a lot—when she teased him like this. That he saw it as progress, that she'd either developed the nerve or was comfortable enough now to let it show.

Progress toward what, exactly, he didn't know. Or wouldn't admit, even to himself. But somehow, telling himself it was likely just the situation—and that they were married, even if only for the kids—wasn't working as well as it once had.

He took himself off for that walk, if for no other reason than to cool himself down in the chill October air.

Chapter 30

Briony tossed the blouse she'd been holding down on the bed. She needed to stop by her condo after the meeting with the attorney today, after she'd had a chance to ask her advice on what she should wear to the court hearing tomorrow. She was thinking what she called her "meet the client" suit, the most expensive outfit she owned. But maybe that would be too much. Too…showy, or something. Maybe she should stick to—

The whoop from the living area cut off her thoughts. She heard energetic running footsteps that she recognized as Justin's, and the delighted giggle of his sister, and wondered what miracle Greg had wrought this morning to have them laughing and happy already.

The same kind of miracle he worked on you last night?

A little shiver went through her as she remembered that kiss. Every hot, sweet moment of it, but most especially when he'd reached up to cup her face, as if he wanted to be sure she didn't pull away. As if there'd been the slightest chance she would have wanted that impossible pleasure to stop. Ever.

And that he, the ever assured and confident Greg Colton, had felt even a moment of uncertainty in a strange way warmed her, had given her the courage to tease him, in that way he surprisingly seemed to like.

When they were finally on their way to Conners, Greg at the wheel, she turned her focus to keeping the kids in the happy mood Greg had put them in. Since they were to be assessed today by the court's chosen juvenile bereavement counselor, who would then submit a report to the judge, she supposed happy was a good place for them to be.

Even as she thought it Greg spoke. "I talked to my cousin Fletcher this morning."

She immediately thought of the tall, broad-shouldered man who had helped them with the PI, and had brought his charming girlfriend, Kiki, to the barbecue. The memory was quickly shattered by a spike of worry.

"Did he hear something? About the PI or Winston?"

"No," Greg assured her quickly. "I just called him to ask about Judge Thompson. He said the guy's by the book, but fair. And off the record, he doesn't have a high opinion of the Ever After Church."

"So smart, too," she said, relieved.

Greg flashed her a grin. That devastating grin. "Fletch said he overheard him say once, off the record, that calling Ever After a church gave churches a bad name."

A little to her own amazement, Briony laughed. She tried hard to hang on to the mood as they walked toward the lawyer's office, but Jane was fussing and she couldn't help thinking that wasn't a good sign, and what if she wouldn't settle down in front of the counselor? But then Greg lifted the little girl up in the air, making the whooshing sound she seemed to adore, and the fussing became a delighted giggle. Justin only asked if this was the place with the room with all the toys, and Briony said in a loud, mock whisper that yes, it was, and there were rumors there would be cookies. Justin brightened, while Jane piped in, "Cookie?"

As they neared the door to the office, Briony saw there

was a woman standing there, watching them. It wasn't the woman who'd taken the kids into the playroom before, at the first meeting, so she wasn't sure why she was so intent on them, unless…unless she was the counselor. She supposed that made sense, for her to watch them unaware, see how they interacted with the children before settling into a more formal process. But it still made her nervous. She hadn't really thought about the possibility that the counselor could turn in a negative report, that maybe she—

"Hope she's not an Ever After fan," Greg muttered as they got closer.

"I was just thinking that," Briony said, her eyes fastened on the woman even as she took heart that they'd both had the same thought. She managed a smile as the woman opened the door for them, introducing herself as, indeed, the counselor.

Although she tried to pay close attention to the attorney's preparation and instructions for tomorrow, one part of her mind was solidly planted in that room next door. It was only when Greg reached out and took her hand that she was able to focus completely on what the lawyer was saying.

Tanya noticed the move immediately.

"So, how's the marriage of necessity working out?"

Briony felt her cheeks heat and couldn't have spoken even if she could find the words.

"We're good," Greg said, his voice holding that little note of roughness that made her nerves twitch.

But his fingers tightened slightly around hers, and that was all it took for her to be able to meet the lawyer's eyes and say evenly, "Yes, we are. And so are the children."

"And you're really, truly prepared to keep going? To commit yourselves to this?"

She glanced at Greg. He met her gaze and held it, warm,

steady…Greg-like. She looked back at Tanya. "We already have," she said firmly.

The woman seemed to consider that for a moment, then nodded. Then the preparation began as she laid out what would likely happen tomorrow.

"We've done our disclosure to Kraft's attorney, slime though he may be. I suspect he's withholding on our discovery requests, which I can turn on him. Mr. Kraft himself has left me two voice mails that are outside the realm of civility, and I'll be using those. But the most crucial factor is what we all already know—that he had no interest in even meeting his grandchildren until the possibility of a significant amount of money entered the picture."

"Bastard," Greg muttered, then quickly looked at the lawyer. "Sorry."

She smiled and shrugged. "When the shoe fits… Now, since they filed the motion, they get to present first. This is not necessarily bad."

She went on to break down the entire process for them, added a little plan of her own that made them both smile, agreed with Briony's choice of attire, suggested the same for Greg, then focused on him.

"You carry a well-known name in Owl Creek," she said.

"Blessing or curse?" Greg asked, sounding a bit sour.

"Both, given that your family's…shall we say strife is fairly well-known, and will probably be used against you if possible. However, it's also well-known that your father is a solid, stable and upstanding citizen, so if he could be here—"

"He will be. I'll call in the whole darn family if it'll help."

She smiled. "I'd say the owner of the Colton Ranch and the CEO of Colton Properties would suffice."

Greg smiled back, steady now. "Good. Chase owes me one anyway."

"After you helped him rescue Sloan and take down a kidnapper, I should hope so," Briony said.

Tanya's brows rose. "Well, well, more arrows for my quiver. I'll need some details on that."

They spent some time going over things, then repeating it all. Then, finally, the attorney leaned back in her chair and asked simply, "In your minds, what is the best possible outcome?"

"That Rick's father never breathes the same air as those kids," Greg said flatly.

"Agree," Briony said instantly.

"You two seemed to have reached complete accord."

"We have," Briony said. *Well, as far as the kids are concerned.*

There was a split second of silence before Greg agreed, that rough note back in his voice. "Yes. We have."

The memory of that kiss flooded her, sending heat rippling through her all the way to her cheeks, and hardly for the first time in her life she rued the pale complexion that went along with her hair.

"I see," the attorney said, and by the way she was smiling Briony thought she probably did. "All the better. Speaking case-wise, of course."

Briony had never been happier for the interruption of the children coming out of the playroom. Justin ran, as usual, and the counselor was carrying Jane, who was fiddling with the necklace the woman wore, looking at both sides intently.

"Doggy," the child said, as if she thought an explanation was required.

Briony looked at the necklace and saw it was an intricately carved head of what she suspected was a wolf rather than a dog, but that didn't matter beside the child's recognition it was something doglike.

"Close enough, sweetie," she said, leaning in to give Jane a kiss on the forehead before she took her from the counselor's arms. The woman looked at Tanya and nodded, adding, "You'll have my report in a couple of hours."

"Good. I need to get it to the judge. He's being understanding with the timeline because of the rush, but I want it there ASAP anyway."

"You'll have it."

They watched her leave. "So we won't know until tomorrow...what she'll say?" Briony asked, feeling anxious.

The lawyer smiled. "I already know. If there was a problem, she would have asked for a private consultation. Now, that's not to say they won't try to rebut her, but she's well established in this jurisdiction, and has the respect of the court and most attorneys."

"Most? As in not Kraft's?" Greg asked.

"He," Tanya said flatly, "has respect for nothing and no one. And that will help us win this."

Briony drew in a deep breath. Then, quietly, she said, "Rick and Wendy chose their attorney wisely."

That got her a wide smile, and there was a glint in the woman's eyes when she said, "Tell me that again tomorrow afternoon."

Chapter 31

If there was any resemblance between Winston Kraft and his son, Greg couldn't find it. Short, skinny, with a rather pinched face, there was nothing of Rick's height and strength in the man. He'd already known there was no resemblance in mind and heart, or in strength of character, but now he knew it was physical as well. Rick had always said he took after his mother, thankfully. It was obviously true.

But Rick had learned right and wrong from the man, although not in the way nature intended. Rick had always joked he'd known the right thing to do by watching his father and doing the opposite. Never had Greg felt the truth of that more than right now.

Tanya had assured them they didn't need to subject themselves to this after their already long morning testifying and being battered by Winston Kraft's self-aggrandizing lawyer. It would be quick, she'd said. He could only hope she was right. He reminded himself Rick had trusted the woman completely, and Rick was no fool. After all, he'd seen through his own father.

He watched the two men disappear into the judge's chambers along with Tanya.

"He's a repulsive little worm, isn't he?" Briony whispered as the door closed behind them. She glanced at a woman sitting in the gallery of the room. "And she isn't helping."

He had to stifle a laugh, inappropriate in a courtroom setting even if the judge wasn't present at this moment. But the woman who had come in beside Kraft definitely was not helping Kraft's case. She was clearly the much younger third wife, a flashy platinum blonde who had on even flashier jewelry, including a massive diamond on her ring finger, and eye makeup that he'd swear sparkled on its own. She was wearing a dress that looked more suitable for a party than a custody hearing. This was the kind of woman the phrase *gold digger* was invented for. Greg had known the moment he'd seen Judge Thompson give her a studying look this was not going to be the influence Kraft had probably hoped for, perhaps showing how rich he was. Not to take care of the kids, but maybe to make the judge believe he didn't really want all that insurance money.

Briony, on the other hand, looked wonderful. Smooth, professional and competent in her business-style navy blue suit, with only a pair of gold earrings as jewelry.

And her wedding ring.

Sometimes he still had to remind himself.

And he knew he would always treasure the look and the quiet, "My, but you clean up nicely, Mr. Colton," she'd given him when she'd first seen him in the—coincidentally, or fated?—navy blue suit and blue-and-white subtly striped tie Mama Jen had given him for the occasion. She'd suggested some other shoes, but that he'd declined, sticking with his dress cowboy boots.

"I am who and what I am," he'd said, and Briony had given him a smile and nod that had him feeling oddly proud.

Now Briony turned to glance over her shoulder, where a large chunk of his family was seated, siblings and cousins alike. And most importantly his father, sitting directly behind them. Briony was smiling that same kind of smile when she turned back. Her fingers tightened around his, and suddenly he felt calmer, despite the fact that he would have sworn half an hour had passed only to glance at the clock on the courtroom wall and see that it had been barely ten minutes.

When it finally happened, when they emerged after just short of an hour, it was over in a rush. He took heart from the fact that Rick's father did not look happy as he stalked out. At all. And that Tanya gave them a wink and a nod as she retook her seat.

He'd never been much on legalese, and all the quoting of Idaho's Title 15, Uniform Probate Code, was worse than Greek to him—he at least knew a little of that, from a ranch hand they'd once had—but the part that needed to be clear was. He and Briony were appointed permanent guardians to Justin and Jane Kraft, with the determination that they shall work together cooperatively to serve the best interests of the minor children.

They'd won. The kids were theirs. He almost enjoyed watching Kraft and his hotshot attorney storming out in anger.

"Well, that should convince the judge he's right, if he had any lingering doubts." Buck Colton's voice came from behind them, and Greg turned to see both his father and aunt smiling widely. They'd had their own time under questioning and had been a strong cornerstone of their case.

"He already knows he's right," Tanya said. "Not only did they hold back some requested information, a clear violation of discovery rules, they tried to bombard the court with motions, and that's a hot button with any judge." She grinned then. "And then there's the glamour-girl third wife."

They all laughed at that. "She was a bit…over-the-top," Jen said.

"And it says a lot about Kraft's judgment that he thought she would be helpful, showing up like that," Dad said.

"Indeed," the attorney said with a smile. "But the deciding factor, if I know Judge Thompson, and I do, was one simple thing." They all went quiet, waiting. "Winston Kraft couldn't pick either of his grandchildren out of a photo lineup, and he had to admit to the judge he'd never met either of them in person. Which he lied about in the filing papers. Even his attorney was angry at him."

As he watched the brisk, professional woman, after a promise to forward the final papers as soon as they arrived, leave the courtroom, Greg felt a little numb now that it was over. They'd won. They had legal custody of the kids. They'd kept their vow to Rick and Wendy, and their precious children would never have to deal with his con man, grifter father.

When they got outside, he sucked in a deep breath of pure, crisp October-in-Idaho air. It felt cleansing, as if the last of the miasma that clung to Winston Kraft had been vanquished.

"Come on," his dad said. "We've got some celebrating to do. I reserved the patio at the Tides."

Greg stared at his father. The Tides was a high-end restaurant on the lakefront, Owl Creek's fanciest establishment. "You what, assumed we'd win?"

"I did," he said firmly. "Idaho still holds up what's right."

It wasn't until they were walking out to their respective vehicles—it had taken a small fleet to get all the Coltons who offered to come to Conners—that his dad took him to one side and said quietly, "Kraft was pretty mad. I'll put the word out on the ranch to be extra watchful."

"Thanks, Dad," Greg said, meaning it more than ever. "And I don't mean just for this. I mean for everything, ever."

His dad blinked. And Greg was sure that, at least for a moment, he'd seen a little extra sheen in Buck Colton's eyes.

"I…"

Words apparently failed him, and Greg counted that a win. And with the thought of credit where it was due, he added, "I've always felt that way, but Briony said I should make sure and tell you. Often."

"She's a good woman, son," Buck said. "You could do a lot, lot worse for a life partner." His mouth twisted wryly. "Take that from someone who did."

He hated that his mother could still make Dad react like that. "She doesn't matter anymore, Dad. Sure, the family's got to deal with her to some extent, but she doesn't matter beyond that."

It was only when they were headed back to Owl Creek that the phrase his father had used really hit home. A life partner. Briony, a partner for life. And he couldn't come up with any words to describe the feeling that gave him. But he couldn't get it out of his head as they drove the road back home.

"The Tides is that fancy place in town, right?"

Briony's question snapped him out of his musings. "Yeah. You've never been there?"

She shook her head. "Rick and Wendy used to celebrate their anniversary there. I would watch the kids sometimes."

He glanced at her. "I know. I'd watch them the other times."

His gaze was back on the road when he heard her let out a sad little laugh. "Do you think they were…training us? Just in case?"

"I wouldn't put it past Wendy," he answered quietly. "She was always thinking ahead, planning for the worst."

"We had to," Briony said simply, and in that simple exchange he got the best sense he'd ever had of just how bad their childhoods had been.

"It's amazing you both turned out as warm and as caring as you did," he said.

"I do care," she said, very softly.

And suddenly that kiss, the kiss he'd never planned, never expected, was crackling in the air between them. And this time it wasn't that he couldn't come up with any words, it was that he didn't dare say them. Didn't dare say that he wanted to try that again. And again after that.

And maybe even more. A lot more.

So he kept quiet until they hit town, and smothered the thought that he'd actually rather go straight home and indulge in those thoughts as they pulled up at the Tides.

The sparkly strings of lights that marked the patio were on, even though it wasn't even starting to get dark yet. Which was a good thing, since it was barely over sixty degrees now, and once the sun set it would start the dive to about twenty degrees less. But everybody here was dressed accordingly, telling him they'd known this was happening.

A buffet table was already set up, with an array of the foods the place was known for, and Greg spotted a tray of champagne glasses near an at-the-moment-unmanned bar.

"Your dad really did all this?" Briony asked as she stared through the windshield, sounding more than a little awed.

"He arranged it," Greg agreed. "But I sense Mama Jen's fine hand here."

She started to speak, but then hesitated. That life partner thing went through his head again, and it made him say gently, "Say it, Briony. You don't have to hold back anymore."

"I was just wondering…how would you feel if she and your dad got married now?"

He met her gaze as she voiced the secret wish he'd been lugging around for a while now. "Like we had the mom we should have had," he answered honestly.

She smiled at that, and it was amazing how good that made him feel.

It turned out the celebration was more fun than he'd expected. And he welcomed the chance to thank all the family who had turned out in support. He guessed the presence of the CEO of Colton Properties, an FBI agent and a couple of cops, among others, hadn't hurt their cause any. The food was good, and the champagne a rare treat.

Sunset had begun and the patio lights seemed brighter as the sky dimmed. The lake was glowing now as the light that remained hit the angle that made the reflection off the water seem even brighter. Greg was enjoying—he wasn't quite sure why, except maybe it would make life easier—watching Briony across the patio talking with his sister, as she'd earlier been talking with his cousin Frannie, who had arrived with her rather intimidating boyfriend, Dante. During that conversation they'd glanced over at him more than once, which had him wondering just what that conversation had been about.

Soon he saw Briony standing alone on the edge of the patio, looking out over the lake, a very slight slump to her posture, and it struck him that she might have hit her limit on socializing in a large group. Or if she'd slept as badly as he had last night, maybe she was just exhausted.

He walked over to her and asked quietly, "Had enough socializing?"

She gave him a startled glance. "I… Is it obvious?" she asked, sounding worried.

He smiled. "No."

She seemed relieved, which oddly pleased him. The other inference there, that he'd learned to notice even the nonobvious with her, surprised him a little. Yes, he'd spent a lot of time with her, but he'd thought he'd been too focused on the kids to absorb anything else. Apparently not.

She looked back out at the lake. "It's so beautiful here."

"It is. I just hope it's a while longer before the entire outside world discovers that."

"And ruins it forever?"

"Something like that, yeah. My uncle Robert started it, trying to turn us into a tourist destination, and it's already happened more than I like."

"Progress," she said, and he liked the ironic tone she put in it.

"To some people."

They looked out over the peaceful water again, until his father came up behind them.

"Why don't you two take off? It's been a long day for both of you. Jen and I have got the kids. We'll get them home and see to them until morning. Take my truck and give me the keys to the car with the car seats."

Greg turned to stare at his father. There had been… something in his voice, something under the lighthearted words, that made him think he was up to something. He had to be, arranging for them to have a big chunk of alone time. See to the kids until morning? Leaving them a night alone…together?

Whatever Dad was up to, Greg couldn't deny the idea of having some peace and quiet was appealing, and he knew it would be to Briony. When he'd gone, Greg looked at her.

"Want to take them up on that? Escape?"

"Yes," she said instantly. "It's not that everybody hasn't been wonderful," she added hastily, "and it was wonderful of them to turn out for the kids today, but—"

She stopped when he held up a hand. "I get it. It's wearing. Even I'm tired. Let's go."

He pulled out the car keys and gave a whistle that made his dad turn his head. He tossed him the keys. His father grinned, pulled out his own keys and tossed them back along the same arc. He smiled back, a little embarrassed, before they turned and walked toward where Dad's ranch truck was parked.

When they got there Briony looked at him for a moment, and he saw that glint of spirit her rough life had never been able to fully destroy. "I'll drive, shall I? I stopped at half a glass of champagne."

"And I had three glasses," he admitted, and fished out the keys and handed them to her without complaint. It was apparently the right move, judging by the smile she gave him then.

And as they got into the truck, he couldn't help wondering—hoping—that it was just the first of his right moves for the night.

Chapter 32

Briony didn't complain when Greg opened the passenger-side window to let in some of the air that had chilled rapidly after the sun had set. She had the heater blowing on her feet, and she had to admit the brisk, clean air was invigorating. Something she needed as well, considering how little she'd slept in the last couple of days. She wasn't all that used to driving a big truck, and the last thing she wanted to do was to ding up Greg's father's.

She suspected Greg was in the same tired boat. Knowing their entire future had depended on what happened today made for some long, sleepless hours.

Their future.

She'd been so consumed by thoughts of what could go wrong—because in her life, they so often had—and what they would do if they lost, she hadn't spent a lot of time thinking about what would happen if they won. She had no doubt Greg would never hand the kids over to Wendy's evil father-in-law, just as she had no doubts she would be right beside him on that. For the kids' sake. Even if it did mean they had to grab them and run.

That he had felt as she did, willing to give up everything to carry out Rick and Wendy's wishes, told her everything she needed to know about Gregory Colton. He was who he appeared to be.

I am who and what I am.

She could count the number of people she knew that fit that description on the fingers of one hand. And now Greg was one of them.

Ironically perhaps, one of the others was Rick's father, in a very negative way. Because he absolutely was who and what he was, an evil, malicious, immoral con man who wrapped his cons in pseudo-religion and sold it to gullible people who couldn't see who and what he was. That could not make her think any less of him, since she already thought the worst.

But that Greg was who and what he was...that was a new certainty that made her feel a tempest of emotions. She glanced over at him as she stopped the truck and waited for two oncoming vehicles to pass before making the turn on the road that led to the ranch gate.

"You really would have done it, if we'd lost," she said, and it wasn't a question.

He turned his head and gave her a steady look. Steady, that was Greg. "Run with them, rather than let him get his filthy hands on them? Absolutely." Then, after a brief moment, he asked quietly, "Would you really have gone with us if I did, if we'd lost?"

"I would." She said it instantly, and with all the certainty she could put into her voice. "I'd be with you every step of the way."

Something changed in his expression then; something glinted in his eyes that she could see even in the dim light of the truck's cab. Something that made her pulse kick up and wonder exactly why his father had done this.

She drove on, the mood that had seized her growing with every heartbeat. When they reached the ranch gate Greg got out without a word to open it. She pulled the truck through, then stopped as he ran—ran!—to get back in. Her ricocheting brain seized on that simple fact, and no matter how she tried to put it down to just wanting to get home, she couldn't stop herself from wondering if he'd been eager to get back to her.

She drove toward the main house, then up to the spot where she'd noticed his dad always parked. She double-checked the unfamiliar gear shift to be sure it was in Park, then took her foot off the brake and turned off the engine.

Finally, she turned in the seat to look at him.

"Leave the keys in it. Dad always does in case some-one needs it."

The words were prosaic, but there was an undertone to his voice that matched the glint she'd seen in his eyes. He didn't say another word as they got out and walked to their house.

Their house. She was even thinking of the place that way. Their future, their house, and now…their kids. She had a husband and two children. Children she loved.

A husband she could too easily love.

She'd never had an overactive imagination, and what imagination she did have usually ran to envisioning the worst that could possibly happen. She'd never spent much time picturing the good things that could happen, because except for Wendy, in her life they never had.

Until now.

Now she had Greg and the kids. And the kids deserved a life where they could be happy. Where they could re-member Rick and Wendy with love, but not spend every day gutted by the loss.

And what did she deserve? Certainly not a man the likes of Greg, but…she had him. And now that she was certain of who and what he was, she knew he would never walk away from the responsibility he'd taken on.

They were safely inside—interesting, that that was the word that popped into her mind, safe—before he turned to her, grasped her shoulders, met her gaze head on and asked quietly, "What's wrong?"

"Nothing," she said, aware of the shakiness in her voice but unable to stop it. "Absolutely nothing."

She saw understanding dawn in his expression. "And that's what scares you, isn't it? That's what you've never had before."

"There's always been something that just went wrong or is about to sometime soon."

There was a long, silent moment before he spoke again, but he never let go of her. "I had it easier. Mom just walked out, Dad stepped up, and it was over." He grimaced. "Well, it was until her other life came to light." The grimace became a smile. "But we got two pretty great half siblings out of that, so I'm not complaining."

She managed a shaky smile in turn. "Maybe there's no such thing as a life where…nothing's wrong."

The look he gave her then was steady, reassuring and very, very Greg. "If nothing's gone wrong in your entire life, then you haven't really lived it."

She stared at him. "When did you become a philosopher?"

His mouth twisted. "About the time I became responsible for two kids whose lives were just torn apart."

She couldn't stop herself. She reached up to cup his cheek. He looked startled but didn't pull away. In fact, he leaned into her touch.

"Our lives, too," she said.

"I know," he said, more softly than she would have thought a tough, rugged cowboy his size could ever speak.

"But maybe…maybe it's not all bad. Or maybe at least we can make something good out of it."

She couldn't speak; she could only look at him. And she saw what he was asking in the depths of those warm brown eyes. She tried to summon up all the reasons it would be a mistake. But they didn't seem to stack up against all the reasons she wanted this. Had wanted this, if she was honest, for a long time. A very long time.

"Bri?" he asked, his voice barely a whisper as he used the nickname he never had before, that only Wendy had ever used, the only person she'd ever allowed to use it.

Until now. Because in Greg's rough whisper, it was the most beautiful name ever. The most beautiful name in the world.

"Yes," she whispered back.

And then he was kissing her, and impossibly, it was even more incredible than she remembered from before. And for the first time in her life, she threw caution to the wind, because in this moment she wanted nothing more than for this to go on and on. She thought of all the times he'd been there for the kids, and for her, rock solid and unshakable, unlike anyone she'd ever had in her life. Even Wendy, sometimes caught up in her own troubles, hadn't always been able to be there.

Greg had never missed a beat. For any of them, even her when Rick or Wendy had asked, since she never would herself.

But she asked him now. Because she would rather have this memory be of this moment, when they'd won, when they were happy, when things were right, than if they turned to each other in shared misery.

He broke the kiss, but only to shed his jacket. When she reached to tug at his shirt, her fingers already tingling at the thought of what running them over those taut abs would feel like, he put a gentle hand over hers.

"Do you mean what it seems like you mean?" His voice was oddly shaky, and she realized he sounded like she felt.

"I'm tired of being curious," she said, hearkening back to that first kiss.

"So am I," he said, and it came out half relieved, half stirring in a way she'd never heard from him before.

What had begun slowly, tentatively, suddenly became a whirlwind. He couldn't move fast enough for her; she couldn't move fast enough for herself. She wanted to touch every inch of him almost as much as she wanted him to touch every inch of her. When her clothes were tossed aside, she was still unzipping his jeans, and when he reached to cup her breasts, rubbing his thumbs over her nipples, she cried out at the sensation that ripped through her.

"My hands are rough," he said apologetically against her ear as he bent to tease it with his tongue.

"Don't apologize," she said. "They're the hands of a working man." Then, in a burst of nerve that had to be brought on by pure, raging need, she added teasingly, "So put them to work."

He laughed, a low, rough-edged but delighted laugh. And that she could draw that sound from him made her feel more than a little delighted herself.

And then he followed her bantering order, and put those rough, strong, yet impossibly gentle hands to work. And before she could process how it had happened, he had swept her up into his arms and they were in the bedroom. His bedroom, although now hers, too. And his bed, which he'd shared with her, if not physically.

Until now.

Now he was naked and beside her, his body declaring

to her like nothing else could that this was real, that he wanted this. And if it was just a reaction to the opportunity for sex, she didn't care. Right now, she didn't care about anything except that she wanted him more than she'd ever wanted anyone or anything in her life. She reached down to caress surging male flesh and reveled in the sound of his groan of pleasure.

She urged him on, although she did feel a jolt when he turned to reach into the nightstand drawer she'd never opened, dug into the back and pulled out a condom.

"Dad, ever hopeful," he muttered when he saw her gaze follow the movement. She couldn't help her wide smile.

He fumbled with it, as if he hadn't done it for a long time. She offered to help, but he gave her a sideways look that was somehow incredibly hot as he said, "You touch me in the way that would take, and this is going to be over fast."

And then, at last, she was in his arms again. His hands were touching, caressing, stroking, leaving fiery paths along her skin everywhere they went. She heard the noises she was making, sounds that had never been wrung from her before, capped by a cry of his name as he finally, finally slid into her.

It had been so long, and with the way he stretched her, it should have been difficult. The ease of it now only told her what she'd already known—she was hungrier for this man than she'd ever been for anything or anyone in her life. The controlled strength and power of him as he thrust into her again and again made her heart race even faster, and unlike the two other times in her life when she'd tried to find this with a man, with Greg she was able to let go completely, because she knew down to the marrow of her bones that he would never, ever hurt her.

And with that her body unleashed, every nerve coming

to life, her hands savoring the feel of him, her mouth the taste of him, and her ears the sounds he made when he drove deep. She hit the kind of peak she'd never really believed in before and she cried out his name as he drove deep one last time and her body clenched fiercely as a wave of sensation swamped her. She felt him shudder in her arms, heard him say her name as if it had been wrenched out of him.

She clung to him as it slowly ebbed, feeling as if she'd been granted every wish she'd ever had.

Chapter 33

Greg felt as if he'd never move again. Felt blasted on so many fronts he couldn't even sort them out, maybe because she'd fried every circuit in his brain as well as his body. In ways he'd never, ever expected.

Briony. Shy, quiet Briony had just taught him a universe of new lessons in only a few minutes. Minutes that he wanted an immediate repeat of, except for the slight problem that, utterly drained, he couldn't even muster the strength to roll off her.

Oddly, she didn't seem to mind, in fact was holding on to him as if she was afraid he'd leave her and she didn't want him to. As if she wanted him right where he was, his body pressed into hers.

He marveled at the fact that even the idea of that began to stoke that fire again. And the feel of it, the feel of her hands on his backside, holding him against her, felt so unreservedly, totally right.

He told himself no one would have expected this beneath Briony's quiet, reticent exterior. But if he was being honest—and he always tried to be, although sometimes it was harder with himself than others—he wouldn't have expected this kind of explosive combustion from himself, either.

Not that he hadn't had normal urges and needs, and not that satisfying them hadn't been pleasurable, but he'd never felt anything like this. Never known it was even possible. And somehow, he didn't think it was merely because it had been a while since his last casual hookup. Right now, he couldn't even remember when that was, let alone what it had been like.

All he knew for sure was, it had been nothing— *nothing*—like this.

Briony. Of all people, of all women, Briony.

"Greg?"

The slight tinge of her old uncertainty in her voice was enough to snap him out of his floating, blissful thoughts. His head came up, and he saw that same touch of uncertainty in those beautiful green eyes. He hated the sight of it. Hated that she'd had the kind of life that instilled those doubts in her. That she could feel them at all, but especially that she could feel them now.

And he felt a familiar determination building in him, the kind he felt when he had a big task before him but knew it had to be done. A determination that if it was the last thing he did, he'd erase those doubts forever.

But right now, he wanted that look in her eyes gone. He wanted a smile out of her. He wanted to know this had been as amazing for her as it had been for him. So he propped himself up on his elbows, lifting his head so he could look straight into those eyes, and gave her a crooked half grin.

"Son of a gun," he said. "They were right."

She blinked, and puzzlement replaced the doubt. He welcomed it. Besides, puzzlement was a cousin to curiosity, and wasn't that what had landed them here to begin with?

He let the grin loose, holding nothing back. "Rick and

Wendy. They were right all along. How the heck did they know we'd combust like this?"

Her eyes widened, and slowly, so he was able to savor every moment of the change, she smiled. It was like the sun rising over the lake, brightening everything around with an inimitable sparkle.

"Maybe," she said, and that glint he was coming to love lit the green of her eyes, "because together they did and they recognized it?"

"Maybe. Maybe they did. Makes me feel pretty stupid for resisting all this time."

"Not stupid, cautious," she said. "I'm sure a guy like you has to be."

He raised a brow at her. "A guy like me?"

"You know. Someone whose word is gold. Someone who's always ready to help a friend. Who always does the right thing, even when it's hard. The kind of man people mean when they say honorable and principled and…trustworthy."

He understood on some gut level the pause before that last word. Understood that of all things, trust was the hardest for her to give.

Understood that she was giving it to him now.

The knowledge tightened something deep inside him, and he wasn't sure exactly what the feeling was. He only knew he'd never felt anything quite like it before. Like so many things with her. That she would choose those things over the more typical compliments to his looks or his eyes or the prosperous ranch was so…Bri.

He went for a joke to stall until he figured it out. "And here I thought you were going to compliment my backside," he said, tensing the muscles still under her hands.

To his surprise she squeezed back, and the glint was even more obvious when she said, "I thought I already had."

Because he didn't know what else to do, he kissed her again. And again. And before he'd even left her completely his body hardened again, and he set about discovering if it had been a fluke, this conflagration he'd felt, even though he thought he already knew the answer. It hadn't been a fluke.

A few minutes later, as he nearly shouted her name under the force of the climax that hit him, he had his proof.

Rick and Wendy had indeed been right all along.

It was later, as they held each other in the darkness, that Briony whispered, "Do you feel…guilty?"

He'd been about to doze off, but even his sated brain realized this was not something to brush off with a platitude. He dug the fingernail on his index finger into his thumb, a trick he used when he had to wake up in a hurry. The little pain did its job, and the sleepiness retreated, at least for now.

"About what?" he asked carefully.

"Us…being like this. It being so…good, when Rick and Wendy are…gone."

Despite the pleasure of hearing her say how good it had been, a warning went off in his head, telling him that how he answered this was important. He'd come to know a bit about this woman, about the uncertainties that were the source of those moments of doubt, of insecurity. He ached inside for the life she'd had, so much worse than his own, no matter what people thought of his mother and her actions.

In that moment he wished for some of his father's wisdom, and the knack he had for putting his answers and advice in just the right way. Hoping he'd learned enough by just listening, he gave it a try.

"I miss them, every day, more than I've ever missed anyone. But I don't feel guilty. Because this is what they wanted. All these years, this is what they apparently saw and tried to make happen."

He heard her let out a long, slow breath, felt the brush of it over the skin of his chest as she snuggled against him. "I'm glad," she whispered. "We're a little late, but…I think of it as a final thank-you to them both."

He shifted one arm to pull her even closer. "I'm glad, too." He hesitated, then figured he'd done okay so far and plunged ahead. "Can we build on this, Bri? Can we build a family, not just for Justin and Jane, but for us?"

She turned her head, and in the faint light of his—no, their—bedroom, he could see her eyes looking into his. "I should be asking you. You're the one who knows about family. Can we?"

"We can."

"Then we will. Because a promise from Greg Colton is golden."

The warmth that flooded him then had nothing to do with arousal or sex, and everything to do with something much bigger. And for the first time he thought they might just be able to build something else between them.

Love.

Chapter 34

Greg had never really looked forward to the Fall Fest. He'd already been pretty much beyond the kind of games and prizes it offered back when it had first started. And as an adult, sometimes he'd been so hard at work on the ranch that he didn't even realize it was happening until he tried to go into town for something and found it swamped with people.

But today he found himself preparing for it cheerfully, almost with gleeful anticipation, because the kids were going to love it. They were already excited, Justin because of the games and prizes, and the presence of the vendor for his favorite treat, a fried doughnut hole concoction Greg secretly enjoyed himself. Jane, he suspected, was just excited because everyone else was.

He'd overheard Briony chatting to the little girl as she got her ready this morning, telling her all about the festival and what would be there. Jane probably comprehended more than he realized, but all that really mattered to him was that the little girl was happy and giggling back at Bri when she slipped into that high-pitched, teasing voice she used with her.

As opposed to the low, husky teasing voice she used with him at night.

With an inward grin, he thought he was going to either

need to stop remembering those luscious hours or step out into the fall chill to cool off. It had dropped below freezing last night, and even with the fortuitously sunny day ahead, it was going to take a while to warm up. Which meant layers for the kids, shirts, sweaters, jackets, heavy socks and warm boots.

He gave a slightly amazed shake of his head as he found himself thinking in those terms before anything else. The kids really did come first, and it felt as natural as breathing.

"Unca Greg, Unca Greg!"

As if conjured by his realization, Justin came running toward him, carrying the insulated boots that would indeed be warm, but were a bit hard for the little one to get on. He had a sudden vision of the days to come, when maybe someday it'd be this little guy helping him pull on his boots, when he was old and gray. He swept the boy up in that way that never failed to make him laugh and plopped him down on the couch before kneeling down to help with the stubborn footwear.

The boy slid off the couch and stamped his feet as if to settle them in the boots. "We going now?"

"Yeah," he said, "as soon as your sister's ready."

The little boy made a grimace that made Greg laugh in spite of the depths of emotion the kid had tossed him into just moments ago. He heard footsteps behind them and turned to see Briony approaching with Jane in her arms. And something about the image that met his eyes made his throat knot up, as if he were seeing something of such incredible beauty there were no words to describe it.

When she looked up and met his gaze, he knew there was no "as if" about it.

The little one was dressed in layers just like her brother, so that except for the heavier outer jacket, they were ready.

Not to mention that Briony looked amazing in a simple pair of black jeans and boots topped with a soft green sweater that made her eyes seem to glow, and that slid over her, clinging in all the right places.

Places he'd been kissing and caressing not so very long ago.

And if he didn't stop this, he was going to be unable to walk.

"Will Pacer be there?"

He looked back down at Justin, who was clutching the stuffed dog that had been one of the few toys he'd wanted from the house.

"Yes," Greg answered, knowing from his brother Malcolm that the local and state SAR agencies were doing some PR at the festival. "And some more search dogs, too. There will be a special booth where you can meet them."

"Cool," Justin said. He looked at Briony, who was holding his sister. "Can we go now?"

He nearly laughed at the boy's impatient tone and the look he gave his sister, as if she was the reason they weren't already there.

Just wait, kiddo. Someday you'll be waiting for a woman and happy to do it.

That he'd never expected to be that guy himself only made his smile wider.

Briony, as she always did, noticed. "Looking forward to this?"

"Actually," he said, his voice a little rough, "I was more looking back."

He saw color rise in her cheeks and knew she'd gotten his point. Last night had been particularly spectacular, until he'd been afraid they'd wake the kids. What they had done was fall asleep, exhausted, until Justin had walked in on them this morning. It was the first time the kids had found them together in bed and judging by the boy's reaction—or lack thereof—he found it perfectly normal. He'd just been anxious to get going to the "big party" as he called it, and they were delaying him.

Greg was a little surprised at the boy's eagerness, but sadly understood when, in the car on the way, Briony teased him a little about being so excited and the boy said, "Mommy and Daddy will be there. They always go."

"Mama? Dada?" Jane chimed in, sounding hopeful.

Every time it happened it was a punch to the gut. He glanced at Briony and saw the sheen in her eyes, knew it had hit her just as hard. But they had to handle it as they always tried to, with consistency.

Briony turned to look at the children in the back seat. "They won't be there, honey," she said softly, and the pain in her voice made Greg's worse. "They can't ever be anywhere again."

"Oh."

Justin's brow furrowed as he wrestled with concepts he was too young to understand. Greg was almost grateful for that, although it made it harder on him and Briony to have to hear the question and answer it, over and over, every time reawakening the pain that their newly hectic lives managed to mute somewhat.

Only the knowledge that they were doing what Rick and Wendy had wanted, that their beloved children were safe with them, made it bearable at all.

When Justin had gone back to peering out the window, Greg reached out and took Briony's hand in his, squeezing gently.

Will it ever get easier?

I think it'll get easier than it is now, but it will never, ever be easy.

He'd asked that just yesterday, when it had been Jane wailing, and it had taken him a trek out to the barn to see Wick to calm her down. Her quiet response had reminded him she had more experience with loss and heartbreak than he'd had, even with Jessie's—he'd started to correct himself to saying that rather than Mother's—more and more unhinged behavior. And he couldn't honestly say he missed his uncle Robert either, despite what had been a powerful presence. Not after they'd learned how he'd cheated on Mama Jen for years with her own sister.

"Remember the morning after the hearing," Briony said quietly, giving his hand a squeeze in turn.

He knew what she meant, and it made him smile. Justin, with his usual energy, had been up and ready to go and further explore the ranch, and Briony had had to herd him back for some breakfast first. And in the middle of his bowl of oatmeal he'd announced with all the officiousness a four-year-old could muster, "I like it here. We should stay."

That moment gave him such hope, that they could do this, that they could build the life they wanted for the children—and themselves.

When they got to town, it was already bustling. The Fall Fest got a little bigger every year, until it was drawing people from all over southwest Idaho. He knew most of his family would be here at one time or another, and before they'd even gotten to the center of the park area where most of the kids' games were, including the bounce house Justin had his eye on, they'd encountered three cousins and his sister, Lizzy, who fussed happily over both kids, getting them both to laugh. And then Dad and Mama Jen appeared, eliciting squeals of delight from Jane and Justin both.

Lizzy took off to wander the festival just as he spotted Malcolm and Pacer at the booth set up to promote the search-and-rescue teams that served the area. He was talking to a tall Black man with close-cropped hair, who held the leash of another dog, a yellow Labrador who looked as fit and energetic as Pacer. Both men wore similar rugged clothing and what looked like communications gear, as if ready to go into action at any moment. He supposed they had to be.

Justin had already spotted the dogs and was off that way at a run. Pacer's tail was already wagging, and he gave a happy bark as his new, playful companion approached. The dog might be all business on the job, but he could romp with the best of them when off duty.

"He's kind of working here," Malcolm explained to the boy, "so he can't really play right now."

"Working?" the boy asked. "Is someone lost?"

Malcolm laughed. "No, but he has to show people what he can do, so they keep wanting him around."

Justin's brow furrowed. "I always want him around."

"I know," Malcolm said solemnly. "And so does he."

As a visitor to the festival stopped to ask about the dogs, Malcolm began to explain how Pacer was a trailing dog, who followed scents both in the air and on things, rather than a tracking dog who followed actual tracks.

"You mean like on TV when they give the dog something of the lost person's to sniff, and then they start off looking for them?" the visitor asked.

"Exactly like that," Malcolm said, sounding justly proud of his clever, dedicated dog.

"He finds stuff I hide, too," Justin exclaimed, sounding nearly as proud, and the visitor smiled.

With a promise that they'd come back to visit the dogs

again while they were here, Greg and Briony convinced the kids to explore the rest of the festival. As they continued to walk around, Greg watched Briony, savoring the look of enjoyment on her face. He wondered if she'd ever been part of a gathering like this before, a cheerful, happy event where people just enjoyed being in this place at this time. He doubted it. Or if she had, she probably hadn't let it seep into her, not through that protective shell her hard life had given her. Seeing her now, smiling, looking around in somewhat bemused wonder, did his heart good.

They ended up at the enclosure of a small petting zoo that had both Justin and Jane excited. They'd really bonded with many of the animals on the ranch, but these were creatures new to them—a couple of baby goats and lambs, a surprisingly cute little pig, a big pen of rabbits, a smaller one of what looked like hamsters or guinea pigs, a rather sizable tortoise, and a couple of ponies Justin zeroed in on—so Greg wasn't really surprised when they both demanded to go in.

One of the trained attendants offered to go with Jane in case her newly acquired walking skills failed her, so off they both went while Greg and Briony waited at the fence. He wanted to ask her how she was doing, but people kept stopping by to say hello, many saying how nice it was to see him here, and he began to get the feeling Briony wasn't the only one who needed to get used to doing things like this. And not just for the kids' sake.

"Your family really is the backbone of this town," Briony said, sounding bemused.

"Yeah, if you could take a couple of them out of the equation," he said wryly. But then, in a much softer tone and with a smile he added, "They're your family, too, now."

For an instant she looked startled, but then an expression of such happiness and warmth spread across her face that his stomach knotted, but in a good way. So much had changed in the last month; there had been so much pain and upheaval. But there had been good, too. Especially the joy and pleasure they'd found in each other, and that gave him such hope for the future.

They would build that life they'd talked about. He knew that now. And he knew something else, as he stood there watching Briony interact with Lizzy, who had just arrived.

It would be a good life.

A sudden commotion across the enclosure drew his attention. A boy about twice Justin's size had apparently tried to ride the tortoise. Attendants rushed over to wrestle the protesting kid off the poor creature. He didn't envy the parents of that one, judging by his reaction to being told tortoises weren't for riding. And judging by the look on the face of the woman who came to round the kid up, this wasn't new territory.

"Poor woman," Briony said.

"She's got her hands full," Greg agreed.

He was just wondering what he'd do if Justin had tried something like that when Briony grabbed his arm.

"Greg!" At her suddenly sharp tone, his head snapped around to stare at her. "Where are they?"

She was looking around almost frantically, and he put his hand over hers soothingly as he scanned the enclosure. Then he scanned it again, slower. Then, his pulse racing now, a third time. Then the area nearby. Then a three-sixty turn to look all around them.

As he muttered a curse, he heard Briony almost whimper.

Justin and Jane were gone.

Chapter 35

Briony had never felt panic like this, even in the worst days of her early life when she'd questioned her own survival. This was worse. Different, and worse. The thought of Justin and Jane lost, out there somewhere, terribly scared, pierced her to her soul. If she'd needed any further proof of how important those kids had become to her, she had it now. Because she knew she wouldn't stop, wouldn't rest until they were back, safe and sound.

She could feel the same sort of tension in Greg, although once they were certain the kids were nowhere in sight, he'd responded more usefully than her own frantic running about rechecking. He'd gone right to his brother and Pacer. Malcolm in turn had called in the other SAR dog and his handler, Ajay Wright, and the whimsically named yellow Lab, Pumpkin. The two men and their dogs immediately began an organized and obviously professional search.

"We'll call in other teams if necessary," Malcolm assured his brother. "In the meantime, use your phone to keep in touch. I'll be live with Ajay via radio, so I can relay anything."

Word spread fast that two little children were missing, and it wasn't long before every Colton and many others at the festival were searching the grounds and beyond. This eased her panic a little, and she was almost able to breathe normally again. Almost.

"We'll find them," Greg promised her, his strong arm coming around her shoulders, dispelling a bit of the chill that had come over her.

"And him, if he's behind this," said Greg's cousin Fletcher, who had just finished a search of the game booths area with no results.

His words stopped her breath, and Briony looked at the man. She told herself that as a police detective it was only natural for him to suspect the worst. But until he'd said it, she hadn't allowed herself to consider the possibility that Justin and Jane hadn't just wandered off. Hadn't allowed it because it would change everything. Change from two small children who'd wandered off from the crowd and gotten lost to a much more horrible possibility.

They had been taken.

And there was only one likely suspect for that.

She turned back to Greg. "Do you think— Would he— Could he?" she stammered.

"From what Rick told me over the years, I wouldn't put it past him for a moment," Greg said grimly.

"I'll make the call," Fletcher said, and pulled out his phone and hit a single button she guessed was to his colleagues at the police department. Somehow that simple action made the possibility they'd been kidnapped very real to Briony, and it was all she could do not to shatter right here in front of everyone. Only the strength she'd had to develop as a kid in the system enabled her to keep from flying into a million pieces.

As if he'd sensed it, Greg pulled her into an embrace. "We'll find them, Bri. We'll find them."

She felt both helpless and useless as the search expanded.

Malcolm called in more SAR teams, Fletcher had what had to be most of the Owl Creek Police Department out searching, and Greg's father had additional plans for searching on horseback to cover the surrounding forested areas that couldn't be easily reached by vehicle.

Then there was the cousin she'd heard about but only now met, even though he worked on the ranch. Greg had told her of Wade's background as a Special Forces operator, and the explosion that had scarred him and cost him an eye, but seeing the eye patch he still wore drove it home to her like nothing else.

She supposed her silly reaction explained why he was scarce around the ranch. He probably didn't like dealing with people who reacted by staring at him like she had. She felt bad and resolved to find him and apologize when this was over, and Justin and Jane were safely back home.

But when he faded off into the trees to do his own search, she almost hoped that, if it were truly Rick's father who had taken the kids, that this guy be the one to find them. She had the feeling he would not go easy on the man. And unlike law enforcement, he might not feel compelled to hold back.

More time passed, and then more, with no luck or leads. Briony had always thought of Owl Creek as a small town, but suddenly it seemed vast and overwhelming. She felt even more useless after Greg mounted up with his father and expanded the search, but she was ridiculously unprepared for this kind of thing. Only when Greg's aunt took her to the Colton Properties building up on Main Street and sat her down at a desk with a phone and a list of numbers to call did she feel as if she were doing anything.

"Thank you," she said to the woman, almost fiercely.

"We'll call every person in town if we have to, and the searchers will not quit," Jen promised, giving her the kind of warm, motherly hug she'd rarely had in her misbegotten life. "We'll bring your kids home."

Briony liked the way she put that. *Your kids*. Hers and Greg's. She dived into the phone calls, quickly learning that identifying herself as Briony Colton usually got her quick cooperation. She had the feeling she was only starting to understand what it meant to carry that name around here.

But her newfound energy faded as hours passed, darkness fell and they were still nowhere. She had gleaned one tiny bit of information that was further evidence against Rick's father but didn't help to find the children now at all.

She sat in the building that had once housed the hardware store that had begun the Colton success story here in Owl Creek, rubbing at eyes that were dry and stinging. As was her nature, she'd taken to keeping a record of everything that had been checked on, people and places. Word had gone out, so her phone rang every time a searcher finished an area or neighborhood, and she made notes. If nothing else, it might save time by keeping others from duplicating her effort. Time that could be put into actual, physical searching.

It was nearly four in the morning when the front door swung open and Greg came in. She immediately got up, looking at him with concern. He was rubbing at his eyes much as she had been, and she knew he probably had to be even more exhausted than she. At least he'd been out physically looking. And she could tell by his uncharacteristically sapped posture that, just like her, he had no good news to share.

But she would never, ever give up on finding Justin and Jane, and she knew Greg wouldn't, either.

"I've called half the people on this list, and I think your aunt called the other half," she said wearily. "Nobody has seen them or knows anything about where the kids might be. Although," she added, feeling she owed it, "most of them were very kind and concerned and many offered to join in the search." That Colton name again, she supposed. "I did find one thing, not that it helps now."

"What?"

He pulled out the earpiece he was wearing, the one he usually wore around the ranch to avoid startling any livestock with the sound of the phone. He rubbed at his ear as he sat on the edge of the desk she'd been using as she paced, trying to shed some of the edginess she was feeling.

"One of my calls turned out to be the insurance agent that sold Rick and Wendy their policy. He recognized the names immediately and was one of the ones who volunteered to go out and search." She stopped her pacing, halting in front of where Greg was leaning on her borrowed desk. "He mentioned that Rick's father had come to him as a client also. And that the policies for the kids were mentioned, although he swore he gave no specific numbers or amounts."

Greg was zeroed in now. "What did he give him?"

"That the kids would never have to worry about money in their lives."

Greg let out a smothered oath. "All it would take to set Kraft on the hunt."

"Yes," she agreed. "And no surprise, it happened right before he filed for custody."

"Figures." He rubbed at his eyes again. "Malcolm and I—and Pacer—just got back from Conners."

That surprised her for a moment. "Conners?" And then it hit her, that that was where the so-called church was. "You went looking for Kraft."

He nodded. "We went to their...compound, I guess you'd call it. Malcolm said Pacer would alert if he caught any trace of the kids having been there recently. He didn't. And," he added with a grimace, "we overheard one of the…cult members—and now that I've seen it, there's no doubt in my mind that's what it is. Those people are living like poor refugees, while Acker, Kraft and the rest of the leaders—probably including my mother—" the words had a bitter tone "—live like royalty."

She wished she could think of something comforting to say, but couldn't, so resumed her pacing as Greg went on.

"While we were there, we overheard one of them saying Kraft didn't show up for last night's services. And that Markus Acker was none too happy about it. Implication being he doesn't know where he is, either."

Her breath caught in her throat. She stopped her pacing again and turned to face him, her fingers curling into her palms, nails digging hard, as if the pain could change the obvious.

"So we were right, Kraft grabbed them," she said, tears starting to sting anew. "And has them…somewhere."

He nodded. "And apparently somewhere other than the compound."

She tried to think, to figure out what this would accomplish in Kraft's mind. Her accountant brain said *nothing*. "How does he think kidnapping them is going to get him access to that money?"

"People don't successfully build cults like Ever After by being timid or uncertain," Greg said sourly. "I'm sure he thinks he's smarter than all of us put together and will figure out a way. Rick always said he looked down on other people, called them stupid and gullible."

"And set out to prove it, apparently," Briony said, unable to stop a touch of bitterness creeping into her own voice. "Thinking if he can help bilk hundreds of people out of their life savings, he can surely get his hands on that insurance money."

"Probably," Greg said, rubbing at his unshaven jaw. "Or maybe…"

His voice trailed away, and she sensed he'd thought better of what he'd been about to say. "Maybe what?"

"Nothing."

"Greg, there's nothing you can say that's going to make this worse."

He let out a long, audible breath. "Don't be too sure of that."

"What?" she demanded.

He hesitated again, then finally said it. "Fletcher was wondering if he was one of those guys who just can't lose. Will do anything to avoid it and gets into that self-centric mode of…if I can't have them, nobody can."

Nausea hit her in a rush, and she wished she hadn't pushed him to say it. Because she'd had secondhand experience with a case like that, where a drug-addict mother had stolen her three children from the foster family who had been granted temporary custody. The foster family she and Wendy had been with at the time.

She'd murdered all three.

Chapter 36

He wished he hadn't said it. She looked as if the words had broken her. It took him a while to coax the story out of her, that horrific tale of three innocent children, one even younger than Jane, who had met an ugly end at the hands of a parent with just that mindset.

And when he had the story, he didn't know what else to do except hold her. Tight.

"Now what do we do?" she asked, sounding as if she were trying very hard not to let that old helpless, hopeless feeling rise in her.

"We expand the search. So far we've stayed in the general vicinity of where they were, but we've pretty much covered all of town. So now we're heading for the outskirts. Malcolm and I will be starting on the eastern outskirts as soon as Pacer has a chance to rest and eat."

"What about you?" she asked. "You need some sleep."

"I'll sleep when they're home safe." He met her gaze steadily. "About the same time you will."

She hugged him. His arms went around her immediately, and they stood there for several long, silent moments, and Greg felt oddly as if, somehow, they were giving each other a strength neither had alone.

And he vowed they would build that life they'd talked about. As soon as Justin and Jane were home safe. But now, the search had to go on.

Time ticked by, and Briony could swear she heard every click of the clock on the wall as her desperation grew. She dialed and dialed and dialed. Some people were gruff or even angry, but most were kind and concerned, many even offering to join in the search. Because it was the way her brain worked, she found herself calculating how long it would take to talk to every permanent resident in Owl Creek. Each call took three to five minutes, sometimes more, times the population divided by households, say an average of two to four people per, except places like the ranch where there were many more, which threw her figures into disarray—

Stop it! It's going to take two days to call everyone, so you've got a day to go, just keep dialing!

When she woke up with a start and realized she'd fallen asleep at the desk, she felt both guilty for sleeping and shocked when she realized it was dark outside. Night was here, and still no word.

"I'm glad you slept a little," said a kind voice from behind her. Greg's aunt, back to be helpful again.

"You should have woken me up," Briony said, getting to her feet.

"I was here if any calls came in."

"They're still searching, aren't they?"

"Of course. Even if everyone else quits, the Coltons will never give up, and there's a fair number of us."

Briony shook her head in wonder. "But so many of them barely know the kids, or me."

"But they know Greg, and Coltons stick together." She

frowned. "Not to mention none of us are fond of that cult they call a church, for various reasons."

"You've been…wonderful, when you have your own… complications to deal with."

The frown became a grimace. "My charming sister, you mean. Yes, she's one I would not include in that loyal group."

Briony almost asked about Robert Colton, Jen's late, adulterous husband who had a years-long affair and two children by that sister, but decided it wasn't the time or the place, and none of her business to boot.

The little bit of sleep she'd gotten—last she remembered looking at the clock had been two hours ago—seemed to have helped. She was able to think a little, at least. She picked up her phone and texted Greg.

Your aunt's here. She says everyone's still searching?

It was a moment before he answered, and she wondered where he was.

Yes. We're rotating now, so people can get some rest, but still searching.

Where are you? She would have asked about him getting some rest himself, but she knew he'd meant what he'd said about resting when the children were home safe.

Just finishing a grid search of the woods at the south end of the lake. Malcolm's taking a break to rest Pacer, then we're heading back out in a couple of hours.

Jen, who had come over to check on the status, said quietly, "I can handle the calls here for a bit. Why don't you both get some rest? Neither of you will do the kids any good if you're so exhausted you miss something."

"I wish he would, but he won't go home until the children are found."

Jen gave her a sideways look. "You still have a place here in town, don't you?"

Briony practically gaped at her. That told her more than anything could how tired she was—she'd never even thought of her little condo just a mile or so away.

Or it tells you how much you've come to think of the ranch as home.

That surprised her even more. Because it was true, she did think of it as home, despite her misgivings about living around so many people. She just hadn't had any experience with living around so many kind, helpful people. One of the kindest was standing beside her now, with yet another solution to a problem.

"Thank you, that's a great idea," she said, and started to type out a response.

"Take my advice," Jen said with a wry smile, "just tell him to meet you there, not why. No one more stubborn than a Colton man on a mission."

"I think I will always take your advice," Briony said, meaning it. And when she saw the pleased look on Greg's aunt's face, she was glad she'd said it.

She did take that advice. She'd get him inside, make him sit down while she did…something, and hope what had happened to her here at the desk would happen to him and he'd sleep a little despite himself. Maybe it would be easier because the children had never been there, so it wouldn't seem quite so…empty.

She was close enough and the coffee shop was open so she stopped and bought some things, knowing her kitchen at the condo was bare. When she got there and let herself in, it felt…strange. She'd lived here for nearly three years, been proud of her first real estate purchase, and yet she'd barely thought of it in the last three weeks. Hadn't even thought much about what she was going to do with it, because the kids sapped all her spare time and energy.

And oh, she wanted them back doing that again, wanted their noise, their needs, their silliness. And she wanted those moments with Greg when they both looked at them and then each other, exchanging in a glance the weary delight of parents everywhere.

Greg had only been here once, to help her pick up what she needed for the move to the ranch, but she had no doubt he'd find it again easily. And just ten minutes after she'd arrived, he was there. He greeted her with concern, clearly wondering why here, and she regretted adding to his worries when he looked so utterly dead on his feet. But she got him inside and sat him on the couch while she brought over a delicious-smelling pastry and a cup of thick, rich hot chocolate—the caffeine-laden coffee could come later—and he ate it quickly, his body probably demanding the nourishment while his brain was still busy elsewhere.

"I just thought we needed a few minutes of quiet, to think," she said as she sat beside him. "Especially you. You've been running at full speed for nearly twenty-four hours now."

"And you've called nearly the entire town," he said after he swallowed the last bite of fruit-filled decadence.

"With little results," she said wearily.

"You found more proof that it's likely Kraft," he pointed out. "Now we just have to figure out where he'd take them."

"I would have thought the compound."

"Me, too. But Acker was angry enough at him for vanishing that he let us in, and Pacer would have let Malcolm know if there was any trace of them anywhere."

"Then he could have taken them anywhere," she said, fear bubbling up anew.

What if he'd left the area, maybe even the state? How would they ever find them? The kids must be terrified by now. First, they lose their loving parents, then they have to move out of their home in a rush, they just get settled in at the ranch and now this, all in the space of three weeks? How could they possibly deal with that?

She tried to focus on the goal of coming here in the first place. She excused herself to use the bathroom. When she was done, she splashed cold water on her face, grimaced at her tired, bloodshot eyes, then ignored them because his were worse. She grabbed a towel to dry her face and hands and took her time about it. She tried to divert her mind by thinking about what to do with the place. Sell it, rent it out?

Finally, she tiptoed quietly back to the living room and found, to her relief, that it had worked. Greg was still sitting upright, but his head was back against the couch cushion and he was asleep. She watched him for a long time, feeling such a tangle of emotions she couldn't sort them out. Emotions she'd never expected to feel, rising out of things she'd never expected to have.

A husband and two children she loved with all her heart.

Chapter 37

Greg was stunned to realize he'd actually slept. And when he took the cup of very black coffee Briony held out to him, and got a good look at her face, he knew.

"You planned this, didn't you?" he said before taking the first sip, which had quite a kick.

"I accidentally slept a couple of hours back at the desk, and it made a world of difference. And I knew you had to be even more tired than I was, out there trekking around all over."

"And I need to get back at it." He felt guilty just having taken this couple of hours, when the kids were out there somewhere, no doubt scared, and maybe worse.

"I know," Briony said quietly.

He downed the caffeinated brew, hoping it hit hard and fast. He stood up, acknowledging he did feel a little better. Or at least ready to start again. He looked at the woman who'd thought to do this because she was worried about him.

He put down the now-empty cup and pulled her into his arms. Just a few seconds, he told himself. Just a few seconds and then he'd get moving. He held her close, and feeling the way she hugged him back made him feel like he could go on forever.

When his cell phone buzzed, had it been in any other

circumstances, he would have delayed answering it to savor her closeness a little longer. It was strange; he'd never felt as if he had a big hole in his life until she had filled it. Only then had he realized how much he'd needed this.

Needed her.

The phone signaled again. He was still reluctant, but when he pulled it out and looked at the screen, the decision was made.

"Malcolm," he said. "He'd just text if it wasn't important."

Briony went still. He swiped to answer the call.

"Bro, I've got something." Malcolm's words came quickly, and he could sense the tension in his brother's voice. "East side, up at the end of the gravel road past the bank. Remember that old mobile home that's been parked up there forever?"

"Yeah?"

"We were out in the trees above it when Pacer went nuts. Breeze was coming up from there, so I stopped and watched. Didn't see anything, no movement, lights on, or anything, but he never settled. He's totally zeroed in on that place, and you know what that means."

Greg did indeed know what that meant. He had as much trust and faith in that dog as his brother did, because he'd seen all the times it had been Pacer who'd found the quarry, from injured hikers in the mountains to children lost in the woods. If Pacer signaled he'd found something, he had.

"You alone up there?"

"At the moment, yes. I called it in, but if you're still at the headquarters in town, you're the closest."

"On my way."

"Armed and ready?" his brother asked.

"Damned straight," Greg said, thinking there was nothing he'd like better than to take out the person who'd grabbed the two kids who were now his own in all but blood.

He ended the call and looked at Briony, trying to decide how much to tell her. He didn't want to get her hopes up, only to have them dashed if the kids were no longer there.

"Malcolm's dog found something up in the hills above town. I'm going to help him check it out."

"Found what?"

"We don't know for sure yet, he just signaled on a place."

"I'm coming with you."

"Briony, just wait here. I'll let you know as soon as I do, I swear."

She shook her head. "I'm coming with you," she repeated.

"It may be nothing," Greg said, antsy to get moving.

"You're saying that dog would ever make a mistake?"

Pacer had, in fact, never made a mistake when it came to finding things connected to a scent he had cataloged in his brain. Greg remembered once when a hiker he'd found came to thank them, and Pacer had instantly reacted to the familiar scent of the woman.

But it wasn't Pacer he was worried about right now.

"Don't get your hopes up," he cautioned.

"Greg Colton, do you really think I don't know how to handle disappointment? I'm going, so quit wasting time."

He knew she was right. There was no more time to waste.

"We have to take my truck," he said, heading out at a run. Briony was on his heels. He passed on his usual chivalrous opening of the passenger door for her, since she was already there anyway.

"Where are they?" she asked as she slammed the truck door shut.

"Up behind the bank on Main and Cedar," he said as he started the truck and they began to move.

"But didn't the searchers already check all around there?"

"He's a lot farther up the hill than they'd reached yet. That's why Malcolm was up there."

He hesitated. Briony reached out and put a hand on his arm. "I can't tell you what it means to me that you want to protect me from whatever pain we might find. No one, except Wendy, has ever done that for me in my life. But for Wendy, I have to do this. Tell me the rest."

He took one hand off the wheel and put it over hers for a moment. Everything they'd become to each other since that awful night was in that touch. And he knew she was right. He went back to driving and answered her.

"There's a gravel road that's really overgrown, and it ends way up top where there's an old mobile home parked. That's where Pacer went wild on him."

"A mobile home?" Her voice went up a notch. "So they could be inside?"

"He hasn't seen any movement or signs it's occupied," he cautioned.

"It's practically the middle of the night—there wouldn't be, would there?"

"Maybe," he agreed cautiously. "Bri, if this is something, you have to stay here in the truck until we know it's safe."

"If the kids are there—"

"I mean it, Briony. If it is Kraft and he has them there, who knows what he might do. This could get dangerous, and I can't focus on getting the kids away from him—" he glanced at her again "—if I'm worried about you getting hurt."

When he said those last words, something flashed in her green eyes for a moment. But she only said, in a determined voice he'd come to know, "I'll stay out of the way, unless I can help. Or there's a chance to get the kids, one or both, out of there. There's two of them—there should be two of us."

He found he could not argue with that. But he still wasn't happy about the idea of her being in a possible line of fire.

"He could be armed," he said warningly as he turned his attention back to driving, silently glad there was virtually no traffic at this predawn hour.

"He probably is," she agreed, much more easily than he would have expected. Then she gave him a slightly crooked but definite smile. "Do you really think I didn't figure out why we had to take this rather than the car with the car seats?"

He gave her a sideways glance. "I told you, it's a rough road."

"So this has nothing to do with it?" She reached up to touch the stock of his rifle in the rack above their heads.

He looked back at the road, not sure how to answer. "That bother you?"

"Not if that's what it takes to get the children back safely."

"Good."

"Not saying I hope you have to shoot him to end this."

"But end it I will."

"I know."

There was something in her voice he hadn't heard before. They were nearing the turn now and he couldn't look at her, so he just spoke her name. The nickname she'd told him only Wendy had ever been allowed to use, before him.

"Bri?"

And then, in the darkness of his truck's cab, she said what neither of them had spoken aloud yet.

"I love you."

He felt as if his chest had taken a lot of blows today, but this was different from any of them. For a moment he simply couldn't breathe. The street was deserted so he risked a glance at her. She was staring down at her hands in her lap, a look half wondering, half scared on her face as she rubbed at her wedding ring.

And he somehow knew she'd never said that to a man in her entire life. He couldn't begin to tell her what that meant to him. Not now, anyway, because they were almost there. They'd reached the start of that gravel road, and for just a moment he stopped the truck. She looked up at him, and he reached out to cup her cheek. And admitted what he'd known for days now.

"I love you, too, Bri."

Her eyes widened, as if she truly hadn't expected him to say it. He saw in her expression a trace of the courage it had taken her to be the one to say it first, and regretted that he hadn't done it, to make it easier on her. He wanted to make her entire life easier from here on out. And as soon as Justin and Jane were back safely with them, he would set about doing that.

"Be careful, Greg. Please, please, be careful."

He heard what she wasn't really saying. That she wasn't worried only about him having to shoot Kraft, she was worried about him maybe getting hurt in the process.

And that gave him a feeling he would carry with him up this hill as if it were armor.

Chapter 38

She didn't regret telling him, and that surprised her. She'd expected to soon be wishing she'd never said those words, never admitted to him how deeply she'd fallen.

She had never expected him to say them back. Especially when she had to stack that up against her certain knowledge that Greg Colton did not lie.

He meant it. He really meant it. It wasn't just a reflex answer; she knew that by the way he'd taken a few seconds of their precious time and stopped, touched her cheek as he'd said it.

He loved her.

She felt a chill go through her when he stopped the truck, parking it across the gravel road, and realized he was doing it to block Kraft—she was ever more certain they were dealing with Rick's twisted, evil father—from escaping in a vehicle. She felt another chill when he reached for the rifle, apparently checking to be sure it was loaded, although she wondered why he had to, given it was his. But she also knew she knew nothing about weapons, so let it go.

He took out his phone, and a moment later was talking to his brother. He'd put his earbud back in, so she could only hear his side, but it told her enough.

"Blocked the road," he said, confirming her guess. "Any

change?" A moment of silence for her as he listened to Malcolm. "Got it. I'm going to move in closer from below." Another pause. "Yeah, slow and quiet from here on."

The call ended, and he looked at her as he spoke in a whisper. "No movement yet. But he got a call back from Fletcher. He's on his way, but also had some info. That place is owned by a member of Ever After."

She sucked in a quick gulp of air. "It's him," she said, her voice even quieter.

Greg nodded as he reached back and grabbed his cowboy hat. "Agreed. Question is, is he alone?"

She hadn't even thought of that. Another shiver went through her. "There's only one car parked up there," she said, "but that's not proof."

"Doesn't matter. We're getting them back, right now." Greg settled the hat on his head, and at her look said, "So Malcolm will know it's me from a distance."

"Oh." That made sense, even as it made her shiver even harder at the reason that was necessary.

She looked up the hill to where she could see the large, rectangular shape of the mobile home. Even in the faint light it looked worn and tired, with moss or water stains leaving darker patches against the lighter structure. It was a stark contrast to the expensive-looking car parked near the front end of the battered house trailer. The car without any license plates that she could see, at least from here. Maybe it was brand-new. That would fit.

"I can't imagine the father Rick and Wendy talked about in a place like that," she said. "Comfort and flash—like that car—were always his first priorities. Not necessarily in that order."

"I know," Greg said, and his tone was grim now. "If it's a sign of how off the rails he is…"

He didn't finish the thought as he opened the driver's door. He didn't need to. They were dealing with a grifter and a swindler, a kidnapper and…maybe a murderer. And that *maybe* was getting fainter and fainter as certainty began to replace it.

She wobbled a little as her feet hit the ground beside the truck. She met him in front, the heat from the motor radiating from the grille in the chilly air.

"He could really have been behind Rick and Wendy's crash," she whispered.

Greg only nodded. Then he looked at her. "Want to take back that hope?"

She knew he meant her hope that he didn't have to kill the man. "No. I don't want you to have to do it, but if it happens, I won't be sorry."

He leaned over and kissed her, quick, light, but full of promise. But then he went straight to instructions. "Stay right behind me. When we get closer, you stay behind the tree line while I move in. If you see any movement in the trailer, freeze, and text me."

Her brow furrowed. "Will you have time to look and see it's me?"

He gave her a crooked smile then. "I'll know." For an instant she wondered what it was, but then his gaze narrowed intently as he added, "And if I yell run, you run. And don't stop until you're down in town again. Then call my dad."

She blinked, but before she could react, he'd slung the rifle over his shoulder and they were moving, slowly, off to one side but definitely uphill. She kept close, but remained aware of staying behind and out of his way. She knew her job now was to be there just in case, for the kids, nothing more. This might not be Greg's bailiwick either, but he was

a lot more capable than she was of dealing with a dangerous man like Kraft.

But when he crept into the small clearing where the
trailer sat, she felt useless. Worse than useless. But she did
her assigned task: she watched the mobile home, scanning
it front to back. From this closer vantage point, she could
see just how worn-out the thing was, that there were dents,
dings, taped-over broken windows, missing siding—

Broken windows. Including a big one on the end closest to her. The entire space appeared to be covered with a
sheet of heavy plastic duct-taped in place. She edged a little closer, mindful of Greg's words and staying among the
trees. Trees, she now noticed, that grew close enough to that
end with the missing window that branches were brushing
against the trailer.

She crept closer, with a slow care that she'd swear was
more tiring than running. The big cedar tree closest to
the mobile home was her target—the branches were thick
enough and low to the ground enough to easily hide in.
When she got there, she crouched down to slip under the
lowest branches that brushed the ground. It was a healthy
tree, with a lot of growth, so it was a little tricky, but she
made herself a spot that was barely a yard away from the
corner, and maybe four feet from that missing window. The
smell of the evergreen filled her nostrils, and she took a
deep breath just because the fresh, clean scent seemed to
clear her mind.

She waited, crouched down in her little space. And
waited, staring at that back window space, watching for
any kind of change in either light or shadow. And waited,
hearing only the rustle of the branches above in the very
slight breeze. Or was that Greg, moving quietly closer?

She didn't know how long she'd been there, but long

enough for her to want to change position. She didn't, not
willing to risk even the tiny noise that might make. She
stayed, crouched, barely breathing so she could hear— She
smothered a gasp as a tiny sound came from the direction
of that taped-over window.

A sound she recognized.

If you see any movement in the trailer, freeze, and text me.

Hearing counted, too, didn't it? She grabbed her phone
and tapped out a message to Greg.

I heard Jane cry! Near the back. Big window broken.

She held her breath as she waited for an answer. Suddenly realized what would happen when he did and quickly
muted all sound on her phone.

The wait was only about fifteen seconds but felt like
fifteen minutes.

On my way.

Relief flooded her. Greg was on his way. To her, to them,
and everything would be okay. And it didn't even bother
her that she'd never had that kind of faith in a man in her
life. Because she knew, down to her bones, that it was not
misplaced. Not with this man.

She didn't hear him until he was only three feet away,
and along with the little jump her heart gave—which
seemed to happen often with him—she marveled at how
such a big man moved so quietly. He put a finger to his lips
to indicate not to speak, then edged closer to the plastic-
sealed window. As he went, he pulled off the hat and
dropped it on the ground so he could get closer, but he slid
the sling of the rifle off his shoulder and held it across his

chest. He stood with his back against the wall, his head turned slightly, clearly listening.

He stood there for a couple of minutes before he nodded back at her. She felt a rush of relief—she'd been right; he must have heard it as well. He edged back to her, moving with a slow care that told how he'd been so silent. He leaned in close to whisper to her, "I'm going in through that window. I'll hand them out to you. You take them and run, no matter what happens. All right?"

She knew he meant if Winston Kraft discovered him. The thought chilled her, but the kids… Justin and Jane had to take priority here. And their parents—for that's what they now were—would do whatever it took. Both of them. She reached up to touch Greg's cheek as she nodded yes.

He pulled his phone out and started tapping out a text message, a longer one. He held it out so she could see it, as if, she thought with no small amount of wonder, for her approval before he sent it.

They're here. Need a distraction at the front end of the trailer, near the car. Pacer howl on command?

She nodded, feeling a little breathless. He sent the text. The answer came back quickly.

Just listen for him. We're close. When?

Two minutes.

Copy. From now.

Briony stayed close behind him as he edged his way to the back of the mobile home. When they were up against the corner of the structure, he set down the rifle and slid the knife he always carried out of the sheath on his belt. She felt a jolt of fear. Was he going to take on Kraft with a knife? They didn't know for sure if Rick's father was armed, but it didn't seem safe to her to assume he wasn't. Then she saw him slide the blade up to the edge of the plastic, test it with a little cut, and realized it was to slice his way in.

Once more time seemed to have slowed, and no matter how she tried to calm herself, her pulse was racing. *If only the seconds would tick off as quickly.*

She quashed the old fears that tried to rise, that it would go wrong, she'd make a mistake, something bad would happen. It wouldn't. Her life had changed; she had two incredible children and this amazing, wonderful man had her back now. Determination flooded back, and she could almost feel her spine stiffen. They would do this, and when they did, she would never let those old fears sneak in again. She would be the woman Greg deserved to have, and—

The howls that broke the night's silence made her jump and sent a chill through her. They were close enough she heard a harsh, muttered oath from inside, then the sound of hurrying footsteps. Greg was already moving, slicing through the heavy plastic as if it were paper. He caught the lower frame and hoisted himself up in one smooth, powerful motion. Despite his size he made it through so quickly it amazed her, and how quietly he did it amazed her even more. He landed on the inside as if he were wearing sneakers instead of cowboy boots.

Pacer was still at it, punctuating the howls with chains of sharp, loud barking, sounding ferocious instead of like the sweet, caring rescue dog she knew he was. But beneath it all, she would almost swear she heard Justin cry out, "Unca Greg!"

The next thing she knew a wailing Jane was in her arms. She wanted to hold the little girl, to cuddle her and assure her she was safe, but then Justin was there, his little booted feet waving in the air as Greg got him clear of his makeshift prison.

"Briny!"

He reached out to her, and she pulled him against her with her right arm. She'd never tried carrying them both at once, but she'd do it now no matter what. She backed away from the trailer to give Greg plenty of room to jump out. Pacer kept up the racket, but suddenly there was a sound that topped even that.

A shot.

Greg's rifle was leaning against the wall below the window.

You take them and run, no matter what happens.

Briony was caught in a position she'd never been in, never expected to be in. She knew what she had to do, she'd given her word to the man she loved, but that man even now could be hurt, even die inside that run-down hulk. All the bad things she'd been through in her life dwindled to nothing beside the biggest fear she'd ever felt, that the precious, sweet life she'd finally found was going to vanish like everything else had—

No! She was not going there. She started downhill, keeping her word, holding on to the only two who could make her do it. But she couldn't stop the tears the fear for Greg drove out of her, nor could she focus on Justin's jabbering about what had happened or Jane's crying.

And then she heard the shout.

"Bri!"

She spun around, awkwardly off-balance with the weight of the two safe, unharmed children as she saw the man who had seen to that safety running toward them. Running, with those long, strong legs, so fast that he was there throwing his arms around them all before she could catch enough breath to even say his name.

"You're okay?"

They asked it simultaneously, and then echoed each other's relieved laugh that the answer was yes for both.

"Unca Greg punched him, that bad man!" Justin crowed.

"I heard a shot," Briony said, still a little breathless, as if there simply wasn't enough air.

"Along with everything else he sucks at, he's a lousy shot," Greg said, and suddenly the air was there.

She looked back toward the mobile home. "Is he—"

"Fletcher got here. He's in handcuffs now, where he belongs."

She stared at him. "And you still came out that window?"

He cupped her cheek, and she saw everything she could ever have wanted to see in his expression. "It was closer to you."

Then he leaned down to kiss both children on the forehead, assuring them they were safe now. And now Briony saw the other car parked behind his truck on the gravel road, and two more coming up behind them. The troops were here.

It was over.

Epilogue

"**D**on't thank me," Malcolm said. "I taught him to signal when he found something, but it was Seb Cross at Crosswinds who taught him to raise hell on command. I never would have thought of it."

Greg watched Justin and Jane playing with a delighted Pacer, and tilted his beer can toward his brother in grateful salute.

"You got all your people notified we have them back?"

Malcolm nodded. "I finally reached Ajay—that's Pumpkin's handler—and his group, so that's all the search teams."

Greg took a long sip of the cold brew. He didn't indulge that often, but this sure seemed like the day to do it. The kids were home safe, Briony was beside him and holding his other hand like she would never let go, and he was happier than he'd ever been.

They were gathered on the patio by the pool. Even Wade had appeared, albeit briefly since he was working today. Mama Jen had invited everybody who'd been on the search to come out to the ranch, to thank them all for their help, but that would be later.

Greg looked up when his father came out of the house. "Just got off the phone with Fletcher. He says Winston—" he used the name unfamiliar to the kids, who were within earshot "—has been booked for the kidnapping, and they think they have a link between him and the crash. They're investigating that, but he said with luck the guy will never get out."

"Is he talking?" Greg asked.

"Nope. Not about this, not about that so-called church or his connection to Acker. At least, not yet."

Greg had his doubts the man would ever crumble. In those moments in the mobile home, he'd looked into those dark, soulless eyes and known the man was everything Rick had ever said he was and worse.

But they would get to the bottom of this. Of all of it— what happened to Rick and Wendy, and the evil that was the cult Rick's father helped build. They would get to the truth because Coltons never quit.

His dad went over and, of course, sat next to Mama Jen. She reached out and squeezed his hand, and his father got that look on his face he only got around her. Someday, maybe, his secret wish would come true. After all, the wish for himself he'd never even dared voice had, hadn't it?

He turned to look at his wife, wondered if he looked as smitten as his father had. Didn't care, because it was true. And when Bri smiled back at him, a smile full of love, promise and the future, he sent a silent toast to the friends he would never forget, along with a reaffirmation of his vow to see to their children.

"I think," Dad said, "we need to look into expanding that house of yours. You need at least another bedroom and bathroom. Maybe a playroom, too, for wintertime. And a fenced yard area."

"Been thinking about that," Greg admitted. "Maybe two more bathrooms." He had in mind a new main bath, with a big shower and a tub big enough for two. He'd suggested it to Briony, and just the look she gave him put the seal on that plan.

"Hey, we could build a fort out back," Malcolm put in cheerfully.

"That, too," he agreed.

Greg heard the sound of his father's phone and looked that way. Dad gave Mama Jen's hand a squeeze and got up, walking a few feet away on the patio. Greg looked back at Briony as she carefully watched Justin, who had developed an interest in the pool despite that it was a bit chilly for swimming.

"Going to need a fence, since there's open access from our place," Greg remarked. "We had one when we were little but haven't had any little ones around in so long I didn't think of it."

Briony smiled in a way that had him thinking she'd perhaps already had the thought but had been hesitant to say anything.

"Don't do that," he said gently. "Whatever it is, whatever it's about, you can say it, ask it, or if necessary, demand it."

The look she gave him then had him thinking about a quiet night to come and just how they might spend it.

His father turned around to face them. His expression had Greg on his feet in an instant.

"Dad. What is it?"

"Nobody can find Lizzy. And she's not answering her phone."

Jen got up swiftly. "She was searching for the children, too, wasn't she?"

Malcolm, also on his feet now, nodded. "I saw her right after we knew what had happened. She was all in."

Greg was glad he'd only taken a swallow of that beer. Because the Coltons were back on alert.

He looked at Briony, who met his gaze levelly, then looked at her father-in-law. "Where do we start?" she asked.

And despite the newly hatched worry about his sister, Greg knew that his wife was now and from now on thoroughly a Colton.

* * * * *